Tried & True

Books by Mary Connealy

From Bethany House Publishers

The Kincaid Brides

Out of Control
In Too Deep
Over the Edge

Trouble in Texas

Swept Away
Fired Up
Stuck Together

Wild at Heart

Tried and True
Now and Forever

A Match Made in Texas: A Novella Collection

Wild at Heart
BOOK ONE

Tried & True

MARY CONNEALY

BETHANYHOUSE
a division of Baker Publishing Group
Minneapolis, Minnesota

Published by Bethany House Publishers
11400 Hampshire Avenue South
Bloomington, Minnesota 55438
www.bethanyhouse.com

Bethany House Publishers is a division of
Baker Publishing Group, Grand Rapids, Michigan

Printed in the United States of America

Library of Congress Cataloging-in-Publication Data
Connealy, Mary.
Tried and true / Mary Connealy.
pages cm — (Wild at heart ; Book one)
Summary: "In 1860s Idaho Territory, Kylie Wilde is disguised as a man, homesteading for profit so she can live comfortably back East. But love or danger could change her mind"— Provided by publisher.
ISBN 978-0-7642-1178-2 (pbk.)
1. Women pioneers—Fiction. 2. Disguise—Fiction. 3. Frontier and pioneer life—Fiction. 4. Idaho Territory—Fiction. I. Title.
PS3603.O544T75 2014
813′.6—dc23 2014017435

Scripture quotations are from the King James Version of the Bible.

Cover design by Paul Higdon
Cover photography by Mike Habermann Photography, LLC

Author is represented by Natasha Kern Literary Agency

14 15 16 17 18 19 20 7 6 5 4 3 2 1

Aaron, the hero in *Tried and True*, is brave, heroic, smart, honorable, and kind. He ended up being very much like the man I named him for.

If you met Aaron—the real one—you'd find that he's an incredibly likable guy. But when you get to know him, you realize that beneath his charm is great intelligence teamed with wisdom, bound up with a profound work ethic.

It all ties together to make him an extraordinarily fine young man and a wonderful husband for my daughter Shelly. Our family is better for having you in it, Aaron. This book is dedicated to you.

Aspen Ridge
Idaho Territory, July 1866

Kylie Wilde's right hand tightened on the hammer as she stared at her roof. A shingle flapped in the endless summer wind. A storm was blowing in over the Rocky Mountains, blast it. She was going to have to go up there and nail that board down or sleep under a downpour.

She'd slept in the rain before. Nasty. About as nasty as crawling across a steeply pitched roof. Her hand clenched. The hammer rose, and her attitude fell.

The sky was as sullen as her mood with its scudding gray clouds. Rain was coming. She had to fix that roof.

It was a fight to keep from saddling her gray mustang and riding to Shannon's house. Shannon, a year older and softhearted, would help—probably. Kylie had just coaxed her into building a corral around the barn, and a week earlier she'd built the porch. And that was after Shannon and Bailey, the oldest of the three Wilde sisters, built the whole house.

Carpentry wasn't Kylie's greatest gift.

Truth be told, the roof was about the only thing Kylie had done herself, which explained why it wasn't holding together.

Her sisters had hoped she couldn't get in much trouble just nailing boards in place. Of course, Kylie's nailing was more like trying to scare the nails into the wood than pound them in. Her sisters were just plain better at it, and Kylie didn't mind admitting that.

Since the house and barn were done, and with her own homestead to run, kindhearted Shannon had started showing signs of botheration when Kylie tried to wheedle help out of her.

And Bailey, the oldest of the Wilde women, wasn't a tractable woman on her best day. Kylie shuddered at the thought of going to her for something this simple.

The shingle flapped again, and Kylie could swear it sounded like mockery. Her cabin was laughing at her. The wind was blowing for the very purpose of tormenting her. The branches in the forest around her seemed to clap, jeering at the trouble she faced. The mountains stood in judgment, as if to declare that Kylie Wilde was a miserable failure as a homesteader.

Kylie could hear all of this as she stood, hammer in hand, scowling at her roof. It would be fair to say she wasn't a woman happy with the life that had been shoved like an anvil onto her shoulders.

But whether she was happy or not didn't matter one whit. That flapping board had to be nailed back down.

Not only was the wind going to rip it all the way off, but it was right over Kylie's bed. She was in for a miserable soggy night if she didn't act fast.

She could just drag the bed to the side and put a bucket under the leak, but if she didn't go up and fix it now, she'd have it to do tomorrow. Putting it off did no good.

Gritting her teeth, Kylie tried to think of all the ridiculous manly skills her sisters had taught her. Of course, she could only think of how good she'd always been at avoiding their lessons. Now she needed to dredge up a few of them or sleep under a deluge.

Ladder. She needed a ladder. Except, the one they'd used to build the cabin had been borrowed from cranky old Pa. Talk about someone Kylie didn't want to ask for help! Cudgel Wilde would scold and snarl and in the end make Kylie want to jump on her horse and ride off and never come back.

Thunder sounded in the distance. She had to get on with this.

"How do I get up there without a ladder?" she said to herself. Kylie studied the house. The porch roof wasn't real high, but it was steep. Bailey said the Rockies had heavy snow, and the roof needed a steep pitch or it would collapse under the weight.

There was a chimney on the south side, yet it climbed up the outside wall right to the peak of the cabin.

Her gaze slid down to the stovepipe. She'd managed to fetch a real potbellied stove out to her cabin. Her family thought that was foolishness, but Kylie hated cooking in a fireplace.

That stovepipe was fairly solid. It came out of the building through the wall, then curved up through the porch roof. Bailey had done it in that strange way, instead of having it go straight up. She'd said something about retaining heat and preventing sparks and keeping rain out of the stove.

Kylie hadn't really been listening.

Now she was glad it was close to the edge of the roof. Of course, it was close to the south side edge, and the flapping shingle was on the north side. She could pull herself up using the pipe, and then she'd have to crawl the length of the porch roof once she was up there, with nothing much to hang on to. But getting up was harder than staying up.

Since getting up came first, Kylie focused on that.

"Bailey set that pipe. She does everything perfectly. It'll probably hold my weight." And below the stovepipe was her hitching post. "Shannon did a good job with that, too."

She could stand on the hitching post, and if she stretched, she could reach the edge of the roof. But could she get herself up on it?

Kylie gave the hammer a dark glare and shoved it into the large pocket of her skirt. The weight almost pulled her skirt right off.

Shannon and Bailey might wear britches all the time, but Kylie didn't do it unless she absolutely had to—if she was going to see anyone besides her family—which she mostly never did, so she mostly never wore pants. She dropped the handful of nails in another pocket and looked at the rocking chairs on her porch. Shannon had built them both, and she'd called them ladder-back chairs. They even looked a little like ladders, with four nice even slats up their sturdy backs.

The glides on the bottom would rest on the hitching post.

Then when the chair tilted, the high back would reach the support pillar on the porch, and she could climb it like the ladder it was named for. Simple.

Wrestling the chair down the steps, Kylie fumed that she had to do this herself. She was a woman, for heaven's sake. She hadn't ought to be stuck doing manly work.

Flicking her hair over her shoulder, she enjoyed that she'd grown it long despite the dire warnings from her sisters and pa. She smiled every time she felt it bounce around her shoulders. Except now, of course. Not much to smile about right now.

They didn't think she should be in skirts, either.

Well, she was sick and tired of pretending to be a man. In the privacy of her own home she'd dress and wear her hair as she pleased.

Propping the rocking chair on the hitching post, it tilted until it rested solidly on the porch pillar. The chair back didn't reach the roof, but it rested against the column so that if she stood up on the back, she'd be shoulder-high to the eaves.

She wedged the rocker firmly in place. Staring at the makeshift ladder, Kylie went into the house and dragged out another chair. She set this chair on the ground. No sense using the second rocker. Common sense said a chair that didn't rock would be better used as the one she'd set on the ground as her step stool to the hitching post.

Kylie liked to think she had common sense, but as she looked at her chair-hitching-post-rocking-chair creation she was forced to admit that there was serious room for debate on that. She was glad no one was here to take the opposing side, because she'd probably lose.

She climbed up onto the chair and stepped to the hitching post, which held her weight nicely, thanks to Bailey. So far things were going well.

Easing herself onto the rocker, she prayed it wouldn't shift or break. It was well constructed, thanks to Shannon.

She stood upright. The rocker felt steady mostly. She leaned forward to grasp the back of the rocker and, an inch at a time, walked her hands up until she reached first the porch pillar, then the edge of the roof. The chair wobbled, and she clawed at the eaves and let her weight, at shoulder level, rest on them to keep from falling. The stovepipe was straight ahead, a long stretch. She wriggled forward, letting go of the edge of the roof and laying her arms on the roof, reaching for that pipe. She wormed her way forward, now with her belly on the roof and her feet off the chair. At last she grabbed the pipe.

Clinging to the pipe while her feet dangled, Kylie wondered just how she was supposed to get down from here.

Well, she'd worry about that later. She scooted forward until her pocket caught on the underside of the eaves. The hammer was snagged. Kylie squirmed and tried to get the hammer loose. She definitely should have worn pants for this job.

When she couldn't get loose, she let go of the pipe with one hand and carefully reached down, felt around for the hammer, found it, and tugged at it.

She slid and clung frantically to the stovepipe. There was fabric twisted around the hammer, and she was a while wresting it free of her pocket. Finally she got the blasted tool out and set it beside her on the roof with trembling hands. Honestly, she was shocked to see the shaking. Good grief, she'd lived through a Civil War battle. How could climbing on a roof bother her so much?

A crack of thunder startled a shriek out of her.

The hammer slid. She grabbed at it, then put it above the stovepipe to keep it on the roof. Having it fall so that she had to climb down and get it and start this whole mess over again was a dreadful thought. She inched forward again, until finally she was all the way up. Her feet no longer dangling. Nothing left to snag.

She looked sideways over the edge and remembered how much she'd hated being up here when she'd shingled the roof. Bailey had come up with her each time and lassoed her to the chimney. Only then could she work without fear of falling.

Well, Kylie wasn't going back for the rope, and that was that.

Her stomach twisted. It took every ounce of her courage just to hang on. The humid July day combined with her fear. Sweat dripped off her forehead, and the breeze told her she'd soaked through the back of her pretty blue blouse.

Finally, just because it was going to be so hard to go back, she forced herself forward. She tried to get to her hands and knees to crawl but was completely unable to do so.

Instead, she used her elbows to crawl forward in a way that reminded her of staying low on the battlefield.

Slowly she worked her way to the flapping board and used about five nails to secure it. Bailey would have needed one.

A gust of wind reminded her again of the strong possibility of rain. Twisting her head, she looked back to the far side of the roof. It wasn't a big cabin, but that stretch she had to cross to get back to her cobbled-together ladder seemed to be a mile long.

Should she turn around? Should she shove herself backward? Sweat dripped into her eyes, and she swiped her sleeve across her forehead. Fighting a growing desire to cry, Kylie started mentally screaming at her family instead.

Why was she up here?

Why had she listened to Pa when he'd come up with this half-witted scheme to use her war service to find fortune out West?

She knew why. She'd come home from the war exhausted. Traumatized. Pa had said he was going west and demanded that she come along. He'd said he would leave her behind if she didn't come. Like a child who needed her papa, she'd agreed.

A homestead took five years to prove up. But a soldier could take his years of service off those five years. Kylie had served two solid years in the Civil War. She'd thought she was being strong when she laid down the law to Pa. She'd come along and stay until she owned this piece of land in three years and then sell it to him, since he wanted it so badly. Then she'd leave and find a civilized life where no one asked a woman to climb up on a roof and wield a hammer.

Three years. She'd be twenty-three then. That was getting old not to be married and have a family of one's own, though not too old. She could wait those three years to earn that money and set herself up for the life she wanted so desperately. And not with some frontiersman. She wanted a settled country. So she'd put in her time, just like she had served her time in the war, and then she'd get out of here.

Three years and she'd been gone.

Three years until civilization.

Three years to the life she wanted.

Thunder sounded in the distance. She had to get down.

Backward. She'd just do everything she'd already done, only backward. With a disgusted toss, she heaved the hammer to the ground. She didn't have to carry that down with her.

With turtle-like slowness, she eased herself toward the ladder. She hadn't gone far when a crack of thunder sounded much closer. Thunder meant lightning, and here she lay in a prime location for a direct hit from a lightning bolt.

She backed up another foot, then another. Thunder cracked louder, closer. A flash of lightning lit up the noonday sky.

"Pa!" she shouted, something she'd never have the nerve to do if he could hear her. "When I get down, I swear I'll never do another man's chore as long as I live!"

Her voice broke, and her first tears fell. Well, there was no one to bother about that either, so she'd just cry her fool head off if she wanted to.

She cried and yelled and crawled another foot, then another. Glad she was alone so no one could see she was acting like a madwoman. So sorry she was alone, because confound it, she was going to have to figure out a way to save herself.

The thunder came even closer and louder and meaner.

Kylie wondered if this would be a part of her dreams now. Maybe this would push back the nightmares of battle and bayonets and a man's crushing, dying weight pinning her to the blood-soaked ground.

It would almost be a relief to have a new nightmare.

A sprinkle hit the back of her neck. Just how slippery did a roof get? Could she survive a fall? What if she broke her leg? Would she have to lie in the yard until help came? Or wolves came?

"Dear Lord," she cried as she glanced at the dark clouds and spoke past them to God, "don't let me be eaten by wolves because I was too stubborn to ride over to Shannon's and wheedle her into fixing my roof."

The sprinkle turned to an icy cold shower, shocking in the summer heat.

Kylie crawled faster and was nearly there when she slipped.

She froze, all except the tears. Those were falling as fast as the rain from the sky. Her sisters would mock her for crying if they saw it, but if they were here she wouldn't be stuck up on this roof, trying to decide between freezing to death or falling, then lying bleeding but fully conscious while wolves ripped apart her broken body.

She'd never been more disgusted with the Rocky Mountains in her life.

"Three years to earn the life I want," she shouted at the sky, or maybe at Pa, or maybe even at God. She slipped again and was afraid to move another inch or yell her anger to the sky.

God, get me down.

Better to pray to God than yell at Him.

She forced herself to move. She'd done that in the war. She'd learned to after the horror of her first battle and that man, dying, pinning her. She'd been frozen with fear and had never forgotten how useless that was. So the next time she'd kept going, even while she was terrified. Who'd have thought fighting in the war would prepare a woman for climbing down from a roof?

"Three years to earn the life I want." She said it prayerfully, repeating it this time like a true conversation with God. "Three years to earn the life I want."

At last she reached the stovepipe, grabbed it, and hugged it as if she'd found her mother's arms. Then it took her a long while to work up the courage to do what came next.

A crashing thunderbolt rolled across the sky overhead. The clouds had darkened the day, and she saw the lightning even while staring straight down at the wooden roof.

She craned her neck and took a hard look at the rocker, which was only partly visible over the roof edge. It was right where she'd left it, but would it hold? Had the rain made it slippery? Could she find it with her feet while hanging on to the pipe? Everything was harder going backward.

"Three years to earn the life I want." Definitely a prayer now. She needed more courage than she alone possessed to get down from here. And God was the only one here with her.

Swallowing hard, she remembered the battlefield, remembered how to keep going, and eased herself around, fighting with her tangled skirts. She had to stop clinging to the pipe with her arms and only grip it with her hands. Moving with care, finally, with her arms fully extended, her hips reached the eaves. She pushed out and let her legs dangle over the edge.

No chair.

Breathing in and out to calm herself, she searched with her toes, mindful not to kick the chair. Yet she couldn't find any purchase with her feet. She slid down farther, letting her arms stretch to their limit, until her belly was on the roof's edge. Still no chair to stand on.

It hadn't been like this climbing up. She'd grabbed the stovepipe right away while her feet were solidly on the chair, hadn't she? She just couldn't remember now.

Thunder sounded again, shaking the cabin a little. How much farther did she have to go? Had the chair fallen somehow when she had her back to it?

How strong was this stovepipe?

Didn't lightning bolts like stovepipes?

"Three years to earn the life I want."

The wind gusted and drove icy sheets of rain nearly sideways. Her whole body trembled with cold and fear and growing exhaustion.

She had to get down off this roof.

One more inch. Still no toehold. Her weight shifted, and she slipped down yet another inch. A scream ripped from her throat as she clutched the pipe with only her fingertips. The pipe groaned under her weight and began to bend.

Finally her toes touched the chair, but her feet skidded on the wet ladder-back. She flailed with her feet to get her balance and managed to kick the chair. She heard it fall to the ground.

She began losing her grip on the pipe, feeling her fingernails scraping along its length, and then lost her hold completely and fell.

Solid arms closed around her legs. "I've got you, miss!"

She slid over the edge.

The confident hold on her legs stopped her from hitting the ground. Then whoever had her gently lowered her to her feet. Her knees buckled. She sank toward the muddy earth. He swooped her into his arms again and carried her up onto the porch out of the cold rain.

Brilliant blue eyes met hers and echoed with strength and kindness. Looking into those clear blue eyes, she felt safer in that moment than she had since she was eighteen and had put on her britches, sworn her oath, and picked up a musket with her fellow soldiers. *Fellow* being a particularly important word.

She threw her arms around his neck. The only solid thing in the whole wide world. And she cried.

Aaron Masterson had his arms around the prettiest little thing in the whole wide world. And considering she was soaking wet, freezing cold, and crying her head off, that was saying something.

He'd had one good look at her eyes before they'd filled with tears and she'd buried her face against his chest. They were different, deep and haunting. Striped eyes that radiated out brown and green and gold from their black centers, like a flashing starburst explosion used to light up a field during night battles.

And one look at those eyes left him feeling as though his life had just lit up.

He had no wish to let go of her. And since he had no idea what else to do with her, and she was clinging to his neck like hanging on was a matter of life and death, he decided to hang on right back. A sheet of hard-blown rain hit, and he decided he could hang on somewhere other than out here.

He carried her inside the cabin.

A quick look at the tiny room showed a chair in front of a cold fireplace. And why wouldn't the fire be out? It was July.

But she was soaking wet and quaking like an aspen leaf. Juggling her around, he grabbed a chair by the small table in one corner of the one-room cabin and swung it over to the fireplace. He set it down with a thud and bent to put the little filly down.

She squeaked and held on tighter still. He thought she might be scared beyond thinking. It wouldn't be friendly to rip her arms off his neck. Besides, he had no real desire to do so.

There was a neatly made bed close to the fireplace. He dragged a blanket off it, wrapped the soggy little thing securely in the blanket, and settled in to hold her until she warmed up enough to notice a stranger had her.

He wasn't in any hurry.

He'd've liked a fire. He was soaked, too. The rain had caught up with him when he was closer to the cabin than town. So instead of riding back to Aspen Ridge, he'd rushed for shelter here, hoping Kylie Wilde would take him in for a spell, until the storm passed. But where was he? Had he been caught out in the storm and left his wife to . . . what? Climb around on the roof?

When he thought the word *wife*, his head cleared and he sat the little woman up, pulled her arms loose from his neck, and finally looked her in the eyes.

Blinking at him, he swore her long, thick eyelashes would wave in the breeze. Even soaking wet she looked beautiful.

Which wrenched a question out of him. "Where's your husband?"

She blinked again, faster this time as her eyes seemed to focus on him. She smiled, and one glorious dimple popped out on the left side of her face. "I don't have a husband."

Her voice was just a little rusty, and deep. Some of it was from the tears, but he thought some was her usual tone, and it scraped something nearly raw inside him.

Aaron was actually sorry she'd said that, because thinking she was married had cooled him down, and he'd badly needed to cool down.

"You saved me." Those starburst eyes looked at him as if he were a white knight who'd come riding to her rescue. Aaron couldn't remember a time he'd felt so heroic. He liked it.

"I'm glad I came along when I did," he said.

Her dimple disappeared. Her shining eyes dimmed. "I was falling. I could have broken a leg. I could have stayed there in the mud while the rain poured down on me. Wolves could have come and eaten me. I would have died." Her pretty eyes filled with tears, and she flung her arms back around his neck and wept into his shirt.

Well, he was already drenched; a few more tears wouldn't hurt a thing.

He let her cry until she got all that salt water out. When she calmed down, she rested her forehead against his shoulder and was quiet. Leaning on him.

God help me, she feels wonderful.

Finally she gathered her strength and sat up to meet his eyes.

He'd never seen such a pretty streaked mix of colors in a single set of eyes. Green and gold and brown radiating out. His ma had eyes like this color, although not this pretty.

She'd called them hazel. Thinking of his ma cut so deep that he focused all the more on this beautiful woman to distract himself from all he'd lost to the war.

And the distraction amounted to looking at this woman's lips and wondering if he hadn't ought to kiss her. That shocking thought broke whatever spell she cast and finally he blurted out his purpose for being here. "I'm looking for Kylie Wilde."

"I'm Kylie Wilde."

His head jerked back. "What? No, I'm looking for the man who homesteaded this property. Kylie Wilde."

"What do you want with . . . ?" Her eyes shifted left and right for a second. A sneaky look. "With Kyle. My . . . my brother Kyle is the homesteader here."

"You've got a brother named Kyle, and your name is Kylie? That must have been confusing for your family."

Shaking her head, Kylie muttered, "You have no idea."

"So it's Kyle who applied for this homestead using a Union soldier's exemption, is that right? Because I'm sure the paper work has Kylie on it. Not Kyle."

"A simple mistake, I'm sure. What else could it be? Kyle has terrible handwriting. No doubt it looks like he wrote Kylie, but why would he? I mean, he wouldn't. Not when his name is Kyle. Unless he just wasn't thinking. Or he was thinking about me. Daydreaming. Always daydreaming. That's my brother Kyle for you." She was babbling.

Aaron saw the minute she realized it and clamped her mouth shut.

Her shoulders relaxed, and she pressed against his shoulders with both hands. He let go of her reluctantly, and she stood. Turning to face the fireplace, she said, "Let me get this cabin warmed up. It will help your . . . I mean, our clothes dry."

"I'll tend the fire." Aaron moved quickly and started grabbing kindling. He noticed she let him do it without protest.

"We c-call my brother . . . Wilde most of the time to avoid confusion. Wilde got a two-year exemption for his war service."

Aaron knelt by the fire and moved tinder around, then struck a match. "Where did he serve?" The kindling caught and instantly began to crackle. Aaron looked over his shoulder at her.

"He was with the Ninth Army Corps, but they moved him around some because he did espionage. He spent most of the war under the command of General Parke."

Aaron's chin lifted, and his eyes flashed with pleasure. "The Ninth Army was at Vicksburg. I fought there, too."

Kylie swallowed visibly. Her eyes shifted again. "Well, according to my brother there were over fifty thousand men involved in that siege," she said. "I doubt we . . . that is, he . . . *you two* ran across each other."

"I fought with troops from West Virginia at first. My company, though, was all but wiped out and I was reassigned. We may have even met. The name's not familiar, but maybe I'll recognize his face. Espionage, huh? I did a little of that. I'll bet we can trade war stories. Where is he? I'd like to meet him."

"Wilde was on his way to do some hunting this afternoon. He . . . uh, if he gets caught in the rain, he might find shelter and be gone overnight."

"And leave you here alone?"

"I'm used to it."

"When will he get here?"

"I'm not sure. And when he does get here, he may not stay long. I never know about his comings and goings. But I'll tell him I met you. He rides into town occasionally. The next time he goes, I'll tell him to look you up."

"Or I can come by again another time." Like tomorrow. Aaron really wanted to come and see Kylie again.

She bit her bottom lip as if to stop herself from speaking.

"I need to, because I've been asked to help during the land rush."

"Help with the land rush? How are you helping?"

"I'm the land agent for Aspen Ridge."

Kylie seemed to inhale a bit too hard. Suddenly she was coughing, until he began to worry. "I hope you didn't catch a chill up on that roof. What were you doing up there, anyway?"

"Making repairs."

"Your brother left that to you?"

After too long a silence, Kylie replied, "A board needed to be refastened. It came loose after Wilde left. I saw the rain coming. I fixed it, but getting down off the roof about did me in."

"I have to inspect the homestead claims and make sure that after six months, they've got a cabin."

Something flashed in Kylie's eyes that Aaron couldn't quite understand. Anger maybe. With a rather exaggerated sweep of her hand, she said, "Well, you can see he does."

A gust of wind drew Aaron's eyes to the window. The rain had nearly stopped, and he had a long ride in the mud to get back to Aspen Ridge. The trails were none too good.

Besides, he wanted to stay so bad he thought it was probably best he left.

"Let me bring your chairs inside, Miss Wilde." He rushed out and grabbed the rocker. She'd kicked it over in the mud, but he'd seen the precarious way it was leaned against the house when he rode up. Proof positive that Kylie shouldn't be left here all alone.

A chair that matched the other one in her house stood soaking wet beside a hitching post.

Aaron grabbed both of them and brought them under the porch roof. There was a matching rocker on one side of the door, so Aaron put the wet rocker beside it and carried the chair inside.

He turned to see her kneeling beside the fire, adding a few small logs. The ends of her hair had dried, and it too seemed to be a mix of colors. Light brown with streaks of gold and honey where it caught the sun. Starbursts like her eyes. Curls bounced where the ends had dried.

Looking at her made him forget what he was doing, until she finished with the logs, stood and glared at him as if he'd done something to upset her. A far cry from the adoring way she'd looked at first. Somehow he'd gone from rescuing knight to unwelcome intruder in a few seconds' time. He had no idea why, and he was really sorry it had happened.

He decided then and there he'd apply himself to making her like him again, but best to do it while Kyle was here. This seemed improper, and he knew it wouldn't have if he didn't find her so attractive.

"I'll head back to town then, Miss Wilde." He realized he'd like to stay and see just how many shades the woman had in her hair. He knew when he started daydreaming about the color of Kylie's hair, he had to get out.

"Tell your brother to expect me one day soon." Aaron strode out of the cabin and caught up the shining black horse that'd stood ground-hitched all this time. He swung up and saw Kylie standing in the doorway, watching him.

He gave her a little mock salute and was surprised when she snapped a very tidy, very proper military salute right back at him.

Strange woman. Strange and fascinating. Strange and fascinating and beautiful.

He'd be back, and needing to meet Kylie's brother wasn't even half the reason why.

Aaron managed to stay away for a full day and a half. Now he rode for the Wilde homestead while daydreaming about Kylie's hair. He wished he'd stayed long enough last time for it to dry fully so that he knew every curl.

He'd seen enough to know it was streaked light and framed those vivid hazel eyes. It would accent her tanned skin and that one perfect dimple.

He'd seen a lot of beauty since moving to the edge of the frontier. The aspen that grew straight up the sides of the mountains. Pine forests so elegant they looked like a painting. He'd seen bighorn sheep leaping with impossible grace, and mountain grandeur that struck him to the heart.

But Kylie Wilde topped them all. He'd saved her from falling.

Saved her.

Aaron the Hero had rescued the Damsel in Distress. He couldn't wipe the smile off his face.

If her brother Kyle spent a lot of time out hunting, then

it stood to reason Kylie was often home alone. So maybe she needed help lifting something heavy or scaring off a cranky badger or patching the roof some more.

She definitely needed help with that.

Maybe she'd need to be rescued again, and there he'd be.

He'd left late enough that Kyle was probably home, but just in case, he urged his gelding faster. Kylie's pretty face was enough to make any man hurry.

The scent of pine made every breath a reason to enjoy life. It was beautiful in its way and helped him to ignore the deep pain of leaving his beloved Shenandoah Valley.

When he thought of Shenandoah now, he only remembered the ruins, the burned-down houses and barns, the missing livestock.

His family dead. All of them dead.

How had that memory come to him here, on his way to see Kylie? He kicked his horse from a trot to a gallop and bent low over the black's neck, riding recklessly on the narrow path so it would take all his attention.

For a stretch, Aaron clung to the huge gelding, one of the few thoroughbreds big enough to carry a man Aaron's size. That was why he'd taken it to war with him, and why it was still alive. Everything left behind was dead.

Aaron's fingers sunk deep in the shining black mane that flowed like silk. They streaked through the forest in a breeze created by a man running away from his memories. Aaron and his horse coming through the war unscratched, while his family stayed behind, left in their graves.

He raced along the twisting path, not wide enough for a wagon but well worn from horse hooves, and at last found himself at Kylie's house.

The trail he rode on opened up on her small clearing, coming in from the west. He hadn't had much time to look at it last time. In the heavy rain he'd seen Kylie dangling from the roof and raced forward to save her. After that, he'd been unable to look at anything else but her.

Today he could enjoy the pond he'd barely noticed before. It spread out on the south side of the cabin and reflected the green trees and the blue sky. There was a cascade of water pouring out of a rock with a constant rippling splash. It collected in the little rock basin, the water clear and clean. The cabin stood beside it, a small structure which didn't look large enough for Kylie and her brother to occupy. But Aaron knew that was often the case with these homestead cabins. The first buildings were modest to the point of being barely livable.

Though the building was small, it was well constructed and well tended—with the exception maybe of the roof. There was a porch with slender saplings forming graceful spindles that appeared to circle the whole cabin. Two rockers were on the south side, where a body could sit and look out at the pond.

The rockers swayed gently in the cool, early evening breeze. A pot of red flowers bobbed between them. There was a stretch about twenty feet long between the cabin and the shoreline. Someone—Aaron would wager it was Kylie—had created a rock garden full of native wildflowers and pretty stones to fill the gap. It made him want to sit on that porch and rest his eyes on the rocks and listen to the rippling music of falling water.

It was the kind of home that beckoned to a man.

Aaron had ridden in from the west with the setting sun.

The clearing was cast in deep shadows. A set of three steps led up to a front door centered between two open windows, their curtains fluttering back and forth. They were glass, which was rare out here. Not many took the time for curtains or glass, nor did they waste time making rocks into something beautiful.

He dismounted, hitched his horse, and jogged up the steps a little too eagerly. He knocked on the door, but there was only silence. No one was home.

The way Aaron's spirits plummeted told him just how eager he was to see Kylie. He walked around to the south side of the porch, facing the water, and sat on the rocker. He relaxed into the seat, noticing how intricately it'd been made. Wilde was a top-notch carpenter. And he'd poured a lot of time and talent into this homestead and garden. Odd because most around here gave their houses a lick and a promise and set to building barns and corrals, attending to their livelihood before their comfort.

Aaron had visited enough homesteads to see a clear priority repeated over and over, even when there were women and children present.

The porch was so comfortable, the scene so charming, and the summer evening so pleasant, Aaron let the moments tick by in pure pleasure. He didn't consider for a single moment giving up on the missing Kyle—or his sister. He would contentedly sleep right here in this chair if need be.

And then, as the dusk settled in, to his right, the same direction Aaron had come from, a shadow separated from the trees. Aaron stood and watched the shadow form into a man. He was carrying a long gun. A Sharps repeating rifle, if Aaron wasn't mistaken. Aaron didn't make a move for his Colt, always close at hand. Instead, he watched very carefully. The man showed no inclination toward taking aim, and it stood to reason that a man hunting would be armed.

"Hello, are you Kyle?" Aaron made sure he sounded friendly.

"I am," the young newcomer replied in a voice that sounded almost falsely coarse. Then Wilde stepped closer, and there was no way to deny he was Kylie Wilde's brother. The resemblance was so strong, Aaron was struck hard by it.

Wilde had on a wide-brimmed felt hat, pulled down over his eyes. Aaron saw the man was dirty, no doubt from a long day of hunting. Smudges showed on his face and his clothes. He was much broader in the shoulders and an inch or two taller than Kylie, but under all the dirt he had a face almost too pretty to be male. He bore a strong resemblance to his sister.

Wilde stepped up onto the porch, nodded at Aaron without raising his hat brim, then adjusted the rocker unnecessarily before he sat himself down on the other rocker, which was now a good five feet away.

"My sister said you needed to check on the building. Well, you can see it's done." Wilde fell silent. Rocking, his face tilted down, the hat covered him nearly to his mouth. Add the shadow cast by the setting sun, and Aaron wasn't sure if his first reaction about the young man's resemblance to Kylie was accurate.

"Need anything else? It's been a long day and I'm worn clean out." It was also clear that Wilde wasn't prepared to be nearly as friendly as his sister, and he wasn't going to invite Aaron in or shake hands or even remove that hat.

"Your sister said you spent time at Vicksburg. I did too. I had a hankering to talk to someone who'd seen some of the war."

"The war's a memory best left behind." Wilde fell silent again.

Aaron realized the kid wasn't going to say any more. Usually men out here in the West were a little more welcoming. Aaron hadn't been here long, had only come to the area a month ago, but he'd visited a lot of homesteads, and most homesteaders were lonely and eager to sit a spell and talk to a visitor. Of course maybe Wilde was just naturally quiet, or maybe his sister was enough company for any man.

"Your sister lives here with you, then?"

Wilde tensed in a way that sharpened Aaron's attention. Something was definitely wrong with the kid. He'd written his age down as twenty-two. And he'd served two years and been mustered out in the spring of sixty-five. Aaron did some quick math and decided Wilde had probably lied about his age. A lot of sixteen-year-olds enlisted in the Army. Two years of fighting, starting at sixteen, and a year since he'd gotten out and headed west meant the youngster was only nineteen years old. He needed to be twenty-one to file on a homestead.

"Uh, yep."

Aaron wasn't a real stickler for that rule. If a man said he was an adult and did the work of an adult, then Aaron wasn't about to make him prove his age. No way to do that anyhow. A baby didn't have a birth record most of the time. Aaron sure as certain didn't haul a document around with details on it.

But if the kid had lied about his age, it might explain why he didn't like a land agent dropping by to palaver.

Which left Aaron frustrated because he didn't even care about Wilde, or his age, or even his unfriendly manner. He really came out here to visit with Kylie again. That young lady was the prettiest thing he'd seen in a month of Sundays. She was mighty friendly, too. Unlike her brother.

"Where is she tonight?"

The kid gathered himself in a strange way, almost like he was pretending to relax, and Aaron had the strangest feeling that whatever Wilde said next was going to be a lie. Aaron had studied men in the war and considered himself a good judge of truth and lies.

"My two brothers and my pa all homesteaded out here." Wilde's voice wavered strangely. Aaron looked at him closer, trying to see past the shadows cast by his hat and the porch roof. "Kylie is at my brother Shannon's house for the night. She's a big help to us all, and we all welcome her."

Shannon Wilde, another name Aaron had seen on his list. Bailey Wilde was there too, along with Cudgel Wilde. And their homesteads were in a neat row, situated so that they blocked the trail to some fertile canyon land and claimed this fine watering hole. The Wildes were savvy homesteaders. With their 160-acre claims, counting that canyon land, they controlled thousands of acres of prime water and grass.

"So Kylie said you were at the Siege of Vicksburg, is that right?"

Wilde leaned forward, clenched his hands, still tucked into gloves, between his splayed knees and looked at the porch floor. "I was there." He glanced up, then turned right back toward the floor. "I spent time behind enemy lines, gathering intelligence."

"You mean you were a spy? Kylie spoke of something like that."

"Kylie's got a big mouth." The statement sounded loaded with sarcasm. Aaron's eyes narrowed. What kind of man spoke so disrespectfully of his sister? It was easy to study Wilde, since he was doing his best not to look at Aaron.

He'd been a skilled army officer and considered himself a good land agent. He put all his skills together and had a suspicion. Standing, he said, "Well, I'll be going, then."

Wilde didn't rise.

Aaron closed the space between them and thrust his hand out, offering to shake Wilde's. A stretch of seconds went on far too long, and finally a gloved hand came out and took Aaron's hand. With a single jerk, Aaron dragged the youngster up and whipped that stupid hat off.

Honey-brown curls streaked with yellow tumbled down around Kylie Wilde's falsely padded shoulders.

She squeaked and looked up at him, her starburst eyes wide with fear.

I . . . I can explain." Kylie had no idea how she was going to explain.

"No need. I think I see things more than clear." Aaron's eyes flashed with contempt. "You're using your brother's identity to claim a homestead, using the service exemptions to get out of doing your five years. That's fraud, Miss Wilde. A woman is free to homestead on her own; you're just lying about your time in the Army to get out of two of those years. You can go to prison for that."

"P-prison?" Kylie tugged against his iron grip, but it didn't give at all.

"And you can certainly get thrown off this land and be barred from ever homesteading again. Does your brother know that his years of danger and sacrifice are being stolen and used by his lazy, dishonest little sister? Is he in on it or are you cheating him too, on top of cheating your country?"

"Let go of me." She jerked her hand free of his, leaving her glove behind.

Her hands were so obviously feminine, she'd had to keep them covered with the buckskin gloves.

"Did you know that besides being a land agent, I also have authority from the government to make an arrest? I *don't* have to let go of you." He threw her abandoned glove down on her porch floor and grabbed her wrist.

Kylie froze at the word *arrest*.

"In fact, I can arrest you right now and haul you off to jail."

His jaw tightened, and his grip on her wrist hurt. He leaned down until their noses almost touched. "Is your brother even alive, Miss Wilde? Or did he die fighting to preserve the Union, and now, like a vulture, you're profiting from his death?"

"Stop right there." That last part was just too much. "I *did* have a brother, who died in that awful war. Everything I've done for the last five years has been because of Jimmy. I will not let you stand there and accuse me of profiting from his death." She no longer wanted to escape. Instead, she was tempted to blacken his eyes.

"Jimmy? You said his name was Kyle. You said he was at Vicksburg. You said he was a spy."

"My brother's name *is* Jimmy, you idiot. *I'm* Kyle!"

Aaron jerked his face away from hers. "You're Kyle? What?"

"And I was at Vicksburg, fighting with the Ninth."

"But women can't . . . don't . . ."

"Women *can* and *do*, Mr. Masterson. I'm living proof that there were women serving right there alongside the men. I faced all the danger I was called to face, and I earned that service exemption." Her voice grated until it could have ground glass.

Aaron's face was a picture as he lost the last of his anger. She could see his mind working, sorting through the surprises of the last few minutes. "And you couldn't have the exemption because you're a woman."

"You tell me who's being cheated. I say *I'm* being cheated out of what I rightfully earned."

"But women can't earn the exemption. They aren't allowed to enlist."

"Well, I *did* enlist. I used my own name too. I never told a single lie. I dressed as a man, but no one ever asked me if I was one."

"Didn't you have a physical?"

Kylie's snort was purely rude. "The physical was a man looking at me. He said my name, saw me standing upright, and waved me through."

Nodding, Aaron said, "I remember mine. That's how it was."

"I served my country honorably and I will not let . . ." Her voice broke, and then she steadied it. "When my brother died, we . . . I went to fight in his place. He believed in this country enough to give his life to preserve it. And I could do no less." Of course, she'd have never considered fighting, even with her grief over Jimmy's death, if Pa hadn't goaded her into taking up arms.

The prying land agent shook his head just briefly as if trying to shed water, then stepped back and sank into the chair he'd abandoned. Kylie had hoped he'd storm off and leave her. She wanted him to go away. But if he did, he'd go straight to Aspen Ridge and disallow her claim. So maybe she didn't want him to go away just yet.

Not sure what she wanted, Kylie sank into her chair, much like Aaron had.

Whether he'd decided to hear her out, or he was stunned by her revelations to a point that he needed to sit down, at least she still had a chance. She might not be able to save herself, but maybe she could save Shannon and Bailey.

"I say I have a right to that Homestead Service Exemption."

Aaron held up a hand at her. "Just be quiet for a minute."

"I enlisted in the Army and served two full years."

Aaron glared at her. "Will you give me a minute to think?"

She glared right back. "I ended up as an aide to one officer or another. I made a point of moving around every chance I got, hoping they wouldn't realize I was a woman."

"I said be quiet!" Aaron snapped. "If you're trying to convince me to go along with this fraud, let me try and figure out how I can do it."

Since that sounded far more hopeful than Kylie had expected, she clapped her mouth shut.

A furious light flashed in Aaron's eyes. "I just don't believe it."

"You don't believe I served? You think I'm lying?"

"Why wouldn't I? You are lying and have been all along. 'I never told a single lie' is a pile of horse dung, and you know it. If I say I believe you fought in the war, then all that proves is that every man who looked at you for more than ten seconds and didn't realize you were a woman must have the intelligence of swamp moss and the eyesight of a bat."

"Most of the men I worked for were too busy to pay me much mind."

"Whether it's true or not, you have no record of what you've done in the war. None that will stand up to scrutiny, because there is no war service available to women. But I know how to solve this."

Kylie's heart lifted. "You do?"

Aaron nodded. "It's not that hard. Women are allowed to homestead. With two pen strokes I can mark you as a woman and strike through the service exemption. It'll take you five years but—"

"No!" Kylie made a fist and was so tempted to throw it, she wondered if she'd lived disguised as a man for too long. Women didn't go around punching people.

"Why not? You'll be here just the same, working your land."

"No I won't!" Kylie's temper exploded. She flung her arms wide and almost smacked Aaron in the face, which would have suited her just fine. "I will be gone. Long! Gone! Completely and forever gone from this stupid homestead. I'll be living back East in a civilized city, wearing pretty dresses and not having to fight for every bite of food I eat. I hate it here!"

"It isn't that long," Aaron yelled right back. "You can put in two additional years. That's what an honest, decent person would do."

Oh, she really was going to punch him. "Stop saying I'm not honest and decent."

He leaned toward her. "Well, I don't know about decency.

Walking around in those britches isn't what I'd call decent. But you can't even pretend like you're honest. Now settle down and be reasonable about how we can solve this. I'm offering to bend the rules mighty hard to help you keep this land."

"You aren't allowing me to use my years of service. How is that helping?"

"It ignores the fact that your claim is fraudulent, which keeps you from getting tossed off your land and forbidden from homesteading anywhere else in the whole United States of America. Not to mention it'll give you the excuse you need to cast aside those shameful britches. I think that's a mighty big help."

"I told you—"

A rumble sounded from the dusky woods, the sound of hooves . . . a lot of them.

Aaron jumped up, and Kylie did the same. He heard tree limbs snapping, a shout. He whirled to face the trail he'd ridden in on, shoved Kylie behind him, and drew his Colt in a single motion.

Kylie pressed close to his back. She must've been standing on her tiptoes and peeking over his shoulder, because she said in his ear, "What is it?"

Aaron almost forgot those rumbling hooves, as Kylie Wilde's warm breath on his ear was a powerful distraction.

Only almost.

He'd learned to be a mighty cautious man in the war, and his skills had only sharpened since he'd set out across the continent. He'd never carried a gun back home in Virginia. Now he never went out of his boardinghouse unarmed.

Another shout.

"A lot of western men, even evil ones, will treat a woman decent. But if they see you wearing trousers, they might think you're no better than you ought to be."

"I'll put my hair up under my hat again and just be Kyle," she whispered, and Aaron almost turned around to drag her into his arms.

"That's a half-witted idea if ever I heard one. It would take an idiot, and a blind one at that, to believe for more than a few minutes that you're a man." A whip cracked from the forest, followed by a man shouting words Aaron couldn't make out.

"I tricked the entire Union Army for two years."

Another shout was closer still.

"Get inside. Get a dress on. And wash your face!" He could see now that she'd deliberately smeared dirt on her face as part of her disguise.

Yet another shout sounded so close, Aaron knew whoever was coming would be here in a matter of seconds. "A dress just might save your life."

Aaron had commanded men in the war, and apparently Kylie had been commanded, because she snapped to it.

The door clicked shut behind him. He spotted Kylie's Sharps rifle leaning against the porch railing and grabbed it. The cold, heavy iron felt good in his hand.

A desert-brown longhorn steer burst from the edge of the woods into the clearing. It bawled as it charged for the pond beside the house, trampling over Kylie's rocks and flowers. A second longhorn was right behind it, then five more, then too many to count, all crashing and kicking up their heels as they raced toward the water. Dust kicked up until Aaron was breathing in grit. The mooing and thudding of hooves were deafening in the choking dust.

Through the haze he saw the rock garden and flowers destroyed under the pounding hooves. A bull veered straight for Aaron, deflected from getting a drink by the charging mass of cattle. The bull looked to be coming up the steps, through Aaron and into the cabin. At the last second it whirled toward the water, bellowing and shoving smaller cattle aside. Spring calves frolicked among the older animals, kicking up their heels, turning the rush to water into playtime. The cattle crowded together in the narrow space between the cabin and the pond. One of them kicked and smashed a stretch of the south porch railing.

A cow shoved against the porch by the herd, leapt up onto it, and faced Aaron. She pawed the wooden floor with her front hooves and lowered her head to present a stretch of sharp horns. For a tense moment Aaron wondered if the cow, which probably weighed a thousand pounds, would charge him. Then the red-and-white beast turned as if remembering the water and jumped through a hole in the railing, taking another chunk out. She disappeared into the herd. They all had a big C branded on their rumps.

A rider trotted into the clearing, saw him, and pulled his brown thoroughbred to a halt so suddenly it reared. Even in the dimness of the evening, it was the work of seconds to take the newcomer's measure. No doubt this was the man in charge. Though Aaron had never seen him before, he'd been in Aspen Ridge about ten minutes before he'd heard of him.

Gage Coulter, owner of the C Bar Ranch.

Riding the shining stallion he'd brought with him from Texas. It was said he was a man who'd moved here because Texas wasn't big enough for both him and his pa. He owned five thousand acres and controlled fifty thousand more, and from the coldly stunned look on Coulter's face, it was more than clear that he thought he controlled this pond, too.

Coulter dragged his broad-brimmed hat off his head. His overly long brown hair matched his horse so perfectly they seemed to be a pair. Coulter rode straight for the porch while longhorns spread out along the edge of the pond. The first cattle to the water were shoved in with a loud splash that sounded beneath the hooves that near shook the ground.

Others waded in on their own. The bawling eased as the drinking began. The blue water turned to mud.

Coulter's eyes jumped from Aaron to the cabin to the barn and back to Aaron. "What's going on here?" he asked.

The words cracked like a whip, but somehow Aaron was tempted to smile. He had a feeling it was a rare thing for Coulter, one of the biggest cattle barons in the state, to be taken by surprise.

Aaron didn't know the land all that well yet—he was new to the area still—but he'd bet that pond was a mighty dependable watering hole, and one Coulter used regularly. Especially at the height of summer.

As the cattle trampled all the things that had made this tidy homestead so pretty, Aaron lost the urge to smile.

It was clear the man had no idea that someone had homesteaded this little corner of his territory. Aaron holstered his Colt and switched the Sharps to his right hand. Coulter might be a powerful man, even a tyrant, but he was no killer. There was trouble here, yet it wouldn't come to shooting.

The door behind him slammed open, and he already knew Kylie well enough to grab her as she charged around him.

"You get your cattle off my land!" Grabbing her didn't stop her from talking.

Glancing down, he saw the real Kylie for the first time. Not soaking wet. Not dressed like a man. He had no time to enjoy the sight, though it was a fine one.

"*Your* land?" Coulter's light gray eyes—cold as ice—looked at her, then at Aaron, clearly dismissing Kylie's claim of the land being hers. Coulter would want to deal with the man of the family. "No nester is going to come in here and squat right on top of one of my best water holes."

"No cowboy is going to come here and insult me on my own property," Kylie sassed back.

Coulter gave Kylie a look of disgust, then hesitated and looked closer. Coulter shook his head fast, and his eyes went to Aaron. "You and your wife have ten minutes to clear out. Eleven minutes from now I'm burning every building on this place."

"I don't own this land, Coulter, she does. I'm not her husband. I'm Aaron Masterson, the new land agent in these parts." It occurred to Aaron that it might have been wise to claim he was married to Kylie. It might make a difference in the treatment she could expect from Coulter. Now Coulter knew Kylie lived here alone. But Aaron was no liar. "I came out to check if Miss Wilde was following the law."

Coulter didn't react to Aaron's knowing his name. His arrogance was such that he expected to be known . . . and feared.

"Miss Kylie Wilde homesteaded this property all right and legal." Well, mostly legal. "You won't be driving her off or burning her out. I operate under the authority of the United States government, and we won't turn a blind eye to any crimes committed against homesteaders. Now, *you've* got ten minutes to get your cattle out of here. You also owe Miss Wilde for damage done to her property."

A gasp of outrage told Aaron that Kylie was just now noticing what all the thirsty cattle had done. "My flowers! My rock garden! I hiked these mountains for days, digging flowers and transplanting them."

With an unexpectedly agile move, Kylie tore loose from Aaron's grip, rushed past him, and stormed down the steps. She wore a dress now. A real pretty pink one. But her feet were bare, and there was still a little dirt on her face. That didn't stop her from being beautiful to behold. And it made Aaron like her all the more that she hadn't taken time to fuss with her appearance before she came out to defend her home.

"Your cattle broke my porch railing. Do you know how long it took Shannon to make that?" The little spitfire marched right up to Gage Coulter's tall stallion. "Get out, Coulter. You're trespassing."

Her hand balled up, and if her head hadn't come about to Coulter's knee, she might've punched him.

Coulter's eyes flashed with annoyed amusement as he swung down off his horse. "Are you planning to use that fist, miss?"

Aaron jogged down the steps to stand beside Kylie. The strength of the urge to step between Kylie and Coulter shocked him. He wasn't a man to stand by while any injustice was done, and for certain he couldn't let a woman be mistreated, but this need to take care of Kylie went deeper. It went to an instinctive, almost animal depth. Fighting back the desire to step between the two, Aaron tried to let Kylie handle this. Could she do it? It took toughness out West, and she seemed more inclined to blushes and weeping. Of course, in a standoff with Coulter, a pretty dimpled cheek and a few well-placed tears might be just the thing.

Coulter's eyes left Kylie, and he had to look up a couple of inches to meet Aaron's eyes, which gave Aaron smug pleasure. Coulter was a tall man, but Aaron was taller. Coulter's gaze went to the Sharps rifle in Aaron's hand, then his eyes flicked back to Aaron's. "How about you? Are you planning to use that gun, Masterson?"

"This only turns into shooting trouble if you make it such."

The men riding with Coulter were busy tending the herd, but they were listening. They looked like tough western types, who rode for the brand. Aaron figured any shooting trouble that started here would end badly for him. Worse yet, Kylie would be right in the middle of flying lead.

"Mr. Coulter, I own this land. Get your cattle and leave." Kylie plunked her little fists on her hips. She stood there barefoot, her hair flying free.

Coulter studied her far too long before he said in a voice far too friendly, aimed only at Kylie, "Call me Gage."

Aaron didn't like the sound of that. "Coulter, you've got the reputation of a law-abiding man, and right now you're breaking it."

Coulter's icy eyes went back to the cabin and the barn.

"My cattle are thirsty, and they won't be driven away from that watering hole until they've had their fill."

"Your cattle aren't my problem." Kylie wasn't returning Coulter's friendliness, which Aaron appreciated.

"I didn't know anyone'd moved in here. I've used this watering hole ever since I came out here in sixty-one."

"The year the war started." Kylie's tone went from unfriendly to downright cold. "I hear Texas in your voice, Mr. Coulter. What were you doing running for the West while the rest of the South, including your home state, was fighting?"

"That wasn't my war," Coulter growled. "War is for fools, and I had no interest in fighting side by side with fools."

Aaron glanced at Kylie, who looked at him. They stood side by side.

Kylie looked away from him to the milling herd, which was starting to spread out from the water and graze around the edges of the clearing. One of the longhorns chose that moment to swing its ten-foot spread of horns too close to the south porch. The steer snapped off another length of railing, as if it were a twig.

"Your cattle seem to be past their thirst. Get out of here, and if you come here again—unless you're as much a coward about your ranching as you were about the war and you turn to back-shooting—you can expect me to meet you with my rifle blazing. And unlike a coward, I promise I'll look you right in the eye when I shoot you out of the saddle." Kylie had just said words that would make a man go for his gun if another man had said them.

Coulter's gray eyes flashed with fury. Aaron's hand tightened on the Sharps.

That expression passed, which said a lot about Coulter's control. He was a man with a temper, but he didn't let it run him. Instead of rage, Coulter gave Kylie an admiring look. "Doubt it'll come to a gunfight between us, pretty lady. I've got other ways of ruling my range." He gave her a smile. "In fact, maybe it's time I took a wife."

Without waiting for a response, which was just as well because Kylie's mouth gaped open in shock, Coulter grabbed his pommel and leapt into his saddle with a movement so smooth, Aaron felt a spark of envy.

"Head 'em out, men. We'll drive 'em to the stream on east of here."

As if they saw their chance to do damage slipping away, two calves butted heads and staggered into the porch and smashed what was left of Kylie's railing.

He looked back at Kylie and tugged the brim of his hat in farewell. "This ain't over, Miss Kylie."

The cattle bawled and churned up the dirt as Coulter and his men wrangled them into motion. Soon they were gone—men, horses, and cows pushed out of Kylie's yard.

Nothing left but a cloud of dust and utter destruction.

Kylie stood frozen, grim-faced as she watched Coulter's men wrangle the unwilling cows out of her yard. If her Sharps had been full of birdshot instead of bullets, she might've filled Coulter's backside.

They were a while getting the animals to clear. When the last rider's horse vanished into the forest, Kylie's knees gave out.

Aaron caught her or she'd've slid straight to the ground. He swung her up in his arms—the man had touched her more than any other man in her life—and toted her like so much baggage to the rocking chair. One was knocked over; the other had managed not to get hit by a cranky cow and stood ready for her. Expecting him to put her on the chair, Kylie was surprised when Aaron sat himself down and held her in his lap.

"Well, this is as improper as can be." She said it, but her hands were trembling, and her insides were twisted up. She made no move to put an end to the situation.

"Just rest a minute." Aaron held her tight as if to restrain her, though she wasn't trying to escape. "We can go back to being proper when your heart stops slamming."

A dry chuckle drew her attention away from her upset.

"What about any of this mess is funny?" She didn't have the strength or even the desire to push herself to her feet. Instead, she rested her head on his chest.

"I'm thinking of you in trousers. You're a fine one to speak of what's proper."

"How did my life go so terribly wrong?"

"You speakin' of the trousers or Coulter or the homestead fraud or a woman going to war or being in my lap?"

Speaking into his shirtfront, she waved one hand in a hopeless gesture. "It's all of a piece."

He didn't respond to that, and she went on staying right where she was. Finally she gathered enough strength to think. Which led her to ask, "When Coulter said 'this ain't over,' what do you suppose he meant? Of course it's over if he's a law-abiding man."

"All kinds of ways to bring pressure to bear on a situation, a lot of them mostly legal."

"Mostly?" Kylie's voice was as weak as her knees. "And here you are with the power to tear my homestead away from me."

And her sisters' land too, since they were all homesteading under the service exemption. Masterson could probably even take Pa's land if he knew Pa had supported his daughters in their lies. Kylie almost snorted at the word *supported*. It'd been his idea from the start. He'd manipulated and loaded on guilt and, in a roundabout way, promised—if they minded him perfectly—he might even love them someday. They'd all fallen in line with this homesteading scheme, just as they had all marched off to war.

"Yep, and for all the trouble I can bring, still you're sitting in my lap."

Which gave her the gumption to stir. Masterson relaxed his hold and didn't try and keep her in place, which pinched her feelings for no good reason.

She stood.

Aaron moved so she could have the rocker to herself. He flipped the other rocker onto its runners and sat beside her. The dusk had turned to dark, and the moon had risen enough to see the grit that hung in the air and the destruction done by Coulter's cattle.

"What a mess." She sank into the seat, throwing her arms wide, feeling helpless to face the damage. "Those cattle even messed up the pond. Mud's all stirred up."

"It'll settle. And the railing's knocked apart, but the boards aren't broken. I can repair it without much trouble. Then you'll move your rocks back in place and plant more flowers. Some of them are still there, just uprooted. The cow chips"—and there were a lot of them—"even make good fertilizer."

"Ugh. My whole life is turning into fertilizer."

"It can all be fixed."

Neither of them sprang into action. They sat rocking, looking over the stretch of land surrounding the pond. In the gathering darkness they could no longer see the water, but the sound of it cascading still sent up its soothing music. The dust thinned until it wasn't a chore to breathe the mountain air. Even all trampled up, it was a pretty spot.

"So what am I going to do?" Kylie finally felt steady enough to think of the trouble she faced.

"First I rework your homesteading claim and drop the exemption."

"No! I don't want to spend five years out here. I'll be too old to find a husband."

Aaron laughed, and she wanted to punch him. "If it's a husband you're looking for, you can probably round one up without much trouble. And out here, he'll have his own land, and you can just let this go."

"But I don't want to stay out here!" she nearly shouted. She covered her mouth and fought down her panic. Speaking more quietly, she said, "I don't want to live where the nearest city is a lifetime away and there's no such thing as a bonnet shop or ladies who gather for tea parties. I want to go back East. I want civilization."

A small, humorless laugh escaped from Aaron as he rocked and took in the view.

"What's funny about that?"

"Just that I had that. I had a nice farm with a city a short train ride away. My ma even had a tea party now and again. I had civilization."

"How could you stand to give it up?"

"When I went home after the war . . ." Aaron shook his head and turned silent.

A breeze cleared the rest of the dust as they rocked, the only sound the creaking of their runners. Aaron was silent for so long, Kylie decided he wasn't going to say more.

Finally, when she was fighting the temptation to nag him, his rocker stilled. "When I went home . . . I ran headlong into so much hate."

He crossed his chest with one arm and propped his opposite elbow on it, then rested his fist on his mouth as if to stop the words. Again Kylie waited.

"I fought for the Union. Everyone around me split their loyalties. Half the neighbors went with the North, half with the South. Even our land was split between Virginia and West Virginia. The South used the area I lived in to launch attacks on the North. The Union Army finally got tired of it and razed every house within a hundred miles of the border."

"Including yours?"

"Yep." He rocked again for a time. "I still don't know who killed my family. But they were sure as certain all dead. Ma and Pa and two little brothers, who were too young to fight, and two older sisters who were near marrying age before the war ripped away every marriage-aged man in the state. They all stayed home. I thought they were all safe. The boys too young. Pa too old. My ma and sisters too female."

Kylie snorted.

"They all stayed safe at home and died. I went to war and survived. And when I came home, half the neighbors wanted to spit on me for being part of what the Union did, while the other half hated me for not fighting harder for the Union and ending the war before the area was destroyed. The farm was completely leveled, not a building left standing. The thought of rebuilding, alone, was overwhelming. Old friends turned on me. There was one who—"

The abrupt way Aaron quit talking made what he *wasn't* saying seem like the most important part of the story.

"There was one who what?" Kylie asked quietly.

Instead of answering, he said, "I left. I'm doing this job for an old commanding officer, and when it's done I'm going to move farther up into the mountains. Find a nice stretch of land and gather a herd of cattle and live where no one hates me . . . leastwise not for something I didn't do."

"Farther into the mountains?" Kylie felt sick at the thought of a place more remote than this. "You mean you could find a place lonelier and less civilized than here?"

"You use the word *civilized* a lot, Miss Wilde. But I lived a short train ride from Baltimore, Washington, D.C., New York City, and Philadelphia."

Kylie gasped. It was her dream come true. "You did?"

"I sure enough did. Some might call them the most civilized cities in America. But what I saw when I got home was a whole lot less than civilized. I want no part of it."

"New York City, a short train ride away . . ." Kylie felt light-headed.

Aaron didn't respond to that. "There are places farther out than this, and I'm going to find them. As soon as I fulfill my promise to get this land rush settled, I'm going west. I've heard there are some beautiful high valleys no white man has ever seen. I'll set up a ranch in some pretty mountain valley with just me and my cattle and the eagles and the mountain goats. Maybe I'll build next to a pond so full of fish they'll jump right on my line. I'll build a tight cabin against the winter wind, add a porch just like this one, and get myself a rocking chair."

His chair creaked quietly as he stared toward the pond. A contented man.

An idiot.

Kylie's overwrought nerves finally calmed. She heaved herself to her feet, and her knees didn't knock.

She found herself disgusted with men.

One without the wits to appreciate a farm back East.

One without the decency to keep his cattle off her land.

One without the love to let his children live as normal women ought.

She plunked her hands on her hips and glared at the only man close enough to feel her wrath.

"If you mean it about fixing my porch, then get to it. I'm going to get some shoes on and then see how much of my rock garden I can repair." She stomped around to the door, and as she went to swing it shut, she heard that rocking chair still creaking. Aaron hadn't moved at all.

Fine, she'd fix her home herself, even if she had to scare nails back into her porch railing. And if she couldn't, she'd get things fixed up like she usually did. She'd finagle her sisters into doing it.

Kylie stepped out of her cabin—her lonely, stupid cabin—to look at her pond. With Aaron gone, and so far out, she didn't hesitate to step outside in her nightgown. Nearly every night, if the weather was fine, she'd spend a few moments out here and say her evening prayers and do her best to find peace with this lonely life in the wilderness.

Tonight the loneliness was the worst it had ever been. It wasn't just that she was utterly alone; it was how far she had to go to be with someone. Her spending time and being held by Aaron today, even her yelling at Gage Coulter, underlined that.

Her throat ached with unshed tears as she looked at the moonlight casting a bright path across the pond. She would cry until that pond overflowed if she didn't know what a waste it would be.

A breeze rippled across the water and fluttered her white gown. Her hair billowed out as she leaned against a corner post on the porch. Aaron had done a nice job of fixing it, once he'd finally started.

Her head rested against the post.

"God, this can't be the life you mean for me to have." She whispered her words to the wind and hoped God heard them and answered. Some days she felt so far out in the wilderness that even God couldn't possibly find her.

That notion was foolish, and it woke up the need to be closer to God in her soul. There was no other way to be close to Him anyway. Before she could focus her prayers, a strange rustling drew her attention to the woods, in the direction Aaron had come from. Coulter had come from that way, too.

She turned to look, and the rustling stopped.

It was the silence that sent a chill up her spine. There were always noises in the woods, of course; she was used to that. Foraging critters. Bushes and trees swaying in the wind, branches rubbing and dancing.

But the way the noise had stopped when she'd turned her head . . . Goose bumps broke out all up and down her arms. She could see nothing in the dark forest that surrounded her home. But someone was out there, she was almost sure of it. She didn't have Bailey's and Shannon's skills, but she was a decent outdoorswoman. That wasn't the wind and neither was it an animal. Every instinct she possessed told her someone was out there.

Fear shook her as she realized she was being watched.

Coulter? Not Aaron . . . no, it wasn't possible he'd do it.

Kylie strained to see into the impenetrable black. For just a split second, with the shifting breeze and lifting of a sheltering branch, she saw a pair of eyes reflect the moonlight. They didn't glow like a raccoon's or a wildcat's would. And they were at a man's height.

Then they blinked—or did they close?—because they vanished as suddenly and completely as if she'd seen a phantom.

It scared her out of her frozen state, and she ran for her cabin, feeling as if all the hounds of hell were racing straight for her. She dashed inside. Running footsteps gained on her. She slammed the door and threw the heavy brace to bar it shut. Without pausing, she rushed to the windows, one on each side of the door, and locked the shutters.

No one could get in now. Her sisters had built the cabin solid. Taking deep breaths, calming herself, the worst of the terror eased. She tried to think! Had she imagined it all? Had she really seen eyes? Or was there some critter in a tree at a man's height and she'd mistaken it for a man?

Not all wild things had eyes that glowed in the moonlight.

Yes, that had to be it. She'd imagined those footsteps.

And those eyes. She'd definitely seen them, but what man would stand in the dark, watching her?

She had to have let her loneliness fill in something frightful. As her breathing slowed, she thought she heard a sound in the darkness.

"Kylie."

So soft, only a whisper. So still it could have been the wind gusting between the trees.

Shaken, she stood still for long moments. But there was no more sound, until finally she knew it really had to be a trick of her mind.

Looking down at her trembling hands, she knew that as tricks went, it had been a very good one. She'd gone out to stand on the porch without lighting a lantern. Now she knew that to light one might make her visible if someone found even the smallest crack in the logs of her cabin.

Terrified to think of those watchful eyes—eyes that were almost certainly just some forest creature—she went to bed, determined to find a way out of this life before it drove her mad.

Kylie swung off her little gray mustang. She'd ridden to Shannon's first thing when she'd gotten up—wearing a dress. Yes, she was desperate for company, but there was more. Meeting Aaron, meeting Coulter, their both knowing she was a woman, the trouble with her claim, the fright caused by her loneliness last night.

She'd awakened this morning determined to make some changes.

Today was the beginning of a new day and a new life. She felt reborn. She was a woman and she was going to live like one, and no one was going to stop her.

Aaron had left the night before, intent on changing her homesteading papers to disallow her the service exemption. So there was no point to her manly masquerade anymore. Still, she rode astride. It wasn't the first time she noticed that although she longed to dress and behave as a woman, there were a few things she didn't like. Riding sidesaddle was one bit of nonsense by which she refused to abide.

"Kylie!" Shannon's voice whipped Kylie's head around, searching for the source. "Help!"

Shannon was nowhere to be seen.

"Behind the barn."

Her sister wasn't visible now, but Shannon must've seen Kylie ride up.

Kylie dropped the reins of her horse and ran, knowing from the tone of her sister's voice that there was trouble. She rounded the barn to find Shannon neck-deep in the fast-moving stream that ran off her mountain. She was clinging to a fat sheep.

"Shannon, for heaven's sake." Just as Kylie yelled, Shannon's head went underwater.

Kylie picked up speed, sprinting for the stream. Her skirts were heavy enough they'd pull her under. Kylie tore at her buttons and shed her dress while she ran. Next she shed her petticoat. She wore only a shift by the time she reached the water's edge.

Kylie wasn't a strong swimmer, and while the time pounded at her, she took the time to rip her shoes away, knowing anything that held her down might be the thing that cost Shannon's life. Kylie ran into the water and was instantly swept along. Shannon's head appeared again and in the same place. She still held that stupid sheep.

Flailing more than swimming, Kylie hoped Shannon got a good breath while her head was up. "Let the sheep go," she hollered.

"I can't!" Then Shannon went under again.

Can't or won't? Kylie wasn't sure. She knew Shannon's

favorite Bible verse was the one about the good shepherd giving his life for the sheep. Shannon might be taking that a bit too far.

The current swept Kylie along. When she came even with Shannon, there'd be a single chance to grab her, because Shannon wasn't moving. Something had her anchored to the spot, even while the water battered at her and tried to pull her under.

Kylie drove herself, got every ounce of strength out of her arms. A wash of water went over her head just as she inhaled, and she choked as she forced herself forward.

Calm down. Remember the war. Keep going. Ignore the fear.

Why did so much in her life remind her of the lessons she'd learned in the war? That didn't seem fair.

Kylie kicked with all her might and grabbed Shannon's shirt as the water swept her past. Her grip held.

"What happened? Why are you out here with that sheep?"

They both went under. The sheep kicked Kylie in the stomach, and Kylie fought to keep from gasping while she was submerged.

When they broke the surface of the water, Kylie saw that Shannon's skin was white, her fingers wrinkled. How long had she been stuck out here fighting for her life?

"This sheep is saving my life. He's the only thing keeping me from drowning. I fell in and rode the current, and then my foot got tangled in a branch or root or something."

Kylie realized the kicking sheep was swimming, trying to escape but also keeping Shannon from going down for good.

Shannon produced a wickedly sharp knife. "Cut me loose."

Kylie shuddered to think of diving down, maybe getting entangled herself. But there was no choice. She took the knife and clung to it as if it were life itself. Which it very well might be.

"Which leg?" They both sank down, and it was a long time before their heads were above water again.

"My right, at the ankle. I tried to slip my ankle free, but it's knotted up somehow."

Kylie sucked in as much air as she could, using Shannon's body to drag herself down, using one hand so the other could hang on to the blade. Fumbling, her eyes open in the clear water, she saw thick roots twisted tight around Shannon's ankle. They came up from the stream bed. Kylie tried slipping Shannon's booted foot free, but the roots were caught all through the hooks on the boot, until it was impossible to get the boot off. Kylie had to cut Shannon free. Desperately trying to figure out where to start, she caught hold of the root closest to Shannon's leg and slashed. A white nick appeared in the brown coil, a tiny one.

She cut again, hacking and sawing. The wound on the root deepened. Sawing with every ounce of her strength, she added a fraction of an inch at a time.

Her lungs began to protest. The root wasn't going to give way easily.

Kylie was halfway through when, finally, she had to come up for air. She clung to Shannon as she bobbed to the surface. If she got washed downstream, she'd be a long time getting to the bank, walking back upstream and starting this all over again. Kylie came up and was face-to-face with that dumb sheep.

Her conscience nudged her on that. The sheep, with

its thin legs thrashing at the water, was keeping Shannon alive. She was too tired and too battered by the current to keep treading water.

"I'm almost done," Kylie panted—not telling the truth, dragging air into her starving lungs. She prayed for the gumption to go back down there and get on with saving her sister.

Shannon nodded. She trembled all over. Kylie wondered how long Shannon could hang on. Pulling herself down, she chopped and sawed some more with the blade. At last a root gave way, but there were at least two more needing to be cut.

Kylie started again, battling her sister's snare. A second root gave just as she ran out of air again and surfaced. "One more!" She gasped for breath. "I'll have you free the next time I go down." Her heart pounded with exhaustion and fear.

Shannon, who was far tougher than Kylie, barely responded. Her fingers were clamped deep in the wool of the sheep. Even the sheep looked exhausted. Kylie had to do it this time. Shannon had nothing left. The sheep, well . . .

Shaking her head, Kylie inhaled deeply one more time, and then down she went. One last root bound Shannon's foot, this one the thickest yet. It was like hacking through a tree branch. She gouged and sliced, knowing she fought for her sister's life. At the halfway point she knew she'd need more air. But Kylie kept at it, pushing herself to the limit.

Her lungs near to bursting, with a desperate slash her knife snagged on the almost-severed root and tore out of her hand. It was gone instantly, vanished downstream. There was no way to get it back without letting go of Shannon. No way to break free this last root without the knife.

A silent scream slashed Kylie as surely as a knife. Her clumsiness had just condemned her sister to death.

The root was still too thick. Yanking on it frantically, Kylie knew there was no give. The knife was gone. Her air was gone. Above her, Shannon quit moving. A splash told her the sheep was swimming away. Shannon had lost her grip on the animal.

Kylie surfaced to see Shannon's head underwater and pulled her up. She was unconscious, limp. She couldn't even think of letting go, getting to shore, and coming back with another knife. Shannon would drown.

A sharp cry drew Kylie's attention to the shore in time to see Bailey cutting into the water with a shallow dive.

Bailey was here! Bailey would save them both. Tears burned Kylie's eyes, even as she clung to Shannon and both of them clung to life. Within seconds, far faster than Kylie, Bailey reached them.

"Shannon's ankle. It's tangled in a root. I was cutting it, but I dropped Shannon's knife."

Bailey drew her knife from the scabbard she always wore, clamped it in her teeth like a pirate, and vanished underwater.

Before Kylie could even give a thought to Bailey going to work, Shannon snapped free. Because she was holding her, Kylie and Shannon were both swept downstream.

Kylie, with her poor swimming skills, fought to keep Shannon's head above water and used one hand to flail away, trying to get to the shore. The banks got dangerously high before long and would be impossible to climb, so their getting to shore fast was vital.

Then Bailey was there again. She flipped Shannon on

her back and grabbed her under her chin in a way that left Shannon floating on top of the water. "Swim for shore fast, the banks get steep. I'll bring Shannon."

In other words, *Leave. You're useless. I'll handle everything, just like always.*

Kylie was too exhausted to block the pain of Bailey's dismissal. She took the barb straight to her heart, let Shannon go, and struck out for the shore. Bailey got to shore, even dragging Shannon, before Kylie did. Finally, about twenty yards downstream of where Bailey reached shore, Kylie managed to wash up into shallow water. Getting to her hands and knees, she crawled across the small but sharp river rocks. They tore at her knees, but she had no strength to stand.

Looking back, she saw Bailey kneeling over Shannon, who lay facedown. Bailey pressed on her back rhythmically.

The sight of Shannon, unconscious, possibly dead, gave Kylie the strength to get up and run, in stumbling steps, to drop at Shannon's side. Kylie opened her mouth, ready to ask for orders. Bailey would assign her something to do, and Kylie could feel like she was helping. Before Kylie could speak, Shannon gagged, and water erupted from her mouth and spewed onto the rocks. Because she was facing Bailey, the big sister also got a bellyful of water and vomit on her pants.

Bailey did everything well. She even took this bit of unpleasantness without reacting as she continued to press on Shannon's back. Another gush of water came out, and Shannon drew in a ragged breath, then vomited again but only a bit. The breathing became a cough. Each breath sounded painful, but moments passed as Shannon's heaving settled down. Taking steady breaths again, her eyes flickered open.

"Bailey, you came."

Another arrow to the heart. Every syllable Shannon spoke said clearly that Bailey's arriving had been her wish. Her big sister was the one she wanted to see in a time of trouble, not her foolhardy little sister.

Kylie didn't take it as hard as Bailey telling her to leave. She'd found the walls that guarded her heart.

They stayed by Shannon's side for a while. Finally, with feeble movements that told how completely spent Shannon was, she pushed herself to her knees. With Bailey's support on the left and Kylie's on the right, Shannon staggered to her feet. Only then did she notice Kylie, even though Kylie had her arm around Shannon's waist and bore as much of Shannon's weight as she could.

"Kylie." Shannon smiled. Not for the first time, Kylie thought how beautiful her dark-haired sister was. It was said she took after their ma. No men's clothes and short hair could conceal her beauty. "Kylie, thank you. Thank you."

Shannon flung her arms around Kylie's neck. Shannon was the sweetest of the three of them. The mother in many ways, with a soft heart for motherless sisters and woolly sheep. It was like Shannon to think of others and make sure Kylie's feelings weren't hurt. Even if she had been useless.

"Bailey got you cut loose. I couldn't do it." Tears threatened again, but Kylie knew the disdain Bailey had for crying.

Shannon let go of Kylie, rested one hand on her cheek, then turned to Bailey. "You both saved me. Thank you." Shannon's voice broke, but she steadied herself, not one for weeping.

"Let's get you back to the house." Bailey slid an arm around Shannon's waist, just above where Kylie had her. Kylie's eyes met Bailey's, and it was a good moment, the three of them together. Kylie shook away the hurt of Bailey saving the day while Kylie failed. She hoped to one day be strong enough that her sister's criticism couldn't hurt her feelings.

They were so different.

Bailey with her fierce pleasure at living like a man. Shannon with her soft heart and those stupid sheep. Kylie with her love of feminine things, her discontent with their ridiculous masquerade, and her stubborn dream of living near civilization. They did a lot of sniping at each other, but it was over surface things. Where it really counted, they never forgot they were sisters. Their bond had been forged in their lifelong battle with their pa. In their shared sacrifice in the war. In their mourning over losing their beloved big brother, Jimmy.

Pa had become nearly crazed when Jimmy died in the war. He'd always been a curmudgeon, but the family had limped along decently enough—until Jimmy died.

They'd been living with the results of Pa's unending grief ever since.

Kylie knew she'd allowed herself to be manipulated, not just out of Pa's grief but also out of her own. A big part of her had *wanted* to fight the South. She'd *wanted* to avenge Jimmy's death . . . and then she'd faced the reality of war. By the time she had a real notion of the horror of it, it was too late. After her first battle, she'd decided to confess that she was a woman, even though to do so would reveal that she'd lived all this time camping with and living with men.

It would be a disgrace. But before she could confess, she found a way to stay in uniform but avoid battle. So she'd stayed in and served out the duration. She'd found some satisfaction in her work as a spy. She'd endured two years of it before the fighting ended.

The three sisters had been sent in different directions. And now here they were, still living a lie. Until yesterday.

Kylie felt like she'd been born again. She had a chance at a new life and she was taking it. She thought of that awful moment last night when she thought a man had watched her from the dark woods. She had to get out of here before she started jumping at every shadow she got near.

Part of her determination to start a new life included her skirts and admitting she was a woman. She suspected her sisters weren't going to be happy about it.

Once they got Shannon inside, Kylie ran back to fetch her dress and return to decency. Shannon changed into dry things while Bailey shed her wet clothes and sat at the kitchen table, wrapped in one of Shannon's blankets. With her clothes drying by a fire Bailey had quickly built, Shannon warmed up coffee. The three of them sat at the table in silence. Shannon and Kylie regaining their strength. Bailey pouring coffee and generally taking care of all of them like she usually did.

Shannon lifted a steaming cup of coffee to her lips, her hands mostly steady, and took a sip. "Did either of you see if my sheep made it to shore?"

Bailey snorted. "You and those stupid sheep."

"That sheep saved my life. I love them now more than ever." Shannon didn't take offense—she'd heard it all before—but neither would she ever part with her fluffy friends.

Bailey noticed what Kylie was wearing. "What are you doing in that dress?"

"Here's something you're not going to like." Kylie saw no way out of warning them, although she wasn't one to face trouble if she could possibly sneak her way out of it.

"He found out you aren't a man?" Bailey erupted from her chair. "How many times have I told you to keep your men's clothes on, no matter what?"

Kylie didn't share how she'd met Aaron the first time, the leaky roof, the soaking wet dress, the tears.

"I saw him sitting on my porch when I came in. I hung back in the woods until it was dusk. I was dressed right and proper in my britches. He figured it out anyway."

Of course he'd been looking for a woman, so that might have helped him along on his way to pulling off her hat.

"And I haven't told you about Gage Coulter yet." Kylie was surprised to find she was enjoying outraging her bossy big sister.

"Heard of him," Shannon said. She did very little talking; probably a near drowning had worn her clean out. "King of the cattlemen out here, it's said."

Bailey snorted. "For now."

Kylie arched a brow at her sister. "You planning on taking over that title, Bailey?"

"I might." Bailey pulled her cup closer, and a look of ruthless ambition crossed her face.

Kylie shook her head. "You worry me. Back to . . ." Kylie stumbled when she almost said Aaron. She didn't want her sisters getting the wrong idea about her and

Aaron Masterson. "Back to the land agent. He's changing my homestead claim over to one not claiming the exemption."

Saying it out loud made Kylie nearly sick when she thought of spending five whole years out here. She'd already done six months. They'd come out before winter had fallen last year. She'd ticked off six months and seen two and a half more years stretching before her. It had been a length of time she'd been determined to endure. She could do it. Stay in this place for thirty more months, then sell the land to Pa, give him his wish, her part in building his empire in honor of Jimmy, and in exchange for enough money to move away. But now to add two more years?

She couldn't stand for it.

But how to make a life for herself elsewhere? She'd made no secret of the fact that she intended to sell her land the moment she had clear title. And besides, she'd earned that exemption. She'd served her time honorably.

"What about us?" Bailey asked. "Did you tell him that Shannon and I are women?"

"Kylie wouldn't do that," Shannon said in her motherly chiding voice.

"No I didn't." Then Kylie felt like she had to add one more worry. "Gage Coulter knows I'm a woman, too."

Both her sisters narrowed their eyes at her.

"He called me a nester. He'll think the same of you, whether you're men or women. And he hinted that he might be willing to . . . to marry me to get my claim."

Both her sisters slammed their cups down with a loud click.

"Marry you?" Bailey said. "How're you going to keep

him from finding out we're women if you ask us to be bridesmaids in your wedding?"

"You, married to a rancher." Shannon started laughing. Her blue eyes flashed, and pretty dimples popped out on her cheeks. How could anyone believe she was a man? "A big old land baron who's never leaving his land. You'd be trapped out here for good."

Shannon laughed so hard, Kylie wanted to smack her.

"Better than *you* being married to a rancher." Bailey rolled her eyes at Shannon. "You and those lousy sheep. Any rancher worth his lariat would have a conniption."

"You're the one who'd make a rancher's wife, Bailey," Kylie said. "Why don't you marry the cattle king?"

"I'm not getting married." She tossed the comment off, yet there was a darkness to it that Kylie didn't fully understand.

Something had happened to Bailey during the war that she'd never talked about, and Kylie had no doubt her big sister would never marry.

"I got mighty tired of taking orders in the Army," Bailey said. "Mostly orders given by fools who put an infantry soldier's neck on the line for no good reason. And I've had a bellyful of taking orders from Pa. I'm not signing up for a hitch with a husband. I like the way I live, and no man would put up with it."

The three of them looked at each other in silence for a while. Finally, Kylie said, "So if none of us is willing to distract him by marrying him, what are we going to do?"

Aaron looked at Kylie's paper work and hesitated. To make it honest would be simple. He wouldn't have to change a word, except for where she'd claimed the service exemption, and he could deny that by striking a line through it.

It wasn't right. She'd put in her time. She'd fought in the war, and he knew the price a soldier paid. He picked up his pen, then put it down again without making the mark.

She'd written her name down correctly—Kylie—so not an ounce of ink told a lie. He decided he needed to talk to her once more before he denied the exemption. He admitted too that he didn't mind having an excuse to see her again.

Aaron pulled on his suit coat, put the papers in a leather pouch, and headed out. He met Gage Coulter, who was reaching for the door to the land office.

Chafing at anything that slowed him down, Aaron said, "I'm on my way out. Can this wait?"

"No, it can't. I want to see the homestead claims on a

bunch of nesters I've found on my land. I need to find out if their standing is legal and where their property lines are."

"I'm not going to stand by while you harass legal homesteaders, Coulter. So any help I give you comes with a promise to protect these folks."

Aaron knew good and well that Coulter was thinking of Kylie. Wait till he saw where the rest of the Wilde family had homesteaded. There was a land rush on and a lot of claims had been staked. The Wildes, though, had homesteaded in roughly a straight line. Except for Kylie, they'd claimed acres with good meadowland and fine water sources. They'd picked very wisely, ignoring heavily wooded stretches, so there were many miles between the properties. But a knowing eye could see that their holdings ended up cornering a big chunk all along the western edge of Coulter's range.

"I'm not asking you to help me break the law." Coulter waved a dismissive hand in Aaron's face in a way that was mighty irritating.

It reminded Aaron that his family had owned one of the largest, most prosperous farms in Virginia not that long ago, and Aaron had learned how to be arrogant at his father's knee. The war and its aftermath had knocked that out of Aaron, but now here stood Coulter, a man who'd run from war and gotten rich while others died preserving the Union.

And here was Kylie Wilde, and Aaron denying her a service exemption, with Coulter having spent the war years cornering all this western land.

"I want information," Coulter went on, ignoring how

his words affected Aaron, or more likely not caring. "I want to know what I'm up against."

"Nothing fancy to tell, Coulter. Miss Wilde has a legal claim on that land. It's about half lake, and most of the rest is mountains."

"I know my land, Masterson. I don't need you to tell me that. I want to know the exact boundaries. I want to know what other land is open for homesteading and what parts of it I can buy to stop nesters from encroaching. Now let's go look at your maps." Coulter moved toward the door.

With a sudden lack of good sense, Aaron reached out lightning quick and grabbed Coulter's wrist. "I'm closed. I'll be back in the office later." After he'd ridden out to Kylie's for a talk. "Check back then."

Coulter wrenched loose and for the first time really looked at Aaron, who added, "It's too bad someone has to put their hands on you to get your attention. No one's going to file a homestead claim while I'm locked up, so nothing's going to change while I'm gone."

Squaring off in front of Aaron, Coulter glared at him. This wasn't a man used to hearing no. And on the rare occasion someone had the nerve to tell him no, Coulter wasn't likely to accept it.

Well, he'd be hearing it today. Then Aaron's normal good sense warred with his annoyance, especially when that good sense told him nothing Coulter was asking for was illegal or even immoral. A whole lot of Aaron's irritation was coming straight from the way Coulter had looked at Kylie and said, "Maybe it's time I took a wife."

Aaron knew good and well that he could ride out to Kylie's another time. It wouldn't change a thing. Without glancing at his pocket watch, he knew it was close to noon. "Come and eat with me, Coulter, or sit and have coffee while I eat."

Aaron tucked the leather pouch holding Kylie's papers into his inner suit coat pocket, and they crackled with every move he made. He wished now he'd made those changes before there was a chance of Coulter seeing them. Because if he saw them in their original form, he'd have all he needed to accuse Kylie of fraud and get her thrown off her land. And by law Aaron would have to take Coulter's side.

"I can listen while I chew, and I can tell you what I know about homesteading boundaries without my papers and maps in front of me."

Coulter didn't want to come along. He wanted to get in that office and start buying up range land he considered his. Aaron had a feeling Coulter was going to be mighty unhappy when he saw all the homestead claims dotting his property. The Wildes were by no means the only ones.

Aaron would just as soon have this fight on a full stomach.

Finally, maybe because Aaron held Coulter's gaze like an equal, or because Coulter knew it was the best offer he was going to get, or because he was just plain hungry, Coulter quit his glaring and turned to walk down the few steps to the street and go with Aaron to Erica's Diner.

Kylie's papers rustled with every step Aaron took.

"Why do you persist in tending these smelly sheep, Shannon?" Bailey wrestled one of them toward the pen. They weren't interested in being herded.

"A sheep saved her life, Bailey." Kylie had a spring lamb under each arm. She looked down at the one in her right arm, and it looked up and tried to nuzzle her. Kylie didn't mind them so much, but she drew the line at kissing. "You're wasting your time trying to talk her out of loving them today."

They really were cute little things. Stupid and high-smelling, but Kylie understood why a person—her softhearted sister to be exact—might get attached to them.

"You're always wasting your time, not just today." Shannon had tamed them too well. They nearly had to be picked up one at a time and carried into the barn, which she did every night. It was only midafternoon, but due to her nearly drowning, Shannon was worn out. Kylie and Bailey had stayed to help with the sheep.

Shannon had changed into dry clothes, and they'd eaten an early dinner Kylie had thrown together. When Bailey had wondered aloud if Shannon shouldn't leave the sheep out overnight, with the wolves and cougars, Shannon had asked for help getting them penned.

"Ramuel himself saved my life." Shannon almost dropped the small ewe she had in her arms when she pointed to the white ram Bailey pushed along. The fluffy critter was still dark from its soaking swim.

Kylie looked at the high-and-mighty ram and snorted at its stupid name.

Bailey shoved the stubborn male toward the pen, and he let out a ferocious *Baa!*—well, ferocious for a sheep. He leapt forward, lashed out his hind legs, and managed to clip Bailey hard on the leg.

"Ouch!" Growling and rubbing her kneecap, Bailey

goaded the animal forward, her golden-yellow eyes—a brighter color than Kylie's—flashing hot with temper. "He's still a puny thing compared to a normal, respectable animal like a cow or a horse."

Shannon had seven adult sheep and a few lambs. She knew them all by name, which made Kylie wonder how her sister was ever going to eat them.

"You said he fell in after you pulled him out of a mudhole left from the rainstorm." Kylie pointed at the mire in a backwater of the fast-moving stream. "Then you fell in trying to grab him and snagged your foot. He saved you, but he's also the reason you got into that mess in the first place."

Kylie carried the last of the babies inside. "How do you ever manage this yourself?"

Shannon shrugged. "Mostly they just follow me like little shadows. But they're stirred up today. Even if they do give me trouble and I have to carry them in, I like doing it. I like having a few moments with each of them."

Bailey groaned.

"And I sold the wool for quite a bit of money. The market is good enough that I'm going to be able to buy a milk cow." Shannon sounded smug as she swung the gate.

"Now, cattle make sense." Bailey came out of the barn last, fastened the door, leaned her arms on the top rail of Shannon's corral fence, and stood there scowling. "A milk cow's a good thing to have around. But I can give you a milk cow, Shannon. You don't have to buy one."

Bailey had been here since last fall, the same as Shannon and Kylie, but somehow, through hard work, bartering, scooping up a few head here and there when homesteaders quit their claims, rounding up maverick cattle that ran wild in the mountains, and having a nice spring-calf crop, Bailey now owned nearly fifty head of cattle. Add to that, Bailey's claim was right smack on top of the opening to a narrow-necked canyon, a canyon that opened into a vast grassy pasture Bailey said was over five thousand acres. Bailey's claim blocked anyone from having access to the canyon, which made it hers.

If Bailey wanted it—and she did—that canyon would soon be teeming with Wilde cattle. Given half a chance, Bailey would soon challenge Gage Coulter for biggest cattleman around.

And a cattle baron's competitor, who lived disguised as a man, wasn't about to agree to marrying him, so Kylie gave up on that method of solving their problems with Coulter.

"I want a gentle cow." Shannon shook her head good-naturedly. "Yours are all longhorns, most of them wild as deer and mean as grizzlies."

"I've got one I can milk." Bailey always found a way.

"I've seen you do it. It's like milking a tornado." They all laughed at Shannon's very apt description. "I appreciate the offer, but one of your cows would gore me before I got a drop of milk out of her."

"Why don't you try milking your sheep, then?" Honestly, Bailey had raised sarcasm to an art form.

"I heard tell of a man in town with a little red-and-white jersey cow, who had twin heifer calves. I exchanged a note with him, and he said the second calf is taking all the milk the man planned for his family. I have already arranged to buy that calf as soon as it's weaned and I've raised just a little more money. So I'll have a young calf I can gentle from the beginning.

"You won't get any milk out of it for two years." Bailey pulled her gloves on as she headed for her buckskin mustang with its long black mane and tail. It stood beside Kylie's gray, both of them staked in the middle of a circle of grass.

They'd come out here in their pa's covered wagon, pulled by his team of oxen. Bailey had ridden out on her own horse, and before they'd even built their cabins, she'd rounded up half a dozen wild mustangs, broken them to ride, and given her sisters their own mountain-bred ponies.

Bailey had found the perfect life for herself. Too bad it was perfectly wrong for Kylie.

Aaron would have made up an excuse to ride out to Kylie's claim if he'd needed to, but lucky for him—or unlucky, depending on how a man looked at it—a reason presented itself that made the visit necessary.

He leaned lower on his horse and urged it to a gallop. There were stretches of the trail to Kylie's that were fairly worn and safe, and other parts with branches sagging low over the trail and stones studding the ground.

He needed to beat Coulter there and warn Kylie of what was coming, though she seemed like a bright little thing, so she probably already suspected.

And maybe he was a fool to hurry. Maybe Kylie would grab up a proposal from a wealthy, powerful man and never look back.

Of course, Kylie wanted to go back East. And Coulter wasn't about to offer her that.

He came to the clearing by Kylie's house and saw a scruffy blue-roan farm horse tied to Kylie's hitching post.

Then his eyes went past the horse to a wiry gray-haired man, who was dragging Kylie up the porch steps, his grip tight on her arm.

"No! No, I won't do it!" She yanked against the viselike hand, but the man was relentless.

"Let her go!" Aaron shouted.

At the sound of his approaching horse, the man turned. Kylie slipped from his grasp and fell, landing on her backside on the top step. Aaron didn't let up his horse's speed as he closed the distance, racing toward the man assaulting Kylie.

Aaron halted only steps from the ugly old-timer and leapt to the ground, placing himself in front of Kylie, who scrambled to her feet.

"You're under arrest." Aaron had his gun drawn before he'd made a conscious decision to reach for it.

"Don't shoot!" Kylie clamped a hand on Aaron's gun arm.

"Why not?" Aaron looked at her, surprised. Aaron had heard of women who let men abuse them. Was she going to take the side of this low-down skunk?

Kylie frowned. Even with a sad expression she was still so pretty. She had a bonnet hanging down her back. She wore a faded blue gingham housedress, covered by a white apron, and Aaron noticed a small trowel on the ground near some flowers. It looked like she'd been busy replanting her rock garden.

She turned to glare at the old man. "Because he's my pa."

"He's your what?" Aaron said.

The man nodded. "I do what I like with my own child, and no man will tell me different. Now, you ride out of here and don't look back." He spun around toward Kylie. "And you get inside and change back into your britches."

"Pa, this is Aaron Masterson." Kylie sounded weary, like maybe she was used to her father dragging her around and not even all that upset about it. "He knows about the homestead exemption. He found out I enrolled as a man, and he's refused to let it stand. In fact, I suspect he's out here right now with the revised form, looking for me to sign it. Did you change my papers?"

Aaron's heart still hammered, and he was having a hard time letting go of the pleasure of arresting the man who'd been treating Kylie roughly. It might matter a bit that a pa grabbing hold of his daughter's arm wasn't exactly against the law.

And it mattered some that Aaron wasn't allowed to arrest anyone. Finding out someone wasn't obeying the rules of homesteading and disallowing his claim wasn't exactly the same as being a sworn-in sheriff. Still, father or not, this was no way to treat a lady.

Shoving that to the back of his mind, he focused on Kylie's question. He hadn't yet made the changes to her papers. "Kylie, I have to. Coulter was in town, snooping through every scrap of paper. If he'd seen that you'd originally filed as a man, he'd have been out here accusing you of fraud within hours."

"So now I've got to spend five years earning this blasted hunk of rock-infested wasteland?" Kylie kicked at one of her rocks, not a big enough one to break her toe, thank heavens. She reached for the rock she'd kicked, lifted it, and hurled it into her lake. It hit with a plop, with ripples spreading out in a circle.

"I told you to pick a different piece of land." Kylie's pa took a threatening step toward her. "You're never gonna grow nothing out here. And I told you to leave your britches on and keep your hair short."

The man stopped before Aaron had to stop him. Kylie didn't flinch or act particularly afraid. Aaron hoped that meant her pa was all bluster. But there was no denying the old codger was right about the land. This spot was beautiful, but it was no place a homesteader would normally pick. Of course the woman showed no sign of farming or running a herd or even hunting. Near as he could tell, her only livestock was a horse and she hadn't planted so much as a garden. How did she live?

"It's too late." Kylie's shoulders slumped in defeat. "Stop yammering at me, because all it does is make my ears hurt."

She stalked past both of them toward her cabin, climbed her porch, and went to sit on her rocking chair, shoulders slumped, the very image of defeat.

With a deep sigh, she said, "I can't do it, Pa. I can't make it out here five years. I told you I'd give you three and that's almost too long. But five, no."

"You're not quitting on me." Her father charged toward the porch, radiating fury. Aaron kept up. Ready to step between Kylie and her pa if need be. "Not after all the work we've done to build this cabin and take care of you."

We? Aaron could only guess that meant Kylie's brothers and her pa were keeping her here, providing her with food, doing whatever it took to keep this homestead active. And if you added this water source to the land he'd seen claimed by the three Wilde men, it did make a nice stretch of land, very nice.

"Pa, I'll be twenty-five. A spinster. I'll never find a husband if I wait until I'm that ancient. I'll be almost too old to have children."

Since Aaron was twenty-nine, he thought that was a bit unkind. Harsh, even.

"Your ma was twenty-five when you were born. A woman's got a lot of years to have a family."

"Ma died when I was only ten. That's proof she was too old." Kylie looked at her lap. He'd seen her angry. He'd seen her scared. He'd seen her soaking wet and exhausted and crying her eyes out. But he'd never seen her like this, so spiritless. Her pa was draining all the fire out of her.

"We need this piece of land to honor Jimmy. Are you going to betray him, along with your family? If you loved him, you'd want to build a big spread that would be a fitting memorial to him."

Jimmy, her brother killed in the war.

Kylie looked up and studied her father for a moment. He'd come to stand in front of her, between her and the pretty view she loved.

Aaron got the notion that her pa had stood between Kylie and the things she loved most of her life. Yet she didn't seem scared of him, not like she would if he'd struck her. But emotionally he packed a wicked punch.

Kylie's eyes shifted from her pa to Aaron, who stood off to the side. "Aaron Masterson, may I introduce you to my father, Cudgel Wilde."

Aaron had a second to wonder if Cudgel was really the old man's name, or was it a nickname he'd justly earned?

"Pa," Kylie went on, "Aaron is the land agent in Aspen

Ridge. He saw through my disguise. He's rewritten my homestead claim to reflect that I'm a woman."

He hadn't yet, but Coulter had left Aaron no choice.

Her pa looked at Aaron, then at Kylie. "Which means you lose your years of service, to be taken off the five years needed to earn out your claim. Which means, because you're more interested in yourself than your family, you're quitting. Do I have that about right, little girl?" Cudgel's eyes seemed to burn through all of Kylie's resistance.

The old man shifted back to Aaron. "It ain't right, you know. My girl fought in that war. She gave two solid years to it. She deserves that exemption, and what's more, I think you know it. You may stand there all proud of yourself for following the letter of the law, but you're ignoring right and wrong. My girl didn't lie about herself when she enlisted. She even wrote her name down right."

Aaron remembered he'd gone to add the *i* to Kyle's name, but it was always Kylie. She'd written it down right. She'd only said her brother's name was Kyle to confuse him that first rainy night.

"She told the truth when she enlisted and when she filed her homestead claim. Now you'll make her work out the whole five years. How is that right? Why shouldn't she claim her years of service like any man who fought?"

Aaron felt Cudgel using all his skill at guilt and manipulation on him, and Aaron had to admit the man was talented.

"You might be able to convince me to look the other way, Wilde. It doesn't seem right that she fought but gets no credit for it. But I'm not your only problem. Gage Coulter wants her gone. In fact, I talked to him. He wants you all gone. And there are a couple dozen other settlers on land he sees as his. He isn't going to give up quietly. He'll jump on any reason to run Kylie off this land. And finding out she's been passing herself off as male would be reason enough for him."

Cudgel's face turned red, and his fists clenched. "Rich tyrant. Thinks he can tell honest folks how to live."

"Not all that honest, Mr. Wilde," Aaron said wryly.

With his teeth bared, Cudgel went back to badgering his daughter. "Is that how it's gonna be, Kylie? You'd betray your family and your brother's memory 'cuz a rich man, who thinks he's a king, tells you to go? Is a few more years of living on this land too much to ask of you? Where's your loyalty to family? Where's your heart for your brother? You want to go find a man who will marry you, but you betray the only men you say you love, Jimmy and me. What man's gonna love a woman with the heart of a betrayer?"

Kylie's eyes were locked with her pa's. They brimmed with tears. "I don't mean to betray you, Pa. And I love Jimmy."

"Then prove it to me, girl. Stay here and help our family build something big and strong. It'll be all ours, and you can help with that or you can stab us all in the back."

"That's enough." Aaron couldn't hold back the words. He could barely hold back his fists. "Kylie isn't betraying you by—"

"No, Aaron. Stop." Kylie surged out of her chair and stepped as if to block Aaron from swinging.

The old man was half Aaron's weight and a good ten inches shorter. Aaron hadn't really planned on throwing a fist, but Kylie's stricken expression stopped him from saying any more. Most likely a girl didn't like seeing her pa take a beating, no matter how much it was deserved.

"This is between me and Pa. Right now you said I have some papers to sign."

Aaron almost regretted that. He might have been doing her a favor by just declaring her claim a fraud and kicking her off her land. If he had, she'd have no choice but to leave. But she clearly didn't feel she could just abandon this land; she'd said as much. She wanted the title so she could sell it, and she'd planned to have that in exchange for three years of her life.

But five was too much.

"So you'll sign?" Pa came up close to Kylie and rested one hand on her shoulder. She turned to face him, and he smiled. Aaron thought the smile might crack the old codger's face, like it hadn't bent into a smile in years.

He saw the tension ease out of Kylie's shoulders. Aaron had seen enough of Cudgel's manipulation to be sure that going along with him would be far easier than fighting him. Even if going along got Kylie nothing she wanted.

"I'll sign," she said, with a note of grief in her voice.

Cudgel patted her on the shoulder. "Good girl. Get on with it, then. I've got to get back to my place."

Cudgel turned and strode down the porch steps. He swung up on his roan horse and rode away.

"He left me." Kylie could barely breathe for the pain in her chest as she watched her father ride out of her clearing.

"Didn't you want him to skedaddle?" Aaron asked.

Kylie whirled to face him. "That's not the point. My

own pa just rode off and left me here, miles from anywhere, alone with a man he doesn't know. No father does that to a daughter he loves."

Turning back to look at the empty trail, Kylie felt her eyes burn with tears, because it hit her, something she'd denied all her life. Her father didn't love her. Had never loved her. Which left her with a question that haunted her: Would he ever love her?

If she worked hard enough, did as Pa asked, upheld Jimmy's memory, then would he finally love her? The ache in her for her father's love was like a hunger she could never fill, a wound that would never heal.

Aaron rested a hand on her shoulder, close to where Pa had touched. The similarity hit so hard, Kylie had to fight not to whirl back toward Aaron and throw herself in his arms. The hunger was there to grab ahold of any man who showed interest, to prove to herself she wasn't unlovable.

And if she grabbed Aaron, and if he was honorable, which he seemed to be, she could probably bring him along to marry her and, by doing that, trap herself out here forever. With a humorless laugh she wondered if Pa would approve. Aaron had no land, but he seemed like the type to do well. With Aaron around, they might grow faster than with just the Wilde brood.

Of course, if one of his girls married, they would be in the keeping of a husband, which would take a lot of Pa's power away. Kylie suspected Pa would want all his children to answer only to him for life.

Which tempted her even more fiercely to launch herself at Aaron.

Kylie controlled the impulse and turned back to Aaron.

She knew, even if Pa didn't, that her signature on this homestead claim was only as good as her presence here. She was promising to stay in exchange for the land. That didn't mean she couldn't forfeit the land and leave. But she wasn't going to make that decision today.

"You have forms for me to sign?"

Aaron looked at her, reading her expression. She'd been a woman serving in the Army with thousands of men. Even more, she'd been a spy. But this wasn't war, and she wasn't trying to hide her feelings.

"Right here." He reached in his dark suit coat and drew out a leather pouch containing a packet of papers. "I even have ink and a pen in case you don't."

Kylie quirked a sad smile. "Nice to see you weren't missing a chance to ruin my life. Very efficient."

"Let's go inside." Aaron nodded toward the house.

Kylie led the way. "I've got ink and a pen. Believe it or not, I know how to read and write."

"I believe it," Aaron said.

He was right behind her. So close. So strong. So utterly a man she could never have. As she swung the door open and stepped inside, she turned to him.

A flaming arrow slammed into the door inches from Aaron's head. Kylie's years of training kicked in, and she grabbed Aaron by the front of his coat and hauled him inside, throwing both of them to the floor. She kicked the door shut as they fell.

She heard another arrow hit, then a third with a vibrating twang. "Indians!"

Aaron leapt to his feet. "Your cabin will burn!"

She grabbed her Sharps off the hooks over the door.

Aaron rushed for the window to the left. Kylie went to the right.

Aaron drew his gun and smashed the window. She almost yelled. She'd worked hard to get real glass.

Biting back her foolishness, Kylie faced reality but lifted her own window from the bottom, then propped it with a ready-to-hand stick. She took a shot into the woods.

Aaron opened fire an instant later.

The arrows switched from aiming at the door to the windows.

Kylie poked her head out and then quickly jerked it back. A burning arrow tore past her and stabbed into the floor.

"Put it out!" Aaron never left his post. "Then swing the door open wide, standing behind it. You can extinguish the arrows so they won't catch the place on fire without being a target."

Kylie wanted to shoot someone, but keeping her cabin from burning down needed doing.

Jumping for the flaming arrow, Kylie wrenched it out of the floor, rushed to a bucket of water, and tossed it in. A soft hiss and a plume of smoke rose up from the bucket. Another arrow cut through Aaron's window. She picked up the bucket and a heavy dishcloth and doused that one.

Aaron slapped at his shirt, and she saw fire. She quickly tossed water on his left arm.

He glanced at her. "Thanks." Turning away, he kept up a steady rain of lead.

A cry of pain came from the woods. It sounded strange, but Kylie didn't have time to wonder why. She'd left her rifle on the far side of the door. She grabbed it and leaned it against the wall beside Aaron. "Use this until I have a chance to reload for you."

"They've broken off the attack." Aaron's gun fell silent.

Careful not to expose herself, Kylie opened the door to see six burning arrows. With the door pressed wide open against the wall, she soaked a towel in the bucket and made short work of smothering each arrow, leaving them where they were. As she worked, hoofbeats thundered away.

"There are two more stuck in the wall on my side of the door." Aaron looked behind him. "I watched close and didn't see any hit the roof, but I might have missed one."

Kylie's stomach twisted. There may be burning arrows up there, but she couldn't get at them without exposing herself. If all the shooters had ridden away, they might be safe, although what if it was a ruse to make them come out. She'd be risking her life . . . or Aaron's.

Yet if she didn't go, she might lose her cabin.

"They're gone. I think I winged someone."

"I heard the shout."

"It sounded like three horses riding away. Looks as though they're done with their mischief."

"Assuming there were only three." Kylie thought of how many might ride with an Indian war party.

"Soak that towel good and give it to me. Then cover me." He reached across the open doorway to shove the Sharps in her direction.

She grabbed her rifle, checked it was loaded, and gave him the drenched cloth. With her back pressed to the wall, she edged close to the doorframe and aimed toward the woods. "Go!"

Aaron was out and back so fast that Kylie barely had

time to worry. No one shot at him. "It's out. Now I want to go down the steps and make sure the roof isn't burning."

"No. Wait. Listen for a minute."

He surprised her by waiting. Kylie hadn't had much experience with anyone doing as she asked, not her bossy big sisters and for sure not her pa. But Aaron . . . well, she might go so far as to say he obeyed her. It was a heady feeling.

They both stood in a profound silence. They heard nothing but the breeze stirring the trees. There was no sound of crackling flames from overhead.

"We'd hear if the roof was burning." Kylie felt the worst of her tension ease. But she had plenty to spare.

"And smoke would be coming through the rafters." Aaron's jaw loosened, and his shoulders lowered a bit. Even so, he still looked more than ready for trouble. "I'd say we got them all."

Kylie remembered nearly collapsing into Aaron's arms after Gage Coulter had ridden off. She fought to keep from doing that again. It could get to be a habit.

"Have you heard about any Indian trouble around here?" Kylie had never even seen an Indian, but she'd heard stories of the Wild West and knew the dangers.

"They weren't Indians." Anger flashed in Aaron's blue eyes.

Kylie tended to agree, though she wasn't sure why. Something niggled at her. "But arrows—surely that means it was a war party."

"I heard them speaking English. The man I wounded yelled, and it wasn't an Indian word."

"You're right." That's what had bothered her. That shout had been a single curse word. One Kylie recognized.

"But why?" Kylie wheeled to face Aaron. For some reason this was more upsetting than an Indian attack. "I've got no cattle to rustle, no money to steal."

"The very fact that there isn't a burning arrow on your roof tells me this was meant mostly to scare you, not burn you out."

Kylie's eyes went to Aaron's shirtsleeve. It was burnt black, but she didn't see any blood. "Your shirt was on fire. That's a real serious way to scare someone. Come and sit down, so I can take care of your arm."

"I'll have a burn, but the arrow missed. It's not serious. You burned your hands just as badly."

Kylie looked at her reddened fingers. She'd singed them somewhere along the way, and she hadn't noticed until now. Well, she'd burned her fingers before; she'd be fine. So would Aaron most likely. Still, it was a mighty mean business.

"Who wants me scared?" And the answer came so quickly, Kylie didn't need Aaron to answer.

He did anyway. "I know of one man who'd like to see you scared into running off."

"Coulter."

"He's got the reputation of an honest man, but a hard one. If he scared you into abandoning your claim, he might see that as justice. He thinks of this land as his."

"If he and his men did this, then he loses any claim he has to decency."

"No argument there." Aaron scowled at the bucket with the blackened arrows. "I intend to ride over there right now and make that clear to him."

"I'm coming with you."

Aaron stumbled, then turned and crossed his arms. "Absolutely not. Coulter attacked you today. I'm not going to give him a second chance. His men have ridden off now, so you'll be safer here than anywhere."

"No, I'll be safer with you."

"Kylie, no. All four of the Wilde homesteads sit on important Coulter water holes and meadows. If he did this, he's dangerous. We can't know how he'll react when he sees you riding up to his property."

"This attack was on me, Aaron. I'm not going to sit here like a scared little girl while you go off and fight my battles."

"I'm the law when it comes to land in this area. It's my job to fight battles."

"Well, I was in the war, so I fought battles, too. I want to be there. I want to look Coulter in the eye. All the spying I did made me a good judge of character."

Kylie hated doing it, but she smiled and fluttered her lashes just a bit. She'd been practicing flirting for years, but rarely did she try it—not much opportunity for that when she dressed like a man all the time.

"Besides, I'm scared to stay here alone." That part was true. And she thought of the night ahead. Would those men come back? How could she stay awake and on watch all night? This concern added weight to her plea. "Please take me with you."

"You can't come, but you're right that you shouldn't be here alone. What can your father have been thinking to leave his daughter alone like this?"

"No one thinks a thing of a young man living alone in a cabin, and until your interference, that's just what I was."

"Well, Coulter didn't drive his cattle in here and harass

you because you're a woman. Those arrows didn't come flying because you're a woman. Until just a few days ago, no one even knew you were one."

Kylie thought of that frightening night when she felt like someone had watched her from the shadowy woods. Had there been someone there? If so, they knew she was a woman.

"You've got a heap of trouble, Kylie, and it's not safe for you here anymore. I'll take you to the nearest Wilde holding. Your brother Shannon is the closest, right?"

"I'm not going to be left like I'm a child who needs tending."

"Not a child. A woman." Aaron scowled at her. "A very childish woman."

"You can leave me at Shannon's, but I'll just follow you. When you ride off, look behind. I'll be right there. I'm not letting you fight my battles."

"You"—Aaron jabbed his finger right in her face—"are not going!"

"Oh, yes I am!"

"If you say one more word about it, I'm going to arrest you for pure stupidity and haul you straight to the jailhouse."

Kylie jammed her fists into her waist and took a step forward. Let him jab her. No decent man laid his hands on a woman. She'd just see how decent Aaron Masterson was.

With no notion of using her rusty flirting skills, she said slowly, clearly, and without hesitation, "You wouldn't dare."

"Don't you dare—!" The jail cell door slamming closed shut her up.

Finally. The first silence for a lot of miles.

"The man I sent will give word to your pa and brothers. I'll release you to them, *if* and only if they convince me they can control you until after I've talked to Coulter." Aaron didn't figure the silence would last, so he enjoyed it while he could. "Until then, I'm leaving you locked up."

Glaring, gripping the iron bars, she looked so mad he half expected steam to blast out of her ears. She reached for a tin cup resting on a little table in her cell, picked it up, and hurled it straight at Aaron's head.

He was watching her real close, so it was easy to snatch it out of the air, glad it didn't have water in it. He decided then and there not to give her anything to eat or drink that he wasn't willing to wear.

"The closest they have to law in this town is the U.S. marshal, and he has a big area to cover. He just needed a place for his family to settle. We're lucky they even have a jail."

She growled something; he thought it might be some mangled, outraged version of the word *lucky*.

The town of Aspen Ridge was so raw it looked like it'd been carved out of the wilderness a few weeks ago. The few buildings and businesses were standing scattered here and there. No streets, unless a body had a mighty good imagination.

"If Marshal Langley is in town, I'll tell him you're not allowed to have any hot liquids in this cup until you calm down." He tossed the cup lightly in the air and caught it, then set it on the marshal's desk with a sharp click.

He'd found the jail unlocked and the cell open. A key had hung handy on the wall. Not a lot of crime in Aspen Ridge.

A good thing, because it meant Kylie wouldn't have to share the cell, for there was only the one. That could've gotten tricky if there'd been another prisoner who was a man. If Langley did come in with a man, Aaron would have to let her out. And he really didn't want to. Not yet. She was the safest here she'd been since he met her.

"You've managed to wear out the day, Miss Wilde. I'll have to wait until tomorrow to get out to Coulter's. For now, I'll leave you to throw everything else that's not tied down. I'll be back later with a meal from Erica's Diner." Erica was married to the marshal, so he could get food and find out the marshal's whereabouts at the same time. "Maybe if I wait long enough, you'll be hungry and eat it instead of flinging it."

Her furious scream followed him outside. He found

himself grinning. His dealings with the little spitfire were proving more fun than he'd had since before the war.

He set about finding Marshal Langley and hadn't begun to finish searching when a man came tearing into town—young, skinny, and none too tall. The rider, blond and with a tan that was more red than brown on his fair skin, rode a buckskin mustang that was larger than most of the mountain ponies Aaron had seen. The cowpoke galloped straight for the jail, and Aaron knew it was either someone with need of the marshal or maybe a member of the Wilde family.

He jogged across the dusty street of Aspen Ridge just as the cowpoke swung off his horse. Every move was unusually skillful, and Aaron knew he was looking at a frontiersman who would make it in the West.

The cowpoke lashed his reins to the hitching post, and as he strode up the two steps to the wooden walk that fronted the jail, Aaron called out, "The marshal isn't in."

The newcomer turned to face him, and Aaron saw a more finely made version of Cudgel Wilde. This youth had none of Cudgel's bitterness and grief carved into his face.

"I heard Kylie Wilde is in custody." The youngster's voice was unusual. Aaron would remember it. "She's my sister. I'm Bailey Wilde."

Aaron stepped up beside Bailey and gestured toward the door. "Yep, she's locked up tight. More for her own good than for breaking the law, although she resisted my arrest of her."

Bailey grabbed the doorknob and wrenched it open.

Kylie stood, both hands gripping the cell door. "Bailey, you came."

"When have I ever not come to take care of you?"

Kylie smiled. Bailey smiled back. A smile that lit up an otherwise unremarkable face.

Aaron shook his head. "Oh, good grief. You're a girl, too."

Bailey whirled to face Aaron, but her eyes went past him. Aaron glanced back; there was no one there. He moved to close the door, knowing Bailey didn't want the whole town to know.

Before she could say anything, Aaron said, "I'm changing your paper work, as well."

With narrowed eyes, Bailey replied, "That's so unjust, I'm surprised you can speak those words to me without shame."

"It's the law, Miss Wilde."

"Shhh . . . don't call me that."

"It's your name."

"My name is Bailey Wilde." She jerked off her gloves, and Aaron saw her fine-boned hands. Much like Kylie had kept her gloves on when she was disguised, Bailey did too. Their hands gave them away. And now that he knew she was a woman, Bailey's face was really quite pretty.

"I enlisted in the Union Army as Bailey Wilde. I served four years as Bailey Wilde. I did the work and earned the pay and served the United States of America honorably as Bailey Wilde." Bailey jammed her fists on her hips. "What's more, I don't need that exemption. I plan to stay out here for good, so putting in five years isn't a problem for me like it is for Kylie. But it's still unjust. I've got my honorable discharge papers, and I used them to get my exemption. No one ever asked if I was a woman, not once the whole time I served."

Aaron felt his shoulders slump under Bailey's logic. "I can't change the law, Miss . . . Bailey. It's illegal, though, for a woman to enlist in the Army."

"I never told a single lie. No one asked if I was a man."

"Just because the question wasn't asked doesn't mean it's not a written down, fully legal act of Congress that the Army only allows men to serve."

"I don't want that exemption because I need it." Bailey slammed her right fist into her left hand. "I earned it. It's right I should be given it. And because I served four years, I'm almost done. I would own my homestead free and clear in just a couple more months."

Aaron studied her face. "I have no idea how anyone could've thought you were a man for more than ten minutes."

"No one's ever had much trouble believing it. You'd believe it too if you hadn't caught on to Kylie."

"I doubt it. Give up, Bailey. I won't be a party to fraud."

Bailey stared at him. He could see the wheels turning in her head. He thought he might be dealing with a very bright young woman, and he braced himself to stand up to her next argument. It wasn't that easy, because she made a lot of sense. Denying her those years of fighting made him feel like he was the fraud, not her.

"More than the exemption, I don't want anyone to know I'm a woman."

"Too late," Kylie said from the cell.

Aaron turned to her. "You've been pretty quiet. How come you're never quiet with me?"

"Because," Kylie said, "I had a hope she could maybe sway you. No one ever turns Bailey from her path."

"If I can't convince you to give me that exemption, can I convince you to keep your mouth shut about me being a woman? Surely running your mouth all over town about it isn't the same as committing fraud."

"Why should I keep silent? What's the matter with you Wilde women that you want to deny you're female?"

With her jaw so tight it might crack her teeth, Bailey said, "For the reason that my sister is right now locked up in jail."

"It's for her own safety."

"That's exactly my point. I don't want anyone doing anything for my own safety."

"Being a woman is a powerful protection out here in the West. Not too many men will hurt a woman."

Bailey stomped right up to Aaron. "I don't want protection; I want freedom. I don't want some well-meaning stubborn ox of a man slamming a cell door shut in my face for my own good. And being locked up is about as far as a body can get from freedom. I want to fork my own broncs. I want to own my land and run my cattle and do as much or as little as the strength of my back and the wits in my head will let me do."

Since she was close, Aaron snatched the broad-brimmed hat off her head, expecting long curls to rain down like Kylie's had.

They didn't.

Her blond hair was shorter than his. He tossed the hat onto the jailhouse desk. "I can't believe you hacked all your hair off. You're about the strangest filly I've ever heard tell of." Then, knowing it would infuriate her, Aaron smirked and said, "But you're sure a pretty little thing."

He caught the fist she threw with the sharp slap of flesh on flesh. Laughing, he let her go and stepped back, almost all the way to the cell. Not all the way of course. He didn't put it past Kylie to grab him from behind and try to strangle him.

"Now, if we can stop with all this female fussing, maybe you'd like to know that someone tried to kill your little sister today."

And that did stop Bailey. The anger in her face disappeared, and she turned to Kylie. "I should never have let you stay alone once it came out you were a woman."

Aaron wondered why Cudgel hadn't said exactly those words. Instead, he'd bullied and wheedled and gotten his daughter to go along with him, then ridden off, leaving her alone and defenseless with a man Cudgel didn't even know. And then the attack had come. Aaron shuddered to think what might have happened if Kylie had been there alone.

It wasn't like Cudgel wanted Kylie to be in danger; Aaron just got the real strong impression he didn't think of it at all. His life was centered on himself, or maybe it was centered around mourning his son.

The truth hit Aaron, and he wanted to kick himself for being so slow. "Your pa's half mad with grief over the death of his son. His *only* son. And he's trying to turn the rest of you into replacement sons. All three of you. Shannon is a woman, too." Aaron wasn't asking; he was just stating the obvious.

Bailey and Kylie both turned to glare at Aaron, and he knew then he was right. Sighing, he added, "I'm changing her paper work, too. You Wilde sisters are the limit."

With a shake of her head, Bailey seemed to toss away

her annoyance at Aaron. "What does he mean, someone tried to kill you? Tell me what happened."

Kylie gave a brief explanation.

"You're right that it's not Indians," Bailey said. "I've met a few of the Shoshone people in these parts."

"You have?" Kylie straightened.

"I've been trading with them a little. I hope to do more of it. I don't believe this of the Shoshone that I've come to know."

Kylie looked to Aaron. "The only person we know who's upset about me living on that land is—"

"Gage Coulter." Bailey said the word low. Her deep, raspy voice seethed. Where Kylie's voice had a bit of the same roughness, Bailey's was a deeper, darker version. "I haven't had a run-in with him yet, but I'm sure my time is coming. I've heard he used to run cattle in my canyon."

"My canyon?" Aaron said. "Strange you'd think of it that way, Bailey. The land in that canyon is only yours because you homesteaded across the mouth of it. You have no ownership except you can stop a man from crossing your property, and no one knows another way in. You're doing exactly what you hate Coulter for doing."

Bailey didn't respond, as she was busy thinking. Aaron saw the signs and braced himself. A moment later, she pulled her gloves out of her back pocket and tugged them on. She turned to Kylie. "I think Masterson's right. You need to stay here where it's safe."

"Bailey, don't you dare leave me in this cell."

"I'm going out to talk to Coulter and put a stop to this right now."

"Oh, no you're not, Miss Wilde."

Bailey scowled at Aaron, and he could see mistaking her for a man. The woman had the right attitude and the right toughness. But Aaron *hadn't* made that mistake, and he had a feeling Coulter wouldn't either. Then Bailey would be in big trouble, because a woman shouldn't stay out on a holding alone, and how was she going to keep her homestead claim if she couldn't live on it?

Her scowl deepened into a sneer. "I'd like to see someone try and stop me."

The jail door clanked shut with Bailey on the business side of it and Aaron on the free side. Kylie would have just as soon been locked up with a rabid wolverine.

"You're not going to get away with this. When I get out of here, I'm turning the law on you. I haven't done a thing to deserve this!"

Aaron had managed to drag Kylie all the way in from her cabin. He'd had a fight on his hands getting Bailey the five feet from outside the cell to inside it with the door shut and locked. And Kylie thought Aaron might have a black eye developing.

"It's too late to go out tonight," Aaron said in a reasonable tone, completely wasted over Bailey's furious threats. Then he raised his voice until the roof shook. "And you should both thank me."

That shut Bailey up, probably because she couldn't imagine such a stupid statement. Kylie was wondering what Aaron could possibly mean by it.

"I don't know what kind of half-wits you two served with in the war, but I promise you, Bailey Wilde, Gage

Coulter will figure out you're a woman ten seconds after you start talking."

Kylie didn't believe it. Bailey played her role well.

"Does that mean you're not going to tell the whole world I'm a woman?" Bailey got the implications before Kylie did. Bailey had always been fast.

"I think living like a man is a blamed fool idea. But no, I'm not going to tell. I don't like the idea of any of you living alone, but you seem like a mighty tough cowpoke, Bailey. Maybe you can convince folks." Aaron paused, then shook his head. "I doubt it, but maybe. And definitely not Coulter. He'll see through those britches in a few minutes."

Aaron quit talking all sudden-like.

Kylie realized what he'd said and blushed.

Bailey might've blushed a bit too, and she never did much blushing.

"I mean he'll know you're a woman," Aaron forged on, clearly wanting to leave his last statement far behind. "Some might be fooled by you just because you've got a tough way about you, not because of how you look. You're a mighty pretty woman, but you've got the act right. Kylie doesn't. She would never fool anyone for long. Look at her. She got away with her masquerade in the Army, because folks thought she was a real young boy and some of them have a look like hers. I'll bet you even told them you were young, didn't you?"

Kylie would have admitted it, except she was never speaking to Aaron again.

"But now she's got to say she's at least twenty-one to claim a homestead, so she's trying to pass herself off as an adult man. No one will believe it. So she's either got to find someone to stay out there with her or get off that land, because she'll never spend another night alone out there—not while I'm alive. Now, I'm going to go get some supper, and once I've enjoyed a peaceful meal with no females nagging me, I'll be back with food for the two of you."

Aaron had been gone about ten minutes when Shannon stuck her head in the jailhouse. "I can't believe both of you are locked up."

Bailey erupted from where she sat slumped on the cot. Kylie quit her pacing. "He took the key too," Bailey said, "or I swear I'd have you break us out."

"A jailbreak. That's got to be bad." Shannon settled in the wooden chair by the marshal's desk. "I don't want a posse coming after us. I have sheep to tend. How am I supposed to do that if I'm runnin' from the law?"

"He's figured out we're all women." Bailey gave Shannon a dour look.

Shannon shrugged and leaned back in the chair.

Kylie stepped forward. "Aaron sounded like he was willing to keep his mouth shut about you being a woman, Bailey. He'll do that for Shannon, too." She looked at Shannon's pretty face. "The only reason we've gotten away with it as long as we have is because we never come to town. We settled on our homesteads and we spent the fall building cabins and the winter snowed inside. We've avoided town. We all know no one will be fooled. The war was different. We were supposed to be young then."

The three of them looked at each other, silent. Finally, Kylie said, "You're going to have to accept sometime that you're both women, and both pretty. You don't look like men at all. This was all Pa's idea, and he doesn't see us as pretty women, only as the sons he could have had. I like dresses and long hair and making my cabin look nice. Aaron says I can't stay alone, but he can't tell me what to do. I'm going to lose my homestead exemption. He can enforce that, but he's got no real power over me. I'll let him talk to Coulter and try to get to the bottom of the attack. After that, I'm going home."

Shannon sat up in the chair. "What attack?"

Kylie told the story again. By the end, Shannon and Bailey were both frowning.

"He's right, Kylie." Shannon had always had a mothering streak. "You can't stay out there alone."

"Then neither of you can stay alone, either." Kylie glared at her stubborn sisters, knowing they'd never give up their land. Bailey was too ambitious. Shannon was too in love with her sheep.

"Sure we can," Bailey said. "I can hold my own land."

"Against a band of armed men shooting flaming arrows from cover?"

"Yep."

Bailey was probably right. Her sister was mighty tough.

Then Kylie added her real worry—not that flaming arrows didn't worry her. "I told Pa I'd stay out the five years, but I don't know if I can stand it."

"You'll be twenty-five, Kylie." Bailey waved a hand as if dismissing Kylie's worries. "Plenty of time to go back East and find some blamed-fool man to marry."

A blamed-fool man who'd do all the roof climbing, Kylie thought wistfully, while she ran a house and shopped for bonnets and planted flowers. Why was that such a terrible dream?

And speaking of blamed-fool men, Cudgel Wilde picked that moment to crash open the jailhouse door and storm inside, looking at his three daughters with contempt.

As if this was all their fault.

Kylie, possibly emboldened by the bars, muttered so only Bailey could hear, "I've just decided I can't stand it anymore."

Aaron had a family reunion in the jail. If he'd've known, he'd've brought more food.

Erica Langley and her daughter, Myra, ran the diner. She had two grown-up sons, who helped out some, but seemed mostly like layabouts.

Erica told him that the marshal, her husband, was transporting a prisoner and might be gone a full week. Considering that Erica was expecting baby number five at any time, she probably wished her husband spent more time on the trail.

Now here Aaron stood in the midst of the Wilde family. This was Aaron's mess, and he was going to have to clean it up. A simple solution wouldn't work, because all four Wildes wouldn't fit in that one cell.

Which was a dirty shame. A few days behind bars might set their thinking straight.

Cudgel had both hands grasping the bars, as if the old coot could bend them apart and set his "sons" free.

"It's about time you got back here, Masterson." Cudgel Wilde turned on him like a hungry lobo wolf.

Shannon was sitting in Aaron's chair. Well, Marshal Langley's chair, but Aaron figured he had claim on it while Langley was gone.

Setting the two plates of food on the desk, he figured he might as well jump into this mess with both feet, since no one seemed interested in being reasonable.

"You three are about the prettiest women I've ever seen." He was telling the truth. Shannon Wilde was a stunning beauty. He could see her hair was short, but a few dark curls peeked out from under her broad-brimmed hat. Bailey Wilde had a subdued kind of beauty with her skin more burned red than tan because she was so fair. She had a more fiery version of Kylie's eyes, with blond lashes and brows, where Kylie's were dark, yet her face had the delicate look of a woman. Only an idiot would have mistaken her for a man.

And Kylie, well, she was the prettiest of them all. How had anyone believed she could pass herself off as a man? How had she gotten away with it during the war, even if she did claim to be young?

Of course, her hair was long and she wore a dress, so she wasn't trying to disguise herself. But he'd seen her in britches, her hair tucked away, and he'd figured it out in a matter of minutes, and that was in poor light with her hat brim pulled down low. There was nothing that was one speck manly about her.

Cudgel strode straight for him, almost foaming at the mouth. "You let my . . . " His words halted.

"The word you're looking for is *daughters*." Aaron turned furious. What kind of father let this nonsense go on? "*Daughters*. You have daughters, Mr. Wilde. You might want to practice that word. Accept it. They're all adult women. *Women*. A woman is a wonderful thing. She should be cherished and respected and admired, not put in some pathetic disguise."

"My children never told a lie."

Aaron closed the space between himself and Wilde. "You lie with every breath you take." Towering over the old man, Aaron leaned down until his nose almost touched Wilde's. "Don't stand there and act like you're an honorable man. Every word you speak dishonors your beautiful daughters. Every paper you sign defrauds the United States government."

Cudgel backed up to the cell door. "My children are under arrest for no good reason, Masterson. From what I understand, you're trying to get to the bottom of an Indian attack and using that as an excuse to break the law. Let them out. Now."

"Until I believe your daughters have enough sense not to go riding out to face a man who might be trying to kill them, they stay locked up." He looked at the only Wilde sister walking around free. "What about you? Aren't you going to offer to charge out to Coulter's place?"

Shannon raised her hands as if in surrender. "I've a good

suspicion that if I said yes, I'd spend the night in jail. And I've got sheep to tend."

"You raise sheep?" Aaron felt his brows arch nearly to his hairline. "They ruin the grazing. They're always looking for some excuse to die. They're prime wolf food. On top of all that, they stink."

"I'll say they stink," Bailey said.

Aaron had the odd feeling that Bailey Wilde could have been a good friend if she hadn't been a woman . . . and a fraud.

Shannon smiled at him. "My sheep are fine-smelling critters, my grass is holding up well, and I haven't lost one to the wolves yet."

"Promise me you'll go home and not to Coulter's place, and you can stay on the outside of this cell."

"You've got my word," Shannon said, still smiling. Every inch a woman's smile.

It made Aaron want to bang his head on something hard. "Well, there's still some fried venison steaks over at Erica's Diner if you're hungry," Aaron said, feeling a very natural manly need to take care of all these women. What was the matter with their father that he'd stick them each alone on her land, miles from help? He remembered Kylie dangling from that roof and suppressed a shudder.

"I think I'll head on home. I don't eat a lot of meat." Shannon rose in a way so graceful and ladylike, Aaron wanted to punch Cudgel Wilde right in the face.

She left the room in her pathetic manly disguise that didn't disguise anything. In fact, now that Aaron knew she was a woman, those britches were downright indecent.

He turned to Cudgel. "Get on out of here, unless you

want to sleep on the floor. A decent man might think he needed to stay with his girls. Or he might take his daughter home instead of letting her go off alone in this wild country. Especially since there's someone out there shooting flaming arrows."

"Shannon's tough. All my young'uns are." Cudgel stalked out of the jail and slammed the door so hard that dust drifted down from the ceiling.

Aaron wondered if the girls, or Cudgel himself, realized that he had never referred to his daughters as women. He'd called them young'uns and children, being careful not to attach a female word to them. Just how deeply was Cudgel obsessed with making men out of his girls?

"Aaron?" Kylie said his name in such a sweet voice, he almost apologized and let her go.

"What?"

"Is there a second cot?" The little woman fluttered her lashes in a way that made Aaron want to get closer and see the streaks of gold and green and brown in her eyes and tease a smile out of her. Which didn't match with his arresting her at all.

"And more blankets? It's going to be so uncomfortable here overnight." That one pretty dimple popped out when she smiled.

Bailey snorted. Aaron arched a brow at her. That one, he'd have no trouble keeping locked up a while.

"I can get more blankets." He'd give her his own from his room in the boardinghouse if he had to. "But there's no other cot." His bed didn't have the look of something to be easily torn apart and reassembled in here. He wasn't sure his landlady would allow it anyway. "Leastways none

I know of. We've never arrested two people at once before. Well, not in the month I've been here."

Aaron had never arrested anyone. Privately he admitted he wasn't really sure he had the right to. A land agent wasn't exactly a lawman.

"Thank you, Aaron." Kylie gave him that smile that made him itchy, made him want to do anything to see it again.

"I won't be gone long." Aaron left at a fast pace. He only realized how he was hurrying to do Kylie's bidding when the vision of her pretty face faded from his head. It took quite a while.

"I don't know how you can live with yourself," Bailey said dryly.

"I don't have one speck of trouble." Kylie relaxed on the stupid cot. "I'm a sight more normal than you, Bailey Wilde."

Shrugging one shoulder, Bailey said, "Probably right."

"So what am I going to do?" Kylie really couldn't stay at her place again.

They had a plan by the time Aaron got back.

"Hired help?" Aaron sputtered. "You can't live out there alone with a cowhand."

"She'll hire a housekeeper, too."

"We don't have any of those in Aspen Ridge."

"We'll find one before she goes home." Bailey sounded so confident, Kylie figured she probably would find one.

"And we've decided to let you handle Coulter. So you can let us go now. Kylie will come home with me for the night, and we'll set about making her home safe for her." Bailey smiled.

Kylie had never seen Bailey try to be polite and ladylike before. She was really bad at it.

"She's not safe with you, either. All you've done is put two women alone against a band of back-shooters."

"There's a difference," Bailey said, leaning one bent arm against the bars and staring him straight in the eye, as tough and forthright as any man.

"No there isn't."

"I chose my land so no one could come up behind me. I built my cabin with windows so narrow all they're good for is giving me a field of fire. I cut back the woods so no one can get close without me seeing them. I've got food stored up and a spring behind my house so no one can starve me out. I built the cabin of rock so no one can burn me out. I keep a loaded rifle right by the door, and I have enough bullets to start a war, and win it."

"That shows good sense." Aaron jerked one shoulder.

Bailey tilted her head toward her little sister. "Kylie picked her claim because it was pretty."

Kylie narrowed her eyes at both of them when they looked at her.

"You're both still female."

"No one knows that but you, Mr. Masterson. I'm trusting you to keep it that way. All anyone will know is that Kylie is staying with her big brother until she makes her place more secure."

"It'd probably be better if she stayed with her pa."

"No!" Bailey and Kylie said it together at a near shout.

"She's staying with me, and the fact that I'm her sister

instead of her brother is something no one will even know if you keep your mouth shut. And right now no one knows she's been attacked but you, her family, and the attackers. Her family will keep quiet. You keep your mouth shut about it, then if word gets out, we'll know exactly who to hunt by who started the talk."

"Coulter will know about it after tomorrow. I don't see how to question him without telling him what happened."

"You claim he's an honorable man and you doubt he's behind this. See if he'll keep his mouth shut, too. It'll help us catch . . ." Bailey cleared her throat. "I mean it will help *you* catch the varmints who shot at Kylie."

Aaron glared at Bailey for a long time, and then with clear misgivings he set the blankets on the desk and unlocked the cell door. "You can go."

Bailey marched out of the jail and headed for the outside without a backward glance.

Kylie waved goodbye and smiled sweetly. "Thank you, Aaron."

He smiled back.

11

Aaron rode up to Coulter's ranch house, impressed. The man had prospered. There was proof of that everywhere.

The house was log and stone like most everyone's house. But Coulter's place was much larger, with a second floor and real glass windows. Aaron wondered if Kylie would count this as civilized.

And the place sat in one of the most picturesque settings Aaron had ever seen. A mountain rose up behind it on the west. To the south, a broad meadow was dotted with red Hereford cattle in equal parts with the longhorns, placidly cropping grass as their calves gamboled around their mamas. Beyond that a wide stream created a natural barrier to keep the cattle from straying. Aaron heard the rush of water over stone as the creek twisted and bent into thick woodland. A broad porch stretched across the front of Coulter's house, though there wasn't a rocking chair to be seen anywhere. A big log barn stood to the south of the house, with a corral of horses grazing on lush grass. Nearby was a bunkhouse, a hitching post along its front.

Aaron had set out early so he wouldn't miss Coulter. The sun was just rising. Smoke curled out of the bunkhouse. While the mountain mornings could be chilly, it was still too warm to need a fire, so he figured the cowhands were at breakfast.

Chickens pecked at the ground in front of a shed. A sleek hound rushed out to meet him with a bark that Aaron figured wasn't a sign of meanness; instead, it alerted those around the place.

As if to prove that, the bunkhouse door cracked open, and an old-timer carrying a rifle showed himself very cautiously. Another very deliberately made himself and his Winchester visible from on top of a bluff that rose up behind the barn. Well-trained men.

For a moment Aaron felt such envy he could barely keep riding forward. It reminded him of his home in Virginia. Laid out neatly, well cared for, comfortable and safe.

All gone.

Coulter came to the front door as Aaron dismounted and hitched his horse. The brown dog snuffled at his boots but showed no signs of biting.

"Come in, Masterson. I'm just sitting down to breakfast. It must be important for you to have set out before sunup."

"It is." Aaron followed Coulter to the kitchen.

The man had nice furniture. Someone on the place was a fine carpenter. Coulter got a coffee cup and filled it from a pot on the stove. He set it in front of Aaron, then jabbed at the platter on the table that still held a stack of hash-browned potatoes and scrambled eggs. There were biscuits and a bowl of jelly.

"Help yourself. I've got plenty. My foreman usually comes in and eats with me, but he had chores that set him on the trail early. Someone came to the kitchen door and told me after I'd started cooking."

"Who else is in the house?" Surely he had someone keeping the house clean.

"There's no one else."

"Good. I want what we speak of to stay between you and me. I want to ask you some questions, and I'm hoping you'll answer honestly and not tell anyone else what I say."

Coulter narrowed his glittering eyes, which turned more silver than gray when he was annoyed. "There's no one to overhear. And I can keep my mouth shut."

"You've got the reputation of a hard man, Coulter. But no one tells me you're dishonest." Aaron spoke harshly to jolt a reaction out of the man. "Someone tried to kill Kylie Wilde yesterday and burn down her cabin. You're the only man I know who wants her gone."

Those eyes flashed like bitter lightning. "I've never hurt a woman. If you're planning to go around telling folks that lie, you'd better be prepared to face me with guns blazing."

Watching every flicker on Coulter's face, Aaron couldn't find a thing false. "I'm here talking to you, aren't I? I'm not shooting off my mouth in town, smearing your name. I haven't done it, and I won't."

Coulter grunted and ran a hand through his shaggy brown hair, a man too busy to get himself a haircut. Some of that anger faded, and he took a long pull on his coffee cup. "Tell me what happened."

Aaron told him exactly how they'd been bushwhacked.

"Flaming arrows, you say? You're sure it wasn't Indians? I haven't had any trouble with the Shoshone, but I've heard of those who have farther west."

"One of them spoke English."

"What did he say?"

Aaron told him. "He yelled when I winged him. You got any men unaccounted for yesterday in the afternoon? Or anybody with an unexplained bullet wound?"

"There was no one who showed up hurt last night, not here, but I've got crews in line shacks flung wide."

"You said hard things in front of your men about Miss Wilde. Some might think it'd please you to have her run off."

A tight smile barely turned Coulter's mouth upward. "I can't swear to what any man does when he's not under my eyes, but I know my men. Most of them have been with me awhile, and this doesn't sound like a one of them. I've got a few newer hands, but they're men I like. I'll talk to them. Including the ones in the line shacks, though that will take days. I'll make it clear to 'em there's to be no trouble where Miss Wilde is concerned." Slouching back in his chair, he added, "I've thought to solve my problems with that little filly in a friendlier way than running her off."

It was a good thing Aaron's hands were clasped on his tin coffee cup. It kept him from making a fist and slamming it into Gage Coulter's mouth.

Those silver eyes calmed back to gray and glinted with sudden humor. Aaron suspected that his reaction hadn't gone unnoticed.

"What's your story, Masterson? You don't look like the type to run a land office."

The question seemed honest. Aaron came from a wealthy family back East, but one where everyone worked hard to run the farm. Here sat a man from a huge Texas ranch. Both of them had struck out on their own, probably for very different reasons, yet Aaron saw the similarities between him and Gage.

"The war tore through my home in Virginia. Seems like about half the battles were fought right on top of my family's land."

Coulter got up to pour more coffee. "Not much left after a war."

"My folks died, along with my brothers and sisters. They stayed home where it was safe on our farm in the Shenandoah Valley." A place he loved. A place he could never return to, not if he wanted to live. "I was in the thick of battle and managed to survive."

Aaron thought of the Wilde sisters. He was struck by a deep curiosity about what they really went through. He longed to ride straight to Kylie and just sit and talk with her for a long old time.

"My ma had family in the Shenandoah Valley," Coulter said as he sat the coffeepot back on the stove, then returned to his seat. "She'd visited there as a youngster. She said it was the most beautiful stretch of land on God's green earth. She'd never seen its like again. Texas is beautiful in its own way, but where we ranched, south of Fort Worth, it was a harsh beauty. And out here, the mountains are an awesome wonder, but life gets hard, especially the winters."

Coulter eased back in his chair and smiled at the memories. "Ma said Shenandoah was lush and green all the time. The trees were thick, and the water poured cold and clean.

She talked about it from time to time, especially in the summer when it was so hot in Texas the chickens could've laid boiled eggs."

Aaron could see it all clearly. "It's still the richest green you've ever seen, and the trees are still there and the flowing water." That beauty, though, was overlaid with newer, crueler memories. "But my family's gone, our home and buildings burned. The land's pockmarked from cannon fire. And because the damage done was at the hands of both the North and South, the neighbors turned against each other. Virginia went with the Confederacy, but my family's sympathies were with the Union. And that's who I fought for. We never owned slaves and didn't hold with it, so the Southern sympathizers hated me for fighting for the Union. The Northern sympathizers hated me for every atrocity they could lay at the feet of the war. There was nothing for me there but hatred. When my former commanding officer asked for my help out here, I saw a chance to start over. Once I'm done with this land rush, I'm heading into the mountains. I'll stake a claim there in some high mountain valley, where my only neighbors will be bighorn sheep."

The two men sat in silence for a while, finishing their coffee. Aaron saw that Gage was thinking hard about something.

"Are you staking a claim to Miss Wilde?" The question came suddenly, and Aaron suspected Gage was maybe getting him back for Aaron's earlier accusation about the attack on Kylie.

Aaron had to fight back the urge to say yes and warn Coulter away from her. But considering the woman wanted no part of him, it was a waste of breath. "She doesn't like it out here. She wants to live in the city. She's not interested in hitching herself to anyone who's not aiming for the same thing."

Gage's eyes flashed with annoyance. "Why does she want to do a blamed fool thing like that? Who'd live in the city when they can own a mountain and run fine cattle?"

Aaron smiled at Gage's response. "She said something about bonnets and she might've mentioned some nonsense about tea parties. 'Civilization,' she called it."

With a snort that'd do a bull justice, Coulter said, "Civilization is overrated. I'd rather wrestle riches out of the soil any day. And my ma grew up with all that fuss and said worrying about dresses and bonnets was for foolish, idle women who went through their whole lives without doing a single important thing."

"Your ma sounds like a wise woman."

"She could be." There was something in Coulter's tone. Affection for his ma, but something else, too. Something darker. Coulter had left Texas, it was said, because of his pa. Now Aaron wondered if his ma might've been part of it, too.

"What are we going to do about the men who attacked her?" Aaron's instinct was to go to her place and stand guard full time. Not at all proper.

"It can't go on, not where there are decent men to protect her." Coulter set his coffee cup down with a loud *thunk*. "Will she let me send some men over to stand guard?"

"Doubt it. She did talk about hiring hands."

Frowning into the dregs of his cup, Coulter said, "It ain't right or decent for a woman to live alone. And having hired hands only makes it worse . . . a single woman with men around her like that."

"She's planning to hire a housekeeper. A woman. She thinks that'll make it all tidy and proper."

Coulter shook his head. "None of them around. I've tried to hire one. I even managed it twice. But they both got married. No single woman stays single out here, not for long anyway, and that'll probably be true of Miss Wilde."

"She swears she'll never marry, not here."

"We'll see. Though it won't be me. I've little interest in a woman who doesn't want the life I can give her."

Aaron felt exactly the same way. Except he'd held Kylie in his arms, and it wasn't that hard to catch himself imagining how it would be. What he would say to persuade her to come with him into the mountains. Surely she'd change her mind when what she wanted was so frivolous. Tea parties and bonnets? Good grief.

"How about if she hired a married couple?"

"Not many of those around either, and unless she's different than a lot of homesteaders, she's got neither the money to pay them nor the space to house them."

"For now, she's staying with her si . . . uh, brother, on his homestead." Aaron almost stumbled over that sentence, and it irritated him because now he was a liar like the whole Wilde family. "She can't do that for long and not lose her claim, but it'll be all right until we get things settled."

It occurred to Aaron that Kylie, and for sure Bailey Wilde, would be mad as a bee-stung longhorn to learn that two men were planning her future.

"I can send a crew to keep an eye out during the day."

"Won't the other men know you've taken to posting

sentries and wonder what's going on? We're hoping if we keep this quiet, the men who attacked will let something slip and we'll be able to track 'em down. So long as no one knows it but us."

"You have that in mind and still you told me about it, Masterson?"

"I knew we could either trust you or you already knew because you'd been behind the attack. Either way, there wasn't much risk in telling you."

Coulter nodded. "I've got a man I can trust who won't be missed from my work crew. I hire him from time to time when I need someone to scout the high-up hills. Matt Tucker's his name. I'll be a few days finding him. He's a mountain man who comes and goes to suit himself, and he may not want the job. But if he says yes, he'll be the best lookout we could get. He knows the land around here and he keeps his mouth shut, mainly 'cuz he's an ornery cuss who don't like talkin' to nobody."

"You've got time, because I'm going to do my best to keep Kylie with Bailey for a stretch." Aaron stood, knowing he had work to do. Kylie was okay at Bailey's for now. So long as she stayed put, Aaron could do homestead visits and ask some questions at the same time.

And that would give Coulter time to hunt up Tucker.

As soon as he could, he'd head to Bailey's place. He hadn't been out there, and he needed to inspect it. But there was no doubt in his mind that Bailey had a cabin up and was fulfilling all the promises she'd made when she'd filed for a homestead—except the one she'd made about serving in the Army . . . as a man.

Aaron started for the door.

"We'll be talking, Masterson." Coulter walked out with him. "No one's gonna harm a woman on my land."

"It's not your land, Coulter," Aaron said as he mounted up. "It's hers. Try and remember that."

"We'll see." Coulter leaned one shoulder against a post that held up his porch roof. He looked casual, yet his pale eyes remained sharp. "Maybe Miss Wilde will get tired of waiting for her city and her tea parties. Maybe I can help her make that decision right soon."

As Aaron rode away, it struck him that despite assurances that Gage wouldn't stand by while someone hurt Kylie, his parting statement sounded a lot like a threat.

I am not shearing sheep." Bailey slid on her leather gloves and glared at her sister at the same time.

Kylie didn't want to help either, but she left the haggling to Bailey and Shannon. She'd had enough to worry about with getting their breakfast ready that morning.

"It won't take long," promised Shannon. "I already sheared most of them in the spring, but Mrs. Langley's offered to buy more wool, and that will give me money enough to get my milk cow. I warned her that the wool is short still. She didn't seem to care. The woman sounded desperate for more yarn. Her baby's coming in September, and she's got to have most things done by then. She said a little one, plus running the diner and four other children, will leave her little time for knitting."

"Well, I've got a bronc to break." Bailey stood from the table. "I've got to move my young longhorn bull to a different pasture. He's been fighting with an old bull, and one of 'em isn't gonna survive. I've got hay to cut, a fence to mend, and a creek to dam. And I'm hoping to start building a chicken coop."

Kylie felt dizzy. "I can't believe you do all those things. All men's work."

Bailey rolled her eyes.

Shannon was undeterred. "I'll come back with you after the noon meal. I'm not a hand with broncs, but I can cut hay and mend fence. If you give me a half day's work this morning, I'll give you a half day this afternoon. But I need the cash money from this wool."

Bailey let out a sigh. "Fine, Shannon, I'll come. But I'm holding you to the afternoon's work. I'll probably have to burn my clothes and make new."

"The work's not that rough," Shannon said.

"But I'll stink, and that sheep stink doesn't come out easily."

Shannon laughed. She was used to the teasing over her precious sheep. "Thank you. You and Kylie are good help. I know you're not fond of my sheep, but you handle them well."

They made short work of cleaning up the breakfast dishes and headed out. As usual, Shannon started saddling a horse for Kylie.

"Let Kylie do that herself," Bailey told her. "She's got to learn."

"I know how to saddle a horse. I'm just slow, and Shannon's in a hurry."

Shannon smiled. "You'll get faster as time passes. A person can't help learning skills she practices. And I am in a hurry. We've got three days' work to do before sunset. We're going to have to press hard to get to it all."

They were leaving Bailey's place when Aaron rode in. Kylie's heart sped up. She hadn't seen him in almost a week. She'd stayed with Bailey like a good girl, yet she was tired of being underfoot at her sister's, even while she was too scared to go home.

He looked handsome and strong, and she knew he was an honest, kind man. He was everything a woman could want in a husband. It was a shame she couldn't have him. For she wasn't about to spend her life stuck on some mountaintop, not even with such a decent and protective man. Not even if he saddled her horse for her.

"Morning, ladies," Aaron said while tipping his hat.

Kylie saw both her sisters tense up. They were used to acting like men. Kylie felt sorry for them. Here she sat on her horse, wearing her skirts with her hair pulled back in a neat bun at the base of her neck, and there they were in britches.

Bailey seemed to like it, but Kylie wondered about Shannon. With her maternal love of animals, how could Shannon not be unhappy passing herself off as a man? It had to go against her most basic motherly nature.

"I don't want to hear you say anything like that again, Masterson. If you get in the habit, you'll slip."

Aaron smirked. "Where are you pretty little ladies off to this morning?"

A move to Kylie's left drew her attention to Shannon, who had a sweet smile on her face that only someone who knew her really well could tell was not sweet but diabolical.

"Why, we 'pretty little ladies' are off to do a really hard job, and we could certainly use some help."

"I'd be glad to help you, Miss Shannon. What is it you need?"

"I reckon I had this coming," Aaron said to no one in particular.

The ram bleated and charged. He knew the critter wasn't up to killing him, but that didn't mean taking one of those small curved horns in the belly wouldn't hurt.

The ram was the last of them and didn't take to being sheared any better than the others. Aaron figured he deserved this for wanting so badly to see Kylie. He should've just let these contrary women have at their shearing, but he'd said he'd help and he'd be bruised for two weeks, thanks to his big mouth.

He snagged the feisty ram and dragged it into the fast-moving river, where he, fully dressed, began soaping the animal up. After the river had rinsed the ram clean, he hugged it against him and hauled it dripping wet over to a grassy pen. Shannon stood waiting beside the pen, also dripping wet from all the sheep that had shook the water out of their hides. She held her shears ready.

Bailey stood back, scowling.

They'd developed a system that had worked pretty well. Kylie herded a sheep to the water's edge. Aaron grabbed it, wrestled it into the water, soaped it up and rinsed it. Afterward he carried it to Shannon.

It gave him some pleasure to watch her get soaked as each sheep shook its wool somewhat dry.

Yet Shannon didn't seem to mind. She just laughed, her

eyes bright and smiling. All that affection, and it was all for her sheep.

Once she was done shearing, Bailey caught the fleece and rolled it up. Meanwhile Kylie herded in another sheep.

It was like clockwork with sheep slobber.

Aaron envied Kylie her part of the job, which left her hands and clothes as clean as a mountain breeze.

Shannon was drenched and coated in wool fluff and had taken a few cloven hooves to the gut.

And Bailey had a tough job bundling the small fleeces into a roll, as the sheep weren't ready to be sheared. Though Aaron knew little about sheep, he knew that much. Shannon had herself admitted she'd sheared them already in the spring.

The skimpy amount of wool made the bundles fall apart, so that when it was over, Bailey was so tufted she looked more sheep than woman.

But Aaron had come out the worst. He looked like he'd been shoved over a waterfall, then run over by a sheep stampede, which actually described the last hour pretty well. Normally he'd have stripped off his shirt to keep it dry, but he wasn't about to do that with three women watching. So he was soaked to the skin with nothing to do about it but let the air dry him, clothes and all.

Shannon tossed the last fleece to Bailey and then gave the cantankerous short-haired old ram a hug. Aaron looked at Bailey and rolled his eyes. She smiled, then quickly made her lips into a line again.

Aaron and Bailey saw eye to eye on a surprising number

of things, including their dislike of sheep and thinking Shannon had a strange way of behaving toward animals.

"We got done in half the time, thanks to you, Mr. Masterson." Despite tricking him into this, Shannon had thanked him graciously several times.

"Considering I've got bruises in the shape of sheep hooves forming over half my body, I think you can call me Aaron." He picked up his boots and holster and everything else he'd shed when, in horror, he realized what his offer of help was going to amount to.

Shannon grinned. "I think you've earned yourself some coffee and a slice of pound cake, Aaron." She glanced at her sisters. "All of you have. I'd have been days doing this alone, and the three of us would never have gotten it done in one morning. Now we're done early enough I can help you a lot this afternoon, Bailey. I can fix dinner if you've a mind to eat a bit early. I've got eggs and cheese and I baked bread just yesterday."

"I put a venison roast on this morning, Shannon." Bailey began brushing off the tufts of wool on her clothes. "When a woman works her heart out for fifteen hours a day, she needs a little meat to give her strength."

As they walked toward the house, Aaron asked, "How'd you talk with Erica to sell the wool? Are you saying you saw her face-to-face and she came away from that thinking you're a man?"

Shannon's cheeks turned pink. "Um . . . well, no. There was a note tacked on my front door. I figured I'd just take the wool in myself, but you've got me worried about my disguise. So I've been wondering, Aaron, if you wouldn't mind delivering it for me and also fetch my money."

"And while you're there, I've got a list of groceries I need," Bailey said.

The women looked a little . . . well, Aaron had to say it. They both looked sheepish. "Of course I'll do that for you, but keeping my mouth shut about you being women is not the same as taking on the job of helping you hide. I've got work of my own to do, you know."

"Thank you." Shannon smiled that pretty smile of hers.

Kylie patted him on his soggy arm.

Aaron figured he'd probably do about anything they asked.

They got to Shannon's cabin, bigger than Kylie's, smaller than Bailey's and like the other two, very well built. "Did you ladies build these cabins yourselves?"

Shannon waved them to her table while she headed for the coffeepot hanging from a hook in the fireplace.

Bailey threw him a towel, then went outside and washed in a basin. When Aaron was as dry as he was going to get, he pulled on his boots and sat down. He noticed Shannon had four chairs, not two like Kylie. He wondered if that meant this house was more the family gathering spot.

Bailey came back in with clean hands and face, looking only slightly less woolly, and sat down.

"Bailey does the building." Shannon poured coffee as they settled in.

"Shannon does the detail work and the furniture." Bailey picked up her cup and slouched back in her chair, her legs splayed and her hair short. She moved in a manly way most of the time, with long strides, shoulders squared. But Aaron saw her delicate hands and the fine bones of her face and gave a mental shake.

Shannon brought a cake, shaped into a loaf, and began slicing it. "Kylie helps us with everything and makes it pretty."

Kylie laughed. "I do if you two will give me time. You need curtains in here, Shannon. And Bailey, if you'd plant flowers out front of your cabin—"

"Stop with the flowers." Bailey cut her off, but she did it good-naturedly.

Aaron wasn't sure if they'd welcome it, but he was so curious about their war service he couldn't stop himself from asking, "You really fought in the war? You were in battles? How did you survive it? I know you dressed as men but—"

"We got spread far and wide," Bailey said, cutting him off, frowning into her cup, "mainly because we enlisted at different times. I'd hoped me going was enough for Pa. When Jimmy died, he worked us all into a fever. All I could think of was fighting in his place. Getting revenge on the Rebs, who killed my brother. I knew later that Pa had stirred all that up in me, and at the time I was in full agreement with him."

"Bailey told us she'd fight for the family," Shannon said quietly. "Pa was prodding all of us, but she didn't want anyone else to go. She said she'd carry the name into war for the family. I was all worked up too, though not as eager to fight as Bailey. After she left, Pa kept at me until I wanted in. I delayed a year. I was too young, but that's not what stopped me. I hated leaving Kylie. She needed someone there to buffer things between her and Pa."

Kylie smiled like someone who was so used to a sad tale it was simply an old memory now. "Pa liked Jimmy best, and he always goaded us to help outside and not dally with foolish womanly ways. I gave him the most trouble. Part of it was just liking dresses and staying to the house, but there was more. Bailey would take him on, be all direct. Fight him toe-to-toe."

Bailey jerked a shoulder in a smug way. "I never was much afraid of the old coot."

"Shannon was a sneak."

With a casual two-fingered salute, Shannon said, "And proud of it. I learned to agree with him and then go do as I pleased mostly. I think there's a Bible story about that. The son who agreed to help, then didn't, and the son who refused to help and then did. I'm pretty sure I'm on the wrong side of that story, but then so is Pa if he thinks I'm his son."

"I did my best to charm him out of his nonsense to the extent anyone could." Kylie acted mighty proud of that. "I learned to trick a smile out of him and make his favorite foods."

"You should see her bat those eyelashes when she wants her way," Bailey said dryly.

Aaron looked at Kylie. "I think I've come under fire from those lashes."

Kylie just smiled. She got up and refilled their cups.

"About the war, I know what the enlisted men lived like, the close quarters, no privacy. And the battles. To imagine a woman enduring that is beyond comprehension."

That shut them all up, and Aaron remembered the way Bailey had cut him off. It wasn't because she was eager to talk; it was because she wanted to talk about something else. The somber look on their faces made Aaron regret bringing it up.

Finally, Bailey said quietly, "My only answer to that is . . . how does anyone endure it? When in a battle, how is my being a woman any different than the man beside me. The fear is so big that being a woman or man doesn't matter. Maybe some women are weaker than some men, more easily frightened, but this isn't a little thing, like being startled by a mouse or jumping when you see a snake. This is different. This is a monstrous kind of terror. Exploding cannons, flying bayonets. Severed limbs and reloading rifles while lead whizzes past your face. How much sooner would a woman run from battle than a man? All I know is I never did."

"None of us did," Shannon added.

"I did my best to get out of it." Kylie gave them all an impish grin. "I managed to become an aide to my commanding officer. I worked more with my head than a rifle." The smile faded. "I didn't avoid it all, though."

"As for being in close quarters with the men," Shannon said, "I found most of them to be as modest as I was. We didn't bathe really, and we slept in the same clothes we fought in. It was common enough for a man to slip into the woods to find a private place to . . ." Shannon glanced at Aaron, clearing her throat. "To find the necessary. I did the same, and no one thought a thing of it."

Aaron looked between the three women, each beautiful in her own way. While Kylie was the prettiest by far, the others were fine-looking women. For some reason it seemed important for him to know what they'd endured, as if by listening to their stories he could somehow help them. But they seemed neither to want nor need his help.

"Oh, and I solved the little problem of Kylie staying on her own," Bailey said.

"You found a housekeeper?" Hadn't Gage Coulter just said there was no such critter around?

"Yep."

"Where?"

"She should be at my place today."

"A woman, out here?"

"Yep."

Aaron looked at Kylie, who asked a bit nervously, "Well, who is it?"

"She's an outcast from the Shoshone tribe."

"An Indian?"

"Yep."

"You're going to let a strange Indian woman move in with Kylie?" Aaron asked.

Bailey rolled her eyes. "You're from Pennsylvania, aren't you?"

"Virginia."

"Same thing. You know nothing about Indians. I do. I've gotten to know them, and most especially this woman."

"You've only been out here six months, and most of that was winter and you spent it snowed in. You think you know more about Indians than I do?"

"Yep."

Aaron was getting tired of Bailey's *yep*. "How well do you know her? Is she dangerous?"

Bailey gave him a disgusted look. "You think I'd arrange this if I thought for one moment Kylie would be in danger?"

"Who is she?"

"Her name is Sunrise. I've known her since I moved in last fall. She's been married to a trapper from up in the hills for years and raised up a passel of kids with him, all grown now. But picking a white for a husband made her an outcast. Her husband died last winter, and she's been living alone in a small cabin. I asked her if she'd come and stay with Kylie, and she said yes. She can help with everything. She can hunt and trap and sew. She chops wood faster than I do, and she's a mighty tough woman. Sunrise can defend that cabin better than any of us."

"Can I meet her first?" Kylie asked.

Aaron could see she was nervous. He didn't blame her.

"She'll be at my house when we get back. She's bringing her own teepee, so you won't have to find room for her in that puny cabin of yours."

"That's not what I mean. I mean can I meet her before I decide if I want her as a housekeeper?"

"I already told her she has the job."

Aaron shook his head. Now he was going to have to ride back to Bailey's. Then, because he wasn't letting Kylie ride off with a stranger, Indian or otherwise, he'd probably just have to accept that he was gonna get roped into working at Bailey's all afternoon and then ride with Kylie to her house and make his own decision about whether the new housekeeper would kill her in her sleep.

Confound it! He'd signed on as land agent. How had that turned into being caretaker to a bunch of women who couldn't figure out how to dress and act and think like they oughta?

He had a job to do, a ranch to find and claim and build. Instead, he was stuck baby-sitting these Wilde women.

"Hush up, Bert." Myra's quiet command as she entered the room cut through Norbert's moans of pain and shut him up.

A week had passed since Bert had been shot and she'd put it off until now, but Myra finally admitted the wound wasn't going to heal without stitches. And of course it was going to be her job to set those stitches. The thought made her want to empty her stomach.

Archie sat on the floor of the tiny bedroom. There was no furniture, only two pallets where Bert and Archie slept.

Archie was a hand at getting them into trouble, but as always it fell to her to get them out of it.

She got them home after Bert was shot.

She scouted around and slipped them upstairs in secret.

She fashioned a tight bandage on Bert's arm and went to work before her absence was noted.

Now she was going to have to deal with this bullet wound.

Bert lay in bed. The first few days they'd gotten Bert and Archie out the door early so they could spend the day in the woods hunting, as they usually did, which kept Mama from asking questions. But the doctoring Bert needed could no longer be put off.

Myra threaded a needle.

"No." Bert slid toward the wall. "It'll heal up on its own. Just keep a bandage on it."

Myra looked at the cut again, then at Archie. "Have you got it?"

Nodding, Archie pulled a small bottle out of his shirt pocket. Laudanum. "This'll ease the pain."

Bert's eyes went to the bottle. He'd had a taste for such things as whiskey and laudanum from a young age. Archie liked a swig of it himself, though there was no money for it mostly.

Looking at the bottle, Bert glanced at Myra with terror, then back at the small bottle. He licked his lips. Slowly he extended a shaky right hand; his left was curled against his stomach as he tried not to move that arm. "Yeah, a swallow or two should help."

"Good, 'cuz we've gotta leave the stitching to Myra. We don't dare ask Ma for help. There'd be too much explaining to do."

"Don't take too much," Myra warned. She loved her brothers, but had no idea what to do with either of them. "You'll need the rest, and the wound's gonna hurt for a while."

Bert took a swig. Too long a swig, but Myra let him. It'd be best if the poor fool went to sleep for this, because there was no way he could be quiet. And if he made too much noise and was found out, they might all be arrested.

Bert handed the bottle back.

Archie waited until Bert's eyelids got heavy and then finally fell shut. Myra looked at Archie, her eyes shifting between him and the bottle. "Good. There's still plenty left."

Archie nodded. "He'll probably be noisy when he wakes up. The laudanum will keep him quiet. We still got us a chance of driving off the Wilde woman." Archie sounded smug, which was a plumb stupid way to act with Bert lying there wounded right in front of him. "If we can run her off that claim, Myra, then you can jump in and homestead it, then make a gift of it, along with yourself, to Coulter."

Myra ran her hand deep into her wispy blond hair. She knew she was attractive enough to snare a man. Weren't half the cowpokes in town sweet on her? It was just too bad that one of the first men she'd laid eyes on when her stepfather Bo Langley had moved them to Aspen Ridge this spring was Gage Coulter. From the first minute she'd seen him, she set her cap for him and no one else. She thought there was a spark of interest in Coulter's eyes when they'd first met, and she'd done her best to fan that spark into a flame, but he never asked if he could come courting.

She figured this was because of his being busy with the short summer season, and she was calmly waiting until the man made his interest known.

And then she heard the rumors about Kylie Wilde, a woman Myra didn't even know was in the area, and Coulter's interest in her homestead. Finally, Myra discovered the way to Coulter's heart.

Snaring him shouldn't be hard, seeing as how this was the West. Women were so rare, a man would practically marry a copperhead if'n it wore a poke bonnet and could fry up decent corn pone. Myra had the bonnet, and she could cook better than decent.

If she married Gage Coulter, she'd take care of Archie and Bert, too. She'd see they got hired on with him. It stood to reason that Gage wouldn't want the lazy louts around. But Myra was sure a wife could sway her husband.

She'd thought it would be simple to drive Wilde off, but they hadn't figured on that land agent being there. And Myra sure hadn't planned on the man firing back. Big war hero, Myra had heard. A man who was ready for trouble.

Their first try had failed, and Myra might've quit if Archie wasn't so set on trying again. Archie had a mean streak, and if he got riled, Kylie might vanish and no one would ever think a thing of it. Indians, wolves—there were plenty of things that could be blamed.

Yet Myra would know her brother had done something terrible to Kylie. To stop that from happening, Myra needed to get her hands on that homestead. That'd be the safest thing for Kylie and the best thing for Myra.

She'd be a good wife to Coulter, too. All she had to do was figure out a way to make Kylie run.

Sunrise seemed like a steady woman. Not much of a talker, but when she spoke it was in clear, if accented, English, just as a woman would speak after years away from her tribe, one who'd been married to an English-speaking mountain man. And usually whatever she said needed saying.

Aaron helped set up the teepee and found the process

interesting. He decided he'd live in a teepee on his homestead while he got his cabin built.

Once Sunrise had finished, she said, "I hunt now." She picked up her bow and arrows and slipped silently into the woods.

That left Aaron and Kylie alone in the cabin.

Aaron really needed to go. He hadn't done a lick of work yesterday—not counting working like a slave for the Wilde women of course. And now here he was spending another day with Kylie, so he could make sure she was safe with her new housekeeper. Which she most certainly was. Except now Sunrise was gone.

"Are you going to be all right?" he asked.

Kylie shrugged, her eyes wide and worried. "Yes, except what if those men come back and try to burn me out again?"

Which meant no, she wasn't going to be all right.

"I'll stay until Sunrise comes back," Aaron said, which was exactly the opposite of going, and he really should go.

"Someone is always taking care of me." Kylie frowned. "I know I'm a disappointment to my sisters and pa."

He really couldn't go. She needed him.

"They can't figure out why I don't try harder to learn how to get on out here in the wilderness." Kylie looked down at her fingers, twisting them together. "They wonder why I'm not content with frontier life. I can't figure it out either, but it's true. I hate the distance. I hate the hard work to do every simple thing. I had to throw a huge fit to get my stove." She nodded at the small potbellied stove in her kitchen. "My family thinks I should be content to cook in a fireplace, and I should. Mostly I just can't be happy living so completely alone."

Out here where Aaron intended to stay forever.

Kylie looked up.

Aaron looked down.

Their eyes met.

The moment stretched on.

Considering Kylie wanted a life completely different from what Aaron had planned, it was a blamed-fool notion that made Aaron move closer, lean down, and touch his lips to hers.

A blamed-fool idea that felt better than anything Aaron had ever done in his life.

Aaron was having a stern talk with himself about just what a bad idea this was at the same time he slipped his arms around Kylie's slender waist and pulled her against him. He tilted his head and deepened the kiss and quit berating himself to focus on kissing her.

"Stop! We can't do this!" Kylie jerked away from him and pulled him right along with her, as her arms were still tight around his neck.

"You're right. We can't." Aaron obeyed her, mostly, not as fast as maybe he should have, what with having to pry her arms loose and pausing to kiss her another time, or two, or three.

Kisses she returned enthusiastically. Honestly, the little woman didn't seem to want to be let go of at all.

Finally, Aaron got away.

She covered her mouth, although it looked more like she was just touching her lips, remembering how it felt to be kissed and maybe holding that kiss close. With her eyes locked on his, she backed up until she hit the rocks around the fireplace. That seemed to shake her a bit, and she crossed her arms.

And licked her lips, which were pinker than before and maybe a bit swollen. He studied them mighty close to be sure. He noticed too that her hair hung down in those streaked honey-brown-and-blond curls. It had definitely been tied up in a knot on her head. He had a vivid memory of the silk of her hair in his hands and just how slender she was at the waist.

Not a good enough memory, though. He'd like to touch her hair again. He'd pay better attention next time.

The kiss had gone on quite a while, yet at the same time it had ended far too soon.

"Aaron, we can't be kissing like that." Her eyes flickered to his lips.

"There are a lot of ways to kiss. If you don't think we should be kissing like that, we could keep trying until we find a way you like."

"Oh no." Kylie shook her head. "I liked it just fine as it was."

That seemed like an invitation to do it again. Aaron took a step toward her.

She held up her hand, palm facing him. "I'm not staying out here in the West, and you are. We can't be together. I can't let any man turn me aside from the life I want."

"It was just a kiss, Kylie." Aaron knew that for the lie it was the second it came out of his mouth. It wasn't *just* a kiss; it was the finest kiss ever in the history of the world. What's more, Aaron didn't have one bit of doubt that they could improve on it.

Which annoyed him into saying, "After only one kiss,

it's a little early to be talking about me turning you aside from the life you want."

"It's a little early for a lot of things. In fact, it's 'before a kiss should have happened.'" Kylie fluttered those beautiful dark lashes, and her starburst eyes flashed fire. "And now we're firmly into 'after it happened' and settled entirely into 'it'll never happen again.'" She pointed at the door. "I think you should go."

"What about the flaming arrows?"

Kylie quit pointing and covered her mouth again. From behind her hand she asked, "What are we going to do?"

Aaron had an answer to that he figured would only get him slapped. He tried to clear the fog from his brain so he could think about something other than stealing another kiss. He had to figure out a way to convince Kylie to stay in the West with him. Yep, way too early for a lot of things.

Then, under the guise of escape, he got an idea and looked out the window at the forest that came too close to her cabin. "I'm going to go start building you a chicken coop. That'll keep me busy until Sunrise gets back. Have you got an ax?"

"I don't have any chickens."

"I'll get you some. Then you'll have eggs to eat." Aaron needed to do some hard work. Chopping down trees would make a likely distraction.

Kylie pointed to a large wooden box in the corner near the front door. "Shannon made that, and it holds quite a few tools. That's where I found the hammer and nails I used on the roof."

Aaron remembered her dangling from the eaves and had a sudden desire to drag her home with him where he could take care of her forever, too early or not.

"I'm not sure what else they left me. There are some tools in the barn, too."

"Don't you chop wood and split logs?" Aaron headed for the toolbox, swung it open, and found an ax right away.

"I've managed to avoid it. Bailey seems to like swinging an ax for some reason, so she's kept me in kindling."

Aaron dragged the ax out and turned to Kylie. "I'm surprised she agrees to do it. She doesn't seem like a helpful kind of woman."

"I have to put up with some complaining, that's for sure. But Pa wanted me to claim a homestead, although I didn't want to do it at all. So they've done a lot to gain my cooperation. And besides, they've seen me chop wood. They know I'll freeze to death without help."

Aaron hefted the ax, looked over at sweet Kylie, who got people to do her work for her and mostly made them think she was doing them a favor. And now he was joining the group. The difference was that he knew this wasn't women's work, while the rest of her family didn't have a brain in their heads.

Stalking out of the cabin, he went to swing the door shut when she put a hand on it, stopping him from closing it in her face.

"What are you doing?" He needed to put some space between them, and here she was following him.

"I'm always so lonely. I'm not going to sit in the house while a visitor is so close to hand. That would be a waste of your company."

Aaron didn't want her along; at the same time he didn't want to let her out of his sight. "Come on, then. I see a couple dozen aspens that will give us enough lumber for the coop, make your front yard larger, and allow a better field of fire. If I cut back the brush a little farther, those varmints who shot at you—if they try it again—will have to stay out of arrow range."

"That makes good sense." Kylie smiled at him as if he were the strongest man on earth, and blast it if she didn't make him feel like some kind of hero.

"Of course, that's just the front of your cabin. It does nothing for the woods in the back or the side yard. The pond makes for decent protection on the south side."

"So I can only get killed from two directions?" Kylie sounded faint as she clutched her dress's collar with both hands. "Lucky me."

When he imagined himself reaching for her again, he quickly pivoted and marched toward the first tree. He made sure she didn't come too close and yet was a little disappointed to see she stayed well back of him, outside of grabbing range. But he didn't want to accidently whack her with the ax, so it was for the best. He got a firm grip—on the ax, not so much on his mixed-up fascination with Kylie—and swung all his frustration into chopping trees.

It didn't help much. If he kept at it until he calmed down all the way, he'd have the forest stripped all the way to the Pacific Ocean.

Kylie was surprised by how much she enjoyed building a chicken coop. "The little notches fit together like puzzle pieces." The construction work around here had always been either heavy work with big logs or fine work for furniture.

Bailey liked the heavy work, while Shannon liked the fine work.

Kylie liked neither, so she mostly fetched and carried for the two of them. True, she had to put up with being insulted on occasion, but she figured it was a fair trade for getting out of hard work.

But this chicken coop was right in the middle. Not too strenuous, nothing fancy about it. The saplings, about four inches in diameter, weren't so heavy that Kylie couldn't lift them, and the construction wasn't so delicate that she could mess it up. And watching Aaron chop down the trees in a few swift blows was very entertaining. His broad shoulders and the way his muscles rippled beneath his shirt were, in fact, riveting.

Aaron smiled as he kneeled across the small coop from her. His blue eyes flashed. He'd tossed his hat aside. The sweat on his brow had soaked his blond hair to a deeper shade, and his fair skin, already tinged from too much sun, turned pink from the exertion.

They worked their way up, adding aspens, snapping the building together as though it were a toy. It was working out to be about ten feet square, because that was the length of the aspens before they started to taper.

When the walls were just begun, Aaron looked across the top of the building at her. "It's time for the noon meal."

"I'll go put something on," Kylie offered.

Woman's work. It almost made her giddy. She hurried toward the cabin, while Aaron stayed outside and did manly things. Normal life was amazingly pleasant.

Once the meal she contrived was finished, they went back to work and put in a good afternoon's labor. The upper half of the walls went slower, including a doorway and a little ramp for the chickens to walk up.

"I think we're ready to start on the roof," Aaron said. He glanced at the sky, and Kylie noticed the sun was getting low in the west.

"You've got a long ride back to town," she said. She hated to see him go.

He nodded. "You're a good hand, Kylie." He looked down at her mouth, and she could swear she felt the look all the way to her belly.

No one had ever told her she was a good hand before.

In fact, her sisters treated her like she was nothing but a nuisance.

As Kylie stood there, looking at him next to her chicken-less chicken coop, she tried to remember why she wanted to go back East so badly. Not a single reason came to mind.

It was something about bonnets and tea. Honestly, it had been years since she'd had a cup of tea. What did it even taste like?

The snapping of a twig turned Aaron away from her. He rounded the coop and put himself between Kylie and the woods. His gun came up with an easy motion. He'd had his gun holstered, always to hand, but he'd been working steadily and she hadn't even noticed he was armed. But he was, and he was aware of his surroundings and quick to step between her and trouble. His first instinct was to protect her.

Kylie's heart twisted with a pleasure that almost brought tears. When had a man ever protected her? Pa sure as certain never did; he'd sent her to war, for heaven's sake. And Jimmy, well, she'd loved her big brother, but he hadn't spent too much time worrying about his little sister.

Movement from the forest drew her attention. Waving branches transformed into human form as Sunrise emerged from the woods. Her deerskin clothing and long dark braids were so well matched to the woods, she seemed part of them. Sunrise had a bow and a quiverful of arrows hung over her body that crisscrossed her chest. She carried a heavy-cloth bag in one hand.

Sunrise looked over at the new building. "A chicken coop?"

"Yep." Aaron holstered his gun. "I appreciate the warning."

Kylie didn't know what Aaron meant by that.

"I am silent when I choose to be." She held up two sticks, one in each hand, and tossed them aside.

The snapping twig? Sunrise had done that on purpose?

"It's a good notion to warn folks in a land where most everyone carries a six-gun." Aaron turned back to the coop.

"I have dinner soon." Sunrise hoisted the bag. "Quail. Wild chickens that need no building."

"Maybe, but I don't have to hunt in the woods for hours to find a chicken. They're in a pen just ten feet from my back door."

"I like hunting. I have hours." She nodded at the coop. "You build a bit longer if you wish while I cook. I finish the coop tomorrow. No hurry with no chickens." She smiled, but the smile soon faded. "Tracks from those who attacked. I read their story." With that, she headed straight for the cabin.

The sharp interest in Aaron's eyes told Kylie the man wasn't going to be heading for town anytime soon.

It was impossible to keep the smile off her face.

"What're you grinning for? She's going to tell us about who attacked you yesterday."

"I've got three people for the evening meal, and not one of them is related to me." Kylie shrugged one shoulder and smiled even wider. "It's almost like I'm throwing a dinner party."

She rushed after Sunrise to get ready for the biggest social event since she'd moved here.

Aaron split logs for the roof until Kylie called him in for supper. When he walked up to her on the porch, he didn't plan to take her hand, but somehow he ended up doing it anyway.

She paused to look at the simple little building. "I enjoyed working with you, Aaron. You're not as bossy as Bailey. You don't look like you pity me, like Shannon, and you're not critical like Pa."

"Why would I be bossy or treat you like you're pitiful? Your help got that coop a lot further along than I'd have done on my own." He glanced back at the building. "I think you need to know—your family's a bunch of half-wits."

Kylie smiled at that.

He got the door for her and let her go in ahead of him, careful to let go of her hand. No sense letting Sunrise see that. Not that Sunrise struck him as being much of a gossip.

Kylie bustled around setting the table. He could see that working in the kitchen suited her, and he pondered how he could turn her into a woman with normal chores. The best way was to marry her, of course. But he already knew she didn't want the life he could offer. And he wasn't going to treat her like her family and force her to give up her dream by insisting she follow him into the wilderness.

Sunrise set fried quail on the table, along with biscuits, potatoes, and a steaming bowl of gravy.

"It all smells great." His stomach growled as the three of them sat down to the meal.

They ate quietly. After the meal was done and Kylie had poured them each a cup of coffee, Aaron was ready to listen to Sunrise's story.

"Tell me about the tracks," he said.

Sunrise looked from Aaron to Kylie. "Not my people."

Aaron nodded. "We figured as much. Do you know who they were?"

"Three riders. One a woman."

Kylie blinked. "A woman? Are you sure?"

Sunrise gave Kylie a strange look. "Would I have said it if I was not sure?"

Kylie flushed. "I wasn't doubting you, Sunrise. I'm sorry if it sounded that way. I was just surprised. I don't know why I would be." She sounded exasperated. "Women do all sorts of things you'd believe were men's work. And not just in the West."

"They went straight down the trail to town," Sunrise went on. "Three riders may have entered town together after the attack."

"I can ask around and find out," Aaron offered.

"One was bleeding heavily, not the woman. Three riders enter town, one wounded."

With grim satisfaction, Aaron said, "I've got me some clues to follow. What else did you see?"

"Woman has small feet, skinny, not deep prints. Not many women around."

"No, not many at all." Kylie looked at Aaron. "So few that it narrows down who it could be by quite a lot—assuming folks in town know she's a woman."

Sunrise tilted her head, confused. "How could anyone not know that? Even if they dress in manly clothing like your sister, Bailey, anyone with two eyes can tell a woman from a man."

Kylie must've swallowed her coffee wrong, because she started choking.

Casually, Aaron reached over and whacked her between the shoulder blades until she started breathing again.

"Y-you know Bailey is a woman?"

Wrinkles appeared on Sunrise's forehead. "Yes, I know."

"Does she know?"

Sunrise looked confused again. "Do you mean, does your *sister* know she is a woman? You are not sure if she knows? How could she not know this?"

Kylie giggled. "Of course Bailey knows. I mean does she know *you* know?"

Sunrise sighed. "Do you want to hear about those who attacked you?"

"Sorry. Please go on. Although I'm really looking forward to seeing my big sister again."

Aaron noticed a definite smirk on Kylie's face as she went back to drinking her coffee.

"I found hairs from a black mane or tail tangled in a scrub pine. Look for such a horse. The men were of a size. Not long-legged, not heavy. Their boots showed much wear, so look for old boots. The woman wore old boots with a small heel. They attacked soon after they arrived. The horses were tied so they could not graze. The riders had a short stay in mind."

"Two men and a woman. Slender, worn boots, a horse with a black mane." Kylie looked at Aaron, who'd eased back in his chair at the same time Kylie leaned forward. He had intelligent blue eyes, and she could tell he was sorting through all he'd heard.

"I found arrows that had gone wild. Not good with the bow."

"At least one of them was," Aaron said. "The house was hit repeatedly."

"But it was missed, too. I think one of these three has good aim."

"I'm not sure how to test people on their skill with a bow," Kylie said. "But it's another clue to their identity. Surely three people in league with each other will be noticeably friendly in town."

Aaron nodded. "But I'm not going to assume they live in Aspen Ridge just because they rode that way. It's the main trail west from your homestead and it doesn't branch out for a while. There are a lot of homesteaders around, some mountain men, fur traders, including a few who are married."

Kylie thought of something else. Here sat Sunrise, a woman married to a fur trader, eating with two whites. And Sunrise was good with a bow. Could one of the attackers have been Indian? If so, that would explain the English they'd overheard. Kylie knew Sunrise had given them solid clues, but at the same time she'd taken away a few things they thought they were sure of. Frustrated, Kylie didn't know if this was a step forward or back.

"Thank you for the meal, ladies. Sunrise, you've given me a lot to work with. I'd best be getting on." Aaron rose from the table. The days were long, but they'd worn this one clean out. It was already dusk and he had a long ride in the night to get home.

Kylie felt a twinge of fear and had to clamp her mouth shut to keep from asking him to stay.

He went to the door and plucked his hat off a hook, then turned to meet Kylie's eyes, looking worried and so kind. "Can you step outside with me for a moment?"

Sunrise stood and went to the basin on a small cupboard where Kylie washed her dishes. Ignoring them.

Kylie knew she shouldn't go out, because all she could think of was that she wanted a goodbye kiss and she knew she shouldn't be wanting that. She wasn't interested in staying here, and that was exactly what Aaron had planned. Her heart sank to think of how easily she could be persuaded to give up her dreams.

Even with all that in her head, she followed him out the door of the cabin.

Aaron knew he needed to leave her alone, but he invited her outside for a private moment, and did she refuse? Did she tell him to get going and leave her to plan her life back East, where he couldn't bear to return? No. He'd lured her outside, and the little minx had come right along with him.

What he wanted to do was reassure her she'd be safe, maybe even offer to stay. Instead, he pulled her into his arms.

Why was she so cooperative?

Why was he so attracted to this woman?

Why didn't Sunrise come after him with her bow and arrow? Hadn't the woman moved out here to protect Kylie?

Well, she was mighty poor at her job, and Aaron could think of nothing but taking over Kylie's protection. He'd move her to town, arrange for the land to be sold to Coulter, then take Kylie so deep into the mountains she'd never get back East. She'd just have to adjust to life as he laid it out for her.

He'd do his best to keep her happy until she forgot there were such things as tea parties and fancy clothes.

Maybe a few babies would keep her busy. The thought struck him so hard he managed to break off the kiss. Both of his rough hands were sunk deep into her richly colored hair.

The moon shone down on the peaceful pond to the south of the cabin. Standing together in the shadow of the porch, Aaron rested his forehead against hers and tried to gather his wits.

"What are we going to do about this, Kylie?"

A breeze hushed out of the aspens and pines. Kylie was silent for so long, Aaron decided she had no answer. He filled the silence with more kisses.

Finally she said, "Why are you so determined to go on west? You said you left hard feelings behind, but you also left your roots. You left beautiful land and the valley that was your home."

"Not hard feelings. Hate. Soul-destroying, murderous hate."

She had no response to that, and he pressed his lips to her forehead and held her tight.

"I want to be in your arms, Aaron, but the thought of moving even farther from civilization is crushing my heart until there's no room for anyone in it."

"No room for me, you mean." Aaron tried to keep the hurt out of his voice. He fought the urge to clench his hands deeper in her hair and kiss her until she agreed to give up everything, even her dreams, to be with him.

Something he wasn't willing to do for her.

"Do you hate your home so much?"

"I love my home, Kylie. You can't imagine how beautiful

it was. I own hundreds of acres of lush valley handed down through three generations on my father's side. Our cows were fat, and we grew flourishing crops in tidy rows. We had an apple orchard and honeybees, pigs and chickens. It was a prosperous farm. A river ran close along one side, full of fish. Father and I and my little brother used to spend every Sunday afternoon, all summer long, with a line in the water. Mother and my sisters would come out with cake and lemonade, and we'd spend time under an oak tree that'd been huge from my grandfather's earliest memory. Our roots there were as deep as that oak tree. We'd have fried fish rolled in cornmeal for supper, so fresh and crisp it was like heaven to chew.

"No life is perfect, but it was a fine, comfortable life, one I felt was due to the country we lived in. That's what made me fight for the North, to preserve the Union. I saw it as preserving the life I loved."

A sad chuckle from Kylie distracted Aaron from his story. "My life was somewhat less perfect."

He thought of her cantankerous old father and knew that had to be the absolute truth. "Well, my life changed, thanks to that war. When I got home, the farm was gone. My family was dead. There were no graves to visit."

"But the South has been defeated, and you fought for the Union. Surely—"

Aaron cut her off. "I heard different stories from people who might have reason to lie, but I believe the Rebs killed my family because of me. My parents, my two sisters, and my little brothers were killed because I fought for the Union. . . ." His voice became unsteady, and he stopped talking before he shamed himself by weeping.

"Aaron." Her arms tightened around him.

The guilt and pain he carried daily nearly broke him, until it was as if only Kylie's slender but strong arms held him together.

When he felt steady again, he went on. "Our property was one of many farms split when Virginia divided into two states. Some of our land was in West Virginia with the North, but the bulk was with the South in Virginia. The Confederacy used our farm and many other places along the border to attack West Virginia and Maryland. They entrenched themselves and harried the citizens right across the Mason–Dixon line through most of the war."

Kylie eased away from him, and instantly he missed her closeness. Yet he knew she shouldn't be in his arms if they had no future together. Then she surprised him by taking his hand and leading him to her rocking chairs.

They settled in and rocked as a hoot owl cried. Gentle splashing came from the pond as the spring spilled in, sending little waves toward the grassy shore. Ripples on the water picked up the moonlight.

"The day came when the South got their army right up to the outskirts of Washington, D.C. It's said that Abraham Lincoln came out on the balcony of the White House and watched the war. Some said he was within rifle range—that's how close the South got to taking the capitol."

"I heard about that." Kylie reached across the small space between their chairs and took his hand again. They rocked in time under the beautiful evening sky. Aaron loved it out here, so far from those old, ugly wounds. He'd gotten away. He'd escaped the hate. Except, of course, for the memory of it that he still had to carry.

"After the Confederacy nearly overran Washington, the Union decided they had to take back that land, the Shenandoah Valley. They used what they called a scorched-earth attack. They burned everything, killed or captured every man, woman, and child they found, burned every haystack and the crops in the fields, as well as crops that had been harvested and stored. They slaughtered livestock, leveled every building, and left nothing in their wake. They did it so there was no way the Rebs could survive on the land that had been razed. That was what I came home to. My family killed by the South, my land destroyed by the North. Everyone hated everyone. No matter which side you supported, there was plenty of reason to hate both.

"I was determined to start over, even though I had no heart for it. My nearest neighbor had lost everything and everyone too, but he'd fought for the South. He was a friend from childhood."

Aaron fell silent as he remembered that moment when he'd gone to the door of Nev's root cellar, all that was left on his land. Living underground like an animal.

Kylie leaned toward him. "What happened?"

After years in the war, Aaron had thought he was good at covering his feelings, but somehow Kylie realized this was the worst of it, the real reason he'd left the Shenandoah Valley.

Silence stretched for a long few moments as Aaron steadied himself again, and for the first time he tried to put that hurt into words.

"I had a friend, my best friend, Neville Bassett. The two of us and Nev's big brother, Leonard, were inseparable. We grew up together, ran in the woods together, complained about school and chores, swam in the creek. We built a raft and spent hours every chance we got floating down the river and hiking back, pulling the raft on a rope. Every summer we built a bigger raft, a better one. We hunted, played robbers and cowboys, and . . . and war." Aaron's throat went dry, and he had to swallow hard.

Kylie's hand let go of his and slid up his forearm to clasp his arm just below the elbow, as if she wanted to lend him the strength and courage to go on.

"Lenny was the leader of our little gang of outlaws." Aaron couldn't remember it without affection and terrible pain.

Kylie's hand tightened even more.

"When the war broke out, Nev and Lenny fought for the South. They were both in a fury to think the powerful government in Washington would tell the states what to do, said no real American would stand for it. Neither of our families owned slaves, but it wasn't about slaves to them. It was about freedom. But all I could see was a fight over keeping slaves or not. Why would Nev and Lenny risk death to preserve slavery?" Shaking his head, Aaron closed his eyes.

"I still can't believe we fought that war. I kept thinking it would end. To me, saving the Union was a worthy cause, yet what kind of father sends his sons out to fight and kill and maybe die so slavery can go on? I thought for a long time that finally those powerful slave-holding fathers in the South, who were financing the war and pushing for it, would say, 'It's not worth my son's life. We quit. End it now.' But they never did."

"The war was as brutal as it was," Kylie said quietly,

"because both sides were American, and Americans don't know how to lose. Both sides came to the conflict with the thirst for freedom that made this country great. That's why it was fought to the death."

"Ugly, stupid waste of lives." Aaron remembered the worst of it. "The day came when I faced on the battlefield the Southern Army of Virginia, the unit Nev and Lenny were in. I never saw them; I didn't recognize any of the men we fought that day. I hope and pray that no bullet of mine was involved when Lenny was killed. But what difference does that make? I was shooting others from my own state. Nev knew what unit I was in. When the war was over, I went to his home. It'd been destroyed just like mine. I was so lonely and heartsick from my family's death. I hoped we could mourn together.

"Nev told me Lenny was dead. I remember his exact words. 'I swear before God that if you had any family left, I'd shoot every one of them and make you watch, and then I'd finish by killing you.' Then Nev grabbed his rifle and fired. He was in the cellar, and the rifle caught on the door and went off. He was half mad. Maybe more than half. He was dressed in rags, thin to the point of starvation." Aaron paused, again swallowing hard. "I ran. He chased me through the woods near our home for hours. It was a terrible deadly version of the games we played when we were young. I finally lost him and went back home, but he was lying in wait for me there and almost killed me. I knew that if I stayed, I'd die. Or I'd have to kill my best friend. I couldn't stand the thought."

Aaron looked away from the pond to Kylie, and met her gaze. "And if I go back, that's what I'll face. What's worse, if I took you, you might die along with me. Nev wasn't the only one who hated me and blamed everything on me, but he was the worst because we'd been friends. His hatred was what I couldn't bear."

Aaron let out a sigh. "After Nev attacked me, well, before that I'd been blaming the Rebs for my family's deaths. Once I saw Nev, though, I started having nightmares of me killing him, and him slaughtering my family. I still have those dreams. He isn't the only one guilty of hate."

"I have them, too," Kylie admitted, giving his arm a squeeze.

Aaron needed to stop talking and hear Kylie's story. What all had she seen?

They exchanged a long look, and too much passed between them. Too much, at least, for a man and woman who couldn't be together. Aaron looked back to the water.

"I've never said that out loud before, Kylie. That the hate wasn't all on Nev's side. I blamed him and my neighbors for my misery. I grieved for my parents and turned that grief into hate for everyone. Sitting here, in this peaceful place, finally I can admit that—and know that it's wrong."

"War and hate, hard to have one without the other. You need to try and hate a man to make yourself kill him." Kylie's warm hand slid back down to take his. He ran his thumb over her knuckles. Talking about his loss seemed to lighten it somehow.

Frogs sang in the night, and a splash on the pond drew his attention. He watched as a beaver made its way across the water, leaving a widening V behind. It had gotten late as they talked, and he still had a long ride home ahead of him.

Getting away from Shenandoah had seemed like he was

getting away from the feelings, but now he realized he'd carried the hate west.

"There might be places in the Bible that men can debate," Kylie said. "Places hard to understand, and folks differ on the meaning. But not when it comes to hate. It isn't allowed. 'Love your enemies. Pray for those who persecute you.'"

The beaver reached the far side of the pond, the rippling behind it continuing on.

"I haven't for a moment done any such thing," Aaron said.

As the gentle sounds of the night soaked into his mind, he felt the sweet strength of Kylie's presence and the sway of the rocker and found his first prayer in far too long. Cold knots he hadn't known were there eased in the deepest part of his heart and soul.

He prayed he could let go of the hate. Let go of the guilt.

This night, this woman, and a loving God made it possible. A weight lifted from his shoulders as his simple prayer came to an end.

None of his problems were gone. He'd left enemies behind that made it impossible to go back home. And he was coming to care for a woman whose dreams were the exact opposite of his.

If he wanted to go on loving Kylie Wilde—and he most definitely did—he had to convince her to join their lives somehow. But once they were joined, it was even more unthinkable that they'd go to Shenandoah. Because if he did, he'd lead her straight into misery. She might even die if he took her home. He couldn't risk that.

And he had one more problem above all the others. Someone had tried to burn Kylie out, and they hadn't cared much if they ended up killing her. Those varmints were still out there, no doubt plotting to try it again.

Maybe the West was no better than the East.

Thinking of those who had attacked her straightened his shoulders. He needed to deal with Kylie's enemies. And he'd start right now.

"I need to get on home, Kylie."

Her chair stopped so suddenly he wondered if she'd forgotten he wasn't here to stay. She gave him a wide-eyed look, and those hazel eyes glittered in the moonlight. He saw fear, and it was all he could do not to drag her out of her chair and into his lap.

He had to leave before he did just that. "I'll look around in town and ask some questions, see if I can get to the bottom of who attacked you. You're in good hands with Sunrise."

She could probably keep Kylie safer than he could. A humbling admission.

"Come back anytime, Aaron." Kylie gave him a sad version of her beautiful smile.

Admiration for her blossomed into something else, something more. Something he was just going to have to learn to live with . . . or rather learn to live without.

He rose and strode across the porch and down the steps to untie his horse from the hitching post. He mounted the saddle before he did something really stupid, like kiss her goodbye and make promises he might not be able to keep.

Riding away, he looked back just once. He saw that she'd stepped down off her porch and stood there bathed in moonlight, watching after him as he left. Then he turned his back on the prettiest woman he'd ever known.

Bailey showed up before dawn. "I'll make coffee. You put some clothes on."

Kylie shook off sleep and rolled her eyes at her bossy big sister. "Good idea. I probably wouldn't've thought of getting dressed without you telling me." Kylie tossed back her thin blanket. Coffee was boiling by the time she had her clothes on.

Shannon showed up with a dozen eggs just as Bailey poured the first cups. Kylie sliced a rasher of bacon, which Bailey had brought a week ago.

Bailey questioned Kylie about the new coop, making plans to come back tomorrow with a few of her own chickens.

Sunrise came in next carrying three skinned rabbits and a lumpy cloth bag that she dumped out to show some odd roots. "Stew for dinner." The Shoshone woman had already been hunting this morning.

Kylie started the bacon frying while her sisters and Sunrise made rabbit stew and organized Kylie's life. She didn't even mind too much, so long as the food kept coming.

They were close to finishing their breakfast when hoofbeats drew their attention. A quick glance out the window made Kylie gasp. "It's Coulter, and he's not alone."

Bailey and Shannon, both dressed in their manly clothing, rushed to the windows, each taking their own side of the door, staying back so as not to be noticed.

Kylie wondered if their disguises would hold. "You don't have to hide from him. Aaron's already changed your paper work, so the fact that you're women is out now."

Bailey scowled at Kylie, then glanced at Sunrise. Kylie realized Bailey thought Sunrise still believed her to be a man.

Shaking her head, Sunrise said, "I have known you are a woman from the first. I saw no reason to question the clothes you chose to wear."

Bailey looked startled but then went right back to complaining. "It may be written down on paper, but if Coulter discovers we're women, pretty soon all his cowhands will know, and then everyone will know." Bailey drew her gun and edged to the side of the window. "Our chances of living quietly will be gone."

"I know Coulter," Sunrise said. "Hide if you have a mind. I will go out so he will know Kylie isn't alone."

Bailey and Shannon exchanged a look. Kylie knew it didn't suit them to let their little sister take charge of anything, but this once she was right, and here she stood in a dress, no secret life to hide. Besides, they probably trusted Sunrise to take care of things, and the big-sister brigade was here if she needed to call in the cavalry.

Finally, with a jerk of her chin, Bailey said, "You go talk to him, Kylie. Sunrise, stay close to her. Get rid of him."

"Coulter is not easily gotten rid of," Sunrise said, "but we will try."

Shannon returned to the table and poured more coffee for herself. Bailey stayed on guard.

Kylie, with Sunrise right behind, stepped out as Coulter rode up with another man. A wild man from the looks of him, with a full beard and long hair, his clothing made of deerskin. His shirt was beaded like an Indian's, and he had knee-high moccasins on his feet.

"Tucker." Sunrise spoke first, and Kylie realized Sunrise knew everything about this country, far more than the Wilde sisters and most likely more than Coulter, though maybe not more than this man who rode with him.

"Sunrise, what brings you here?" Coulter asked.

"I live here." She hadn't brought out her bow and arrows, which gave Kylie comfort. The woman clearly expected there to be no shooting trouble.

Coulter's mouth twisted. "It appears you're making yourself even more comfortable, Miss Wilde." His eyes wandered to the teepee visible in Kylie's yard, to the trees cut back in the front, and lastly to the new chicken coop standing between the teepee and the cabin.

What had Aaron said last night? Kylie hunted around in her head. "I cut the trees back to give me a better field of fire. Whoever shot flaming arrows at my cabin is gonna have to do it from a lot farther back now. It's all part of settling in on my land."

Coulter grunted. "Who else is here?" He looked at the corral, where Bailey and Shannon had penned up their horses.

No doubt Coulter remembered she only had one horse; the gray mustang was the only livestock to her name.

"My brothers," she said.

"Well, get 'em out here. I want a word with 'em."

"Your business is with me, Mr. Coulter. My brothers respect my ability to handle my own affairs." Oh, how Kylie wished that were true. "I've asked them to stay inside." As if her "brothers" had ever done as she'd asked, even once in their lives.

Coulter narrowed his eyes, obviously annoyed, yet he didn't push. He gestured to the man riding with him. "This is Matt Tucker. He works for me from time to time, and I've asked him to look around and see if he can figure out who attacked you the other day."

"Howdy, miss." Matt Tucker, bareheaded, wore a buckskin jerkin and pants of the same light-brown hide with fringe up the sides. He sounded younger than he looked.

Kylie studied him closer and realized that, sure enough, he was a youngster, probably only a bit older than she was. Even so, he had the hard look of a man who'd lived in the mountains for a long while. How did a man pick such a solitary life at such a young age?

"I have scouted," Sunrise said.

Tucker nodded. "That's good enough for me. Tell me what you found, so I can go hunting the varmints who attacked Miss Wilde."

"Aaron Masterson's already looking into it," Kylie said. "We'll let him handle it."

"I welcome Tucker's help," Sunrise said. "He is good on a trail. *Nearly* as good as I."

Hearing how Sunrise stressed the word *nearly* caught

Kylie's attention, especially when it was followed by Tucker's face breaking out in a smile.

Sunrise smiled back. Kylie had a sudden interest in seeing him without all the fur on his face. She suspected that under that beard was a good-looking man. Not that she cared. If ever there was a man who wasn't interested in civilization, it was Matt Tucker the mountain man.

"Nearly as good, Ma?"

That nearly staggered Kylie. "He's your son?"

No, he couldn't be. His hair was light brown, the ends burned nearly blond from the sun. He had shining blue eyes. He showed no trace of a resemblance to Sunrise with her midnight-black hair and eyes. And hadn't she heard that Indians couldn't grow beards?

"Not son of my blood. His pa and my man hunted together. Tucker became mine when his ma died." Sunrise then said to Tucker, "This is my home now."

Tucker nodded and leapt off his unsaddled horse with the grace of a big cat. He rode a gray mare with a black mane and tail. The horse wore an odd-looking bridle that didn't appear to have a bit.

"How is the Gru?"

"The Groo . . . ?" Kylie turned to Sunrise, wondering what that meant.

Sunrise smiled. "His horse. It's a grew-ya."

"Grulla," Tucker echoed. "That describes her color, but I gave it to her as a name. Ma calls her Gru sometimes. She's a mustang pony I saved when she was young, and she's the best horse a man ever had." He patted her gray shoulder. The mare lashed a hoof at Tucker and tried to bite him.

Kylie jumped. "That's the best you've ever had?"

Tucker laughed. "She's still half wild, and she only stays with me because she wants to. That's the only reason I stay anywhere too, so it suits me fine."

"I would like to show Tucker the tracks I found yesterday," Sunrise said as she walked down the porch steps. "Perhaps there is still something to teach the boy."

Tucker laughed again. The man seemed quite happy. Kylie wondered if being a mountain man was in fact a carefree way of life. It sounded like a lot of hard work to her, and lonely.

Tucker swept Sunrise into a hug that hoisted the short, stout woman off her feet. When he set her down, Sunrise reached up and tugged on his beard. "I thought you shaved this fur in summer. You look more animal than man."

"Reckon that about describes me, Ma. I been busy, but it's time to have at the beard and get my yearly haircut."

"I will see to it for you. You are clumsy, and I do not trust many with a razor close to your throat."

The two of them laughed while walking side by side toward the woods.

"So, I'm not allowed to meet your brothers?" Coulter drew her attention back to him.

From the window Aaron had broken, off to the side so she wasn't fully visible, Bailey said, "I'm Bailey Wilde. Consider me met, Mr. Coulter."

"Two extra horses," he called back. "There should be another brother in that cabin."

"There is, and the other one's less friendly than I am." Bailey had a husky voice, naturally deep for a woman. But she cast it a bit deeper when she said, "Say your piece and be on your way."

It was all Kylie could do not to turn and gawk at Bailey. It appeared her sister was going to let her stand out here alone.

Maybe Bailey's confidence in her disguise had been shaken, with Aaron seeing her for a woman almost immediately, and Sunrise knowing all along. It would be more normal for Bailey to come rushing out, gun in hand, and take charge. Instead, she held back, hiding. But she still tried to run Coulter off, so Bailey hadn't completely lost her nerve.

Coulter smiled at the voice, a cold-edged smile that made Kylie shake in her boots. If she'd had a gun on Coulter, she would've handed it right over and apologized for being so rude.

Bailey was made of sterner stuff. "I said, state your business and go."

That smile faded as his gray eyes focused on the window. Kylie looked behind her, figuring Coulter wasn't paying her any attention anyway. Only a shadowed outline showed, and Kylie couldn't make out a single detail. The way Coulter was staring, she wondered if those icy eyes didn't have a bit more strength than a normal human, because he kept looking even though there wasn't much to see.

Finally, Coulter turned away from the window. His smile returned, warmed a bit as he looked at Kylie. He leaned close, but when he spoke there was no doubt he meant his voice to carry to the window. "I had a mind to ask if you'd like to ride out with me, Miss Wilde. A pretty woman moves in, and a man is apt to wonder if she'd be a likely . . . friend." The silence between the words *likely* and *friend* carried a world of meaning. "But I think I'll hold off on that ride. I've got another notion I want to track down first."

"Notion?" Kylie had no idea what was going on with Coulter, but something was definitely afoot. He struck her as a man who didn't make decisions or change his mind on a whim, so there had to be a substantial reason why he'd come over to invite her to go riding, then changed his mind. That change made her nervous. What's more, she was certain he knew she was nervous and enjoyed it.

Coulter tugged on the brim of his hat, looked back at the window, and nodded toward Bailey's silhouette. "When Tucker gets back, tell him I rode on home. He and Sunrise can figure out how to go about making you safe out here, Miss Wilde. I don't like nesters on my land, and I mean to see you and your whole family gone. You may find you don't like my tactics, but you won't be hurt by them. Well, not *exactly* hurt."

"What does that mean, 'not exactly hurt'?" she asked.

Coulter just smiled, nodded to her and Bailey's shadow again, and turned his horse. Before he could ride away, Aaron came trotting into the yard.

Kylie swung her arms wide. "I've never had this much company in my life."

Riding up, Aaron hopped off his horse as if he owned the place and intended to stay. Coulter's plan to leave was abandoned as he too dismounted and hitched his horse. At the same time, Tucker's grulla wandered off, grazing.

"Who else is here? Where's Sunrise?" Aaron asked as if he thought Kylie was in danger from Coulter.

Kylie wasn't so sure he was wrong.

"Tucker and Sunrise are going over the trail left by those bushwhackers," Coulter said. "I'm going to join them."

When had he decided that? First a ride, then no ride. Then he was leaving; now he was staying. Gage Coulter seemed to be turning downright whimsical.

Aaron turned toward the woods. "I'd like to see 'em, too. I did my share of tracking in the wilderness around my farm back East."

"We'll go together." Coulter slapped Aaron on the back.

"Are you all right?" Now Aaron was looking at her. "Do you mind staying here alone?" Aaron's eyes shifted to the corral, and the tension went out of his shoulders. He recognized the horses.

"Her brothers are inside. Standoffish types." Coulter said it with a strange hint of amusement that made Kylie uncomfortable.

"Let's go, then." To Kylie, Aaron said, "I'll be back before long. I left town with no breakfast, if you've got any to spare."

The two men started heading toward the woods.

"You've met the brothers, then?" Coulter asked in his deep voice.

But Kylie couldn't hear Aaron's reply. Just seconds later, they disappeared into the brush.

Bailey came to the door behind her, still keeping to the side. "That man wants your land, Kylie."

Kylie walked back to the cabin and went inside. "A bunch of strangers are taking over my life. It reminds me why I want to go back East. On the other hand, it's nice to have all this company."

Bailey was still looking at the woods, where Coulter and

Aaron had vanished, probably worrying Coulter might try to sneak back without Aaron with him.

Shannon stood to pour coffee for each of them. "I think he wants way more than the land." She hadn't been watching, but Coulter had spoken up nice and clear, and she'd heard every word. "What else is he after?"

Bailey holstered her six-gun. "I'm sure we'll find out soon enough."

Kylie had the sudden urge to laugh. "You two need to grow up."

Shannon arched one of her pretty dark brows.

Bailey, never so subtle, said, "What?"

"Come away from the door, Bailey. Drink your coffee and let me tell you about how I grew up a few days ago and put on a dress."

Kylie had never felt quite so in control. Shannon gave her that indulgent motherly smile of hers, and Bailey rolled her eyes but conceded to Kylie's request.

Kylie had seen the two of them react to those men. Her sisters, as much as they liked to pretend otherwise, were women, with women's interests. For being the baby of the family, it gave Kylie a spark of pride to realize that accepting who she was had renewed her. She felt like she was starting life all over again. And it wasn't just a renewal of her way of life; it was a renewal of her mind and spirit, too.

There was a Bible verse about being born again, and Kylie knew what that meant.

"Bailey, do you know that I can't remember ever once in my life seeing you in a skirt?"

Bailey clumped across the room in her mannish boots, her hair short as a boy's. She sat with her legs splayed, her every move masculine. Except when she reached for her coffee mug and her hand curled around it. Even with its work-hardened calluses, her hand was purely feminine. She had many of the masculine moves down just because she lived her life in a way that fit such moves, but her hands were graceful and delicate, and belied any attempt at passing herself off as a man.

"I suppose not," Bailey replied. "Jimmy was just a year older than me, and from my earliest memory I was tagging along with him and Pa outside and wearing britches just like them. I don't remember much before I was four. Ma was busy with you, and Shannon was already running with me."

They'd been four in a row: Jimmy, Bailey, Shannon, and Kylie. Four babies born just about as fast as possible. Kylie wasn't sure why, but Ma was always a quiet woman. For some reason, though the older ones ran outside with Pa, Kylie got to stay inside with Ma. And then Ma had died when Kylie was ten.

"You got to put a skirt on once in a while, Shannon," Kylie said.

Shannon nodded. "What are you getting at? It seems to me that Bailey and I have been taking a lot of care of you out here. I'm not sure how that means we need to grow up. I think it might be the other way around."

It didn't even pinch, because Kylie had figured out that being a grown-up man didn't make a lot of sense when you were a woman. "It's time you two figure out you're women, and what's more, buried under all the nonsense you've been taught by Pa, you *want* to be women. You like good-looking men. It comes naturally to want a man of your very own, to want babies of your own. You scoff at it, but it's as natural as breathing to a woman to want these things. And the day I figured that out, I became more of an adult than either of you."

Bailey snorted and rolled her eyes. Yet Kylie had seen the way she'd watched Gage Coulter. Bailey could snort all she wanted to. She'd liked looking. And Kylie had noticed the same with Shannon, who sipped her coffee with a dismissive smile.

Kylie made no further comment. She'd had her say. Her sisters would have to figure this one out on their own. It'd be fun to watch them fight against it, but there was no doubt in her mind they'd lose. Because like it or not, her take-charge big sisters needed to grow up, and outside Kylie's cabin right now were two real manly reasons they might get started with that growth spurt.

Matt Tucker was a man who fought shy of people. Aaron had never met him, but he'd heard stories. When the mountain man materialized out of the woods, utterly silent and looking as untamed as the rest of the Rockies, Aaron knew who he was.

There'd been tales in Aspen Ridge about him. Some said he was part Indian, others a legend, still others a ghost. Now here he stood, in the flesh. There was nothing ghostly about him. Wild, though. Mighty wild.

"This is Aaron Masterson, Tucker." Coulter's voice, deep as a pounding drum, didn't waste much time with niceties.

Aaron gave Tucker a nod. "I've heard a tale or two about you. Coulter and I thought we'd come and poke around the trail Sunrise found."

Sunrise stepped up from behind Tucker. She had the same silent way about her, the same ease in the woods as Tucker.

"You left Kylie at the house?" Sunrise asked.

"Her . . ." Aaron caught himself just in time, before he spoke the truth with the word *sisters*. "Her brothers are still there."

"Brothers." Sunrise rolled her eyes, then looked between the three men with a faint smile. "I will leave the three of you to handle the tracking. Tucker can show you what we have found. Perhaps you can learn more about the cowards who attacked our girl."

Her tone said very clearly that she doubted the three of them together were better than she was alone. Aaron didn't even let it bother him, because she was probably right.

Sunrise left as silently as she'd come.

"Matt." Aaron held out his right hand to Tucker. It reminded him of where shaking hands had come from—a sign of peace, two men offering the hand they used to wield a weapon.

"Call me Tucker." The mountain man reached out and shook Aaron's hand in a good-natured way, as if he'd never seen a weapon in his life. A pretty good trick considering he had a Winchester rifle hanging down his back from a strap over one shoulder, a pistol holstered on his hip, a bowie knife in a scabbard that crisscrossed his chest, a whip looped and hanging from his belt, and Aaron glimpsed another, smaller knife poking out from under the man's sleeve.

Matt Tucker appeared to be a man who was ready for trouble.

"Sunrise talked me through the tracks she found last

night," Aaron said. "I'd like to see them, especially where the horses were tethered. I'm going to look for tracks in town too, so it'll help to lay my eyes on them."

"This way." Tucker held up an arrow. "We found this."

"Sunrise missed that?"

Smiling, Tucker flashed white teeth. "Yes, and I found it. Made Ma mighty humble."

"Ma?"

Tucker nodded. "My own ma died when I was three—birthing a second child, I was told. I don't remember none of it. Pa was living in the high-up hills, wilder than a mountain goat but a good man in his way. He had no idea what to do with me, so he took me to his trapping friend's house. Sunrise's husband, Pierre Gaston. She raised me when Pa was gone, which was most of the time. Pierre was gone mostly, too. They had them a passel of kids, and I fell into calling her Ma, still think of her that way, and her young'uns became my brothers and sisters. We had us a time."

His story reminded Aaron of the fun he'd once had with Nev and Lenny. Running the hills, fearless, their whole lives stretched out ahead of them, too young to worry over the future. Then, before he knew it, he was heading west and running for his life.

"The arrow was in that tree right there." Tucker pointed to a spot maybe ten feet overhead.

Aaron furrowed his brow. "But they were shooting from right here." He indicated the place, which was right below where the arrow had stuck.

Coulter joined them, crouching beside some torn-up ground. "They set up here, only a few feet back of that tree. The trees you cut for the chicken coop were thick enough that they had to get this close or they'd have never gotten an arrow away." Coulter stood, keeping his eyes on the spot. "Even so, that arrow went almost straight up."

Tucker nodded as he stroked his thick beard. "Cutting the young trees makes this safer, but the trees still stand on two sides. Ma thinks she's invincible, but I don't like her being here. She's still one woman against three." Tucker looked over at Coulter. "Three outlaws who may think they're doing your bidding, Gage."

"Well, if that's true, I'll make 'em sorry they thought such a thing. I've already spread the word. I promise you, I'll get a noose on this mess." Coulter drew his six-gun, a Colt Army 1860, the same gun Aaron carried. With a harsh metallic click he checked the load, then re-holstered it with a smooth, practiced move. He looked up to where Tucker said he'd found the arrow.

Aaron figured himself for a tough man. He'd faced down a lot of trouble in the war, but he was glad Coulter was on his side in chasing whoever was harassing Kylie. He wouldn't want to be the focus of Coulter's talent with a gun.

"Whoever it was, he let the arrow go with little skill. Ma found several others gone wild, but she missed this one." Tucker grinned. "I found it."

"So, one among them was good with a bow." Aaron studied the tracks near Coulter. He could see where someone had knelt. He recognized the boot prints Sunrise said were a woman's. He saw the worn-down heels on the men's boot prints. So far he agreed with everything she'd said.

Tucker pointed to a clump of aspen a few paces deeper in the woods. "Here's where they tied their horses. They weren't here long."

More tracks, the ground disturbed and the grass trampled but not eaten. Sunrise said they'd left their horses so they couldn't graze.

"They came, unleashed their arrows, and then rode away. They came to scare her, not kill her." Tucker looked at Aaron. "The fact that you were there hastened their departure. Most likely they'd have stayed long enough to burn down the cabin if you hadn't been there shooting back." He pointed to a black smear Aaron would have missed. "Blood. You hit one of them. It has to have happened back there where they were set up to shoot, but I couldn't find any drops there. If it's hidden by clothes, we may not be able to tell he's wounded, not unless he shows his pain or favors the wound somehow."

"Sunrise told me all this last night. Stay back from the horses. I don't want their hoofprints messed up."

Tucker's eyes showed amused irritation. Good. Aaron figured the man might as well know he wasn't the only one who could read sign.

Dropped to his haunches, Aaron studied the tracks again. Three horses, all of them shod, two mares and a gelding. He saw the long black strand from a mane still hanging from a branch in more than one place. This one horse had been eating from the aspen branches. "The black-mane horse is a small one."

"And based on where the lady's boots are, I'd say she was the one riding it." Coulter came closer, his eyes roving, shrewd enough to look underfoot, overhead, and all around.

"Seems likely," Tucker said.

They were silent for a while, with Aaron still staring at

the tracks. Nothing unusual about them. Shod horses was even more evidence this wasn't Indians, although an Indian may ride a horse with shoes if he'd stolen it or traded for it and the shoes came along.

The hooves weren't all that distinctive, but he hoped he'd recognize them if he saw them again. "I'm not seeing much that makes these prints different from any other horse of medium height and weight. Am I missing something?" Aaron straightened and took satisfaction in towering over the other two.

"I believe I'd recognize them if I saw them," Tucker said. He didn't sound all that sure.

Coulter shook his head, not adding anything.

"So I look for a woman rider and two medium-sized men, one of them wounded in a way that probably doesn't show." Aaron dragged his hat off his head and slapped it against his leg. "And they're probably from Aspen Ridge."

The clues were weak. It'd be pure luck if he could track these varmints down based on what they'd learned here.

"Don't let the direction they rode blind you," Tucker said. "There are lots of homesteaders around."

"Way too many homesteaders," Coulter muttered.

Tucker gave a humorless laugh. "Too many, and more coming all the time—scaring the game, tearing up ground that ain't fit for farming."

"Some with wives and grown-up daughters." Aaron had a list back at the land office.

"Homesteaders are usually hardworking types," Tucker said. "Not a lot of time for scheming when you're trying to wrest a living out here."

"Do you . . . ?" Aaron paused, wondering if he was going

to get a fist in the face, but he had to ask. "Do you consort with the women in town, Coulter? Could there be one who thinks to win your favor by doing such a thing as this?"

Coulter scowled. "There's no one."

"That you know of," Aaron added.

"I can't rightly say about things I don't know about." Coulter's fist clenched, but he didn't seem inclined to plant it. "But there is no woman in that town I've given attention. I'm too busy, and the women are too ugly."

There was a moment of stunned silence.

Tucker cracked first. Aaron felt a ripple of laughter and tried to fight it. When Tucker near bent in half laughing, Coulter gave him a shove that almost knocked him on his backside, but that only left Tucker laughing harder. Aaron lost his fight and stepped back, out of shoving range, until he could lean against an aspen and howl. Coulter gave them both an icy look before his control slipped and he laughed, too.

The three of them, laughing like fools, found a strange bond. Different men with different ideas of how to go about living but united in Coulter's assessment of the slim pickings among the women of Aspen Ridge.

The other two might've been laughing because of Coulter's rude comment, and that was part of Aaron's amusement, but there was more. Aaron laughed because he knew neither of these two had seen the rest of the Wilde family.

Aspen Ridge had about fifty people living in town. Aaron went over his paper work and the few buildings in the ramshackle town all day and night and could come up with only twelve women besides the Wilde sisters. Those twelve didn't include wives of homesteaders.

Because however he chased ideas around, it made no sense for anyone to want Kylie's claim, except that it could get her Gage Coulter.

The claim was in a poor spot, with no grazing, no land for farming. The water was good, but on its own no one would want that claim enough to steal it. There were much better claims available, though the land was filling up fast.

Aaron just couldn't figure out which of those twelve women, running with two men, would attack Kylie. Two worked abovestairs in the saloon. No reason they'd want land, but neither did Aaron expect that those women were as honest as they ought to be, so they might team up with some varmints to cause trouble.

Setting aside his sorting of the Aspen Ridge women, he wondered how in tarnation to find out if anyone was talented with a bow and arrow. It was a skill that needed a lot of practice, and Aaron had never heard a whisper of such a thing, nor had he seen a bow and arrow in town. It was a weapon so associated with the Indians that white men rarely used one. Aaron and his friends had played with bows as kids, built their own, and gotten to be a pretty decent aim. They didn't cost anything and were as silent as the tomb, which made them a good thing for young'uns. But most pioneers carried guns and used them for protection and for hunting.

The Wildes had all been in Kylie's cabin this morning. Aaron tried to wheedle breakfast out of Kylie after scouting for her attackers, but he could tell right off that she wasn't inviting him in. He knew why, too. If she let him in, she'd have to ask Coulter and Tucker in as well. And she didn't trust her sisters' disguises to hold up. So he got run off right along with Coulter and Tucker. It still stung, especially since Tucker hadn't ridden away. Instead, he stood off to the side, talking with Sunrise.

It left Aaron frustrated to the point he was tempted to take it out on someone. He had no idea who, though. Maybe he oughta arrest every single woman he saw. That'd make sure he didn't miss the guilty party. Honestly, Aspen Ridge was a raw western town; most of the folks here had something they were running away from back East. He should just round up the whole town.

A half-wit idea if ever he had one.

He wandered to Sandy's Livery and Blacksmith to check for horses with black manes. There were plenty. He was finding no natural skill for detective work and he was sick of trying. He hoped Sunrise was taking care of Kylie, and he worried about it until he wanted to punch someone.

"Howdy, Masterson."

Aaron looked away from the corral. Matt Tucker rode up on his grulla mustang. It had a black mane and tail.

A smile broke out on Aaron's face. Tucker reminded Aaron of the sheep he'd helped shear at Shannon's place the other day. "What happened to you?"

Tucker's face was scraped raw. A nick showed on his square chin, and a line around his neck was pure white to match his face.

"A shave and a haircut happened," Tucker said. Bareheaded, he ran a hand over his hair that'd been cut nearly to bristle length. "After you left, Ma sat me down and barbered me half to death."

Aaron chuckled at the thought of Sunrise bullying this tough mountain man. "My ma had a knack for making me sit down and do as I was told, too."

Thinking of his mother, who'd still been a youthful, pretty woman when Aaron had left for war—the last time he'd seen her—took the pleasure out of the moment.

Aaron turned back to the corral. "I've been going over the women in town and around the area. While there aren't many, I still can't pick out which one was involved in the attack. After looking over the livery horses, I plan to wander around town to see who's putting their own horses up at home. If we find the ones with black manes and check which of the horses are ridden by women, we might be able to narrow our search to here in town."

Tucker grunted. "I reckon they're from town. Why would a homesteader want to drive another homesteader off her land? They can't buy it and can't homestead it. Unless they've got a personal problem with Kylie, it makes no sense."

"Did you stay and eat at Kylie's?" Aaron tried to sound casual, but he saw Tucker's eyes sparkle.

"I ate, but it was outside while sittin' on the porch rocker. Ma sat with me, but Kylie barred the door from me just like she done for you and Coulter."

"Coulter didn't come back and harass her, did he?" Aaron's temper rose. He trusted Coulter not to attack, yet he also knew Coulter wanted that land and he'd find a way to get it unless Kylie was careful, and some of Coulter's tactics might not be pleasant.

Tucker didn't stop a smile this time. "I rode over with Coulter this morning. I had a notion Coulter was riding over there to sweet-talk Miss Wilde into spending time with him."

"What?" Aaron spun toward Tucker. "I need to ride out to Kylie's right away and warn her."

"Hold up, Masterson. Coulter changed his mind before you got there."

"Why'd he do that? What man would see Kylie Wilde and not want her?" That was saying too much, and Aaron knew it even before Tucker's smile widened.

"I didn't ask. I only saw Gage again while you were there, but he sure enough didn't have Kylie with him and he didn't stay after we went tracking. The man has good instincts about people, so I'm guessin' he saw it was a wasted effort and decided on a new way of going after what he wants. I work for him every now and again, and I know the man well. One thing you can be sure of: He ain't giving up that pond. That's one of the most dependable water supplies in the area, and he thinks it's his. And we're heading into a dry summer. One pretty little lady nester isn't going to turn him aside, at least not easily."

"There's law in the area now. Coulter isn't going to get away with breaking it like that."

"I reckon he knows that as well as anyone. Which'll make him more careful. But there're ways of getting through to a woman without breakin' the law. He won't turn aside from his plans." Tucker looked out at the corral and the herd of horses, resting his arms on the top rail of the fence out back of Sandy's Livery.

Half of the dozen horses had black manes. "Some of these Sandy owns," Aaron said. "He rents them out by the day. Some belong to others and he boards them."

A stocky old man, mostly bald, came out of the livery stable. He walked with a rolling gait, as if his knees pained him.

"Howdy, Sandy," Tucker said.

"Tucker, I ain't seen you in town in an age."

"I haven't needed much a town could give me."

"Can I help you?" The old man's eyes shifted to Aaron. "Or you, Masterson?"

Sandy knew the riders, the horses, and the town a whole lot better than Aaron. And Aaron boarded his horse here, so they'd talked many times.

"We got us some questions about these horses, Sandy." Tucker hooked his thumbs in the waistband of his fringed buckskin pants.

"Come on in. I had a quiet morning, so I used the forge fire to make coffee," he laughed.

The old man's laugh was on the ragged edge of a giggle. A strange old bird, but he took good care of his stock and was the town's only blacksmith. And in a town full of horses, that made Sandy one of its leading citizens.

He was just the man they needed to talk to.

Myra had ridden out here several times in the last week, and for a while she thought they'd done it—driven Kylie off. Now here she was back again, and since she'd come there'd been others coming and going constantly. Kylie had a good scare, but instead of giving up her claim and running, she'd just surrounded herself with help.

They were going to have to scare her worse.

Today she was here, and there wasn't a passel of folks around. Finally.

Myra had spent much of the war—after all the money was gone—hunting in the swamp around their home, and she was better than fair in the woods. She'd done a sight of exploring in this new northern land. If she wanted to be a rancher's wife, she needed to figure out how all her swamp skills translated to the pine forests and mountain peaks.

Besides, staying in the miserable rooms they lived in had become downright unbearable.

Archie hissed and caught her arm. She froze as a squat Indian woman stepped out of the cabin, rounded it, and disappeared between the house and pond.

Myra and Archie had left wounded Bert back in town. He wasn't up to being much help anyway. But without him, they couldn't use burning arrows again. Neither she nor Archie were skilled enough, though Myra intended to start practicing soon. She couldn't do it now, though. Someone might notice and start asking questions.

"What's an Indian doing in there?" Archie whispered. They saw the woman emerge from the far side of the cabin, stride across an open stretch, then vanish into the thick woods to the east.

They'd seen the forest cut back from the front door and had slipped up on the side across from the pond. Archie had a gun, but Myra wasn't going to be party to any killing. While she wanted this land, she'd seen a man hung once and had no wish to die in such an ugly way. She'd get this homestead without turning to murder. But she wasn't opposed to scaring someone.

"You're sure this will work?" Archie held up the writhing burlap bag Myra had handed him.

"I'm sure it'll scare her. Added to the worries of the Indian attack, it oughta move her along."

"There's no window on this side of the cabin. How do we—?"

"Hush!"

Archie obeyed. She could see it riled him that he had, but still he kept his mouth shut.

The door swung open, and a young woman showed herself. Kylie.

Myra hadn't gotten a good look at her before; she'd been on the porch the first day they'd come, mostly standing behind Masterson. Kylie walked down the steps and stood facing the pond as if enjoying the view.

What a waste of time, staring at water.

"Give me that bag." Myra hated touching it, yet she didn't trust her brother to do things right.

He seemed eager to hand it over, and who could blame him? Myra untied the rope that fastened the burlap, clutching the bag tight to keep it closed.

After a long old time spent staring, Kylie walked around the cabin.

"Wait here." Myra rushed for the cabin, quiet as she could manage, darted up the front porch steps, doing her best not to make them creak, opened the front door and, with a wild fling, shook the bag so it opened and the contents emptied onto the floor.

Myra had lived close to the swamps in Alabama and learned many things, including a skill that'd come in handy today. Keeping hold of the bag, she quickly closed the door and ran back into the woods.

She snapped at Archie, "Let's get out of here!"

She was no killer, but what she'd just done could end up with Kylie scared out of her wits, and that was the goal.

Sprinting to their horses, Myra was in the saddle and racing for town without even looking back for Archie. But he was a dependable coward, and she knew he'd keep up with her.

Kylie thought about the little talk she'd had with Shannon and Bailey this morning. It was all part of her claiming her new life. She'd told them to stop dressing and acting like men and start planning to round up a husband. It was the bossiest thing she'd ever done. They'd taken it well.

Either that or she'd left them speechless.

Once they'd left, she'd helped Sunrise finish the roof of the new chicken coop. Now Sunrise had gone into the forest to gather firewood while Kylie piled up the chunks of kindling left from their building by the side of the cabin. That wood needed to dry before it would burn well. As Kylie stacked it, she thought of all the company she'd had lately. Why, it was almost a social whirl! Then bossing her sisters, and now finishing a building.

It had been a fine day.

Kylie headed for the cabin, pleased with her accomplishments. Walking up the steps, she swung the door open and hurried across to the stewpot, hoping to get it warmed up as soon as possible so they could eat. The morning's work had left her famished.

She pulled the pot forward, then turned to the woodbox and reached for a piece of kindling to stoke the fire.

A rattlesnake lashed out at her from the woodpile.

A shriek tore from her throat and she leapt back. She tripped over her own feet and fell, screeching.

The snake went straight for her, its hissing head quickly pivoting as it got ready to strike. On her backside, she spun to face it and clawed away, afraid to turn her back. The snake lunged forward, and she felt the impact on her boot.

Though she felt no sharp fangs cutting her skin, the snake's six-foot-long body coiled around her skirts. She screamed again, scrabbling along, desperate to escape, but she brought the snake with her. It wrapped tight around her ankles.

She slammed hard against the cupboard. Pulling herself to her feet, her hand landed on a knife. Her butcher knife. She grabbed it, turned, and aimed for the snake's head and slashed it hard, severing its head.

Thankfully her boots were made of thick leather and had protected her from venom, as well as the knife.

She ripped the snake from around her legs. Even headless the snake hung on. As she struggled with it, her eye caught another, larger snake slither out from the cold fireplace. It hissed at her, gathering itself to strike.

The door flew open. Aaron stepped in, gun drawn. His eyes followed her gaze. He spun, saw the snake, and blasted it.

"Rattlesnakes!" Kylie screamed. "Two of 'em. Careful, there might be more." She whirled around, looking in every corner. "Get me out of here!"

Aaron rushed to her, relieved her of the butcher knife by tossing it on the table. Then he ripped the dead snake loose from her body.

Just as the coils finally let go of her, Sunrise came running in. She entered with an arrow notched in her bow, surveying the bleeding snakes and then Kylie.

Breathless, Kylie sprinted for the door, but Aaron caught her and hoisted her into his arms. "I won't put you down until we're sure there aren't any others."

Kylie threw her arms around his neck and nodded.

"This is a good cabin. Tight, well built." Sunrise's calm voice penetrated Kylie's panic just a bit. "These snakes did not crawl in."

"Someone put them here." Aaron stated it as an absolute truth. "Just like the flaming arrows."

Hearing their voices soothed Kylie, and although she was by no means calm, she was able to think again. "Someone wants me dead."

"No," Aaron said. "These aren't poisonous snakes."

"They are. They're rattlers. I've seen rattlesnakes before."

"They look like rattlers, but they're gopher snakes. Whoever did this wasn't trying to kill you."

"They're not . . . deadly?" Kylie tried to get herself under control. All she could think of was to run and never stop running.

"No, Kylie. They're big and ugly and startling, but not dangerous. They're just here to scare you out of your wits."

"Scare me out of my cabin, you mean. And off my land." Kylie lifted her eyes to meet Aaron's.

"That's right," he said with an angry tone. "Whether he ordered it or not, this is because of Coulter." Aaron's arms tightened around her, and she felt like he was the only solid thing in her whole world.

"As soon as you're calm, I'm going to go see him and demand some answers, and this time I'm not leaving until I get some."

"No!" Kylie said. "You can't leave me."

Kylie wouldn't let go. Her breathing sped up, but her lungs seemed unable to grab ahold of air. Pinwheels of light exploded in her head. The world darkened at the same time she saw bright explosions. Her vision was like looking down a long tunnel.

"I can't stay. I can't . . ." Her voice rose to a near scream.

A sudden splash of cold water against her face startled her out of the panic. She blinked and saw Sunrise holding a tin cup, now empty.

"Better now?" Sunrise asked. Though the water seemed cruel, Kylie quit gasping and panting. It had worked.

But it didn't change a thing. "I can't stay here!"

Aaron took her by the hand. "Then come with me to Coulter's."

"You go," Sunrise said. "I will stay and make sure there are no other snakes in the cabin. Then I will hunt the real rattlesnakes, the ones who put these beasts in here."

Kylie didn't like that plan at all. "No, you shouldn't stay in here, Sunrise. Who knows what these folks will do next? Forgive me—I never should have asked you to come out here when I knew I was in danger."

"Don't worry yourself. I know how to handle all kinds of snakes, rattlers, or men. Do you need more water thrown in your face?" The strong response from Sunrise made Kylie feel safer, just as Aaron's arms did.

Kylie shook her head. "I feel a little better now, thank you."

Sunrise rested a hand on Kylie's shoulder, and some of the woman's strength seemed to help steady Kylie's wobbly spine. Sunrise said quietly, "I stepped too far away, my girl. I am sorry I was slow to come."

Kylie reached up and clasped Sunrise's strong hand. It was all right. No one could watch over her every minute of the day and night.

She would let Aaron take her away. She would leave Sunrise to clean up the mess and chase after evidence of who had done this latest attack. What she wouldn't do is ever sleep in this cabin again. Not for a single night.

Whoever wanted her gone had won.

Aaron carried Kylie out of the house and straight to where his horse stood, unhitched. He lifted her into the saddle. No snakes up there.

"Watch her while I saddle her horse, Sunrise." Aaron wasn't sure Kylie would let him go, but she managed it. It felt wrong to take even a step away from her. He wanted to hang on. Every time he shut his eyes, he heard her screams.

When Kylie's mustang was ready, he helped her onto her horse and mounted up himself. As they were about to head out, Sunrise said, "Send Tucker if you can find him. He might be at Coulter's." Then she melted silently into the woods.

Though he'd put Kylie on her own horse, Aaron kept wanting to pluck her off and carry her in his lap, hold on to her tight, soothe her. She startled at every dancing limb and each time a shadow flicked ahead of them on the forest trail. She rode so close to him, her horse bumped his several times.

He didn't want her so scared and defeated when they faced Coulter. Aaron was positive she'd just tell Gage she was leaving and the land was his. That didn't give Aaron much power to strike a bargain.

The trail widened into a mountain meadow of lush grass, swaying in the breeze. He spotted a tumble of boulders piled near the base of a bluff along the meadow's edge.

There was a tranquility here. It was so open there wasn't much to frighten anyone.

"Let's sit a spell," he said.

Kylie looked at him, her eyes wide. "Have you never heard the words *snake in the grass*?" She glanced down at the thick grass, as if the ground were crawling with rattlers.

"It'll be all right. We'll sit on those rocks over there."

"Don't snakes sun themselves on rocks?"

Aaron decided to stop talking. He took her reins and guided both horses toward the rocks. Dismounting, he made quick work of switching to a halter on both horses and staking them out to graze. He went to help Kylie off her horse, but she had her hands gripped on the pommel so hard her knuckles were white. With some resistance she finally let go.

He carried her to a big flat rock off a ways from the others. "Look at this boulder, Kylie. No place for a snake to hide." He toted her like a crate of vegetables, in a complete circle around the slab of stone, and he had to give her credit for obeying him.

"Are you okay?" he asked. "Can we sit here awhile?"

Kylie shrugged, and he took that as a yes and set her on the boulder. It was hip-high to him, waist-high to her. Her feet dangled so they didn't reach the grass should a snake be hiding there.

Together they listened to the shushing of the wind and the quiet cropping of the grazing horses. An eagle shrieked overhead, drawing his eyes upward. The noble bird with its shining white head played on the drafts of air, rising and swooping until, a few moments later, it soared out of sight.

Aaron turned to the pretty woman beside him. She'd

been watching the eagle, too. The tension that had gripped her since she'd jumped in his arms back at the cabin had finally eased some. Her color was better, her shoulders less rigid.

"What do you want to do, Kylie?"

Turning away from the vivid blue sky, she looked at Aaron. Her hair, usually coiled neatly at the nape of her neck, had come loose during her desperate fight with the snake. He slid his fingers into its lustrous strands shot through with a hundred shades of blond and light brown, and his eyes moved to her lips. He knew what he wanted to do, what he had to do. There was no longer much choice.

"I can't go back there," she said.

The dead certainty of her words only made it more definite. He was done fighting what had been obvious since the first moment he saw her, when she'd fallen off that roof and he caught her.

He put his arm around her shoulders, and she leaned against him, resting her head on his chest. Aaron didn't trust himself to speak. He had to claim Kylie Wilde, make her his in every way possible. He knew this might not be the life she wanted, but maybe it was time to do what was best for her. What was best for the two of them, together.

He suspected her family had been handling her like that, ignoring her wishes, for the better part of her life, and she was used to it at the same time she hated it.

"I have an idea, Kylie." He had no idea what to say at a time like this, but no man did. No man made a habit of proposing. If he did it right, he did it once in a lifetime. So how could he expect to get any practice?

She managed a smile for him. Her lips trembled a bit, but the smile held. "I'm listening."

Before Aaron said anything, he leaned down slowly, holding her gaze. He saw such vulnerability in her eyes that he couldn't resist. He touched his lips to hers and then eased her closer to him. Her hands slid up his chest. At one point she hesitated, and he thought she'd push him away, but then she wrapped her arms around his neck and held on tight.

A minute later, he was holding her on his lap, just like she'd been the night they first met. He should have recognized his fate and just hauled her to town and married her then and there.

When their next kiss turned fiery, Aaron ended it while he still could. Moving his hands to her shoulders, he gently pushed her away from him. She straightened, cleared her throat. He thought maybe her terror had finally subsided. The worst of it, anyway. With a slight shake of her head she focused her eyes, and it looked like she was back to her old self again.

"I can't go back, Aaron," she repeated. "I just can't. I've been trying while we ride to work up some backbone. I thought I could live out here for three years. I probably could survive on a homestead if no one was trying to shoot arrows at me or bully me into leaving. I'm worthless at frontier skills, but I'd do it for my family so long as my sisters kept the food coming and did my repairs. And if I had Sunrise there to do all the things I can't. But now, after the snakes . . ." She shuddered.

"I hate that you had to go through that, Kylie. How did you ever survive the war?"

Kylie's chin came up. Her jaw tightened, and her eyes flashed with renewed spirit. "That's the right thing to say to me. When the going gets tough, I remember the war. I survived when many didn't." She sat up straighter. "I let the snakes get past my defenses, and only now when you asked about the war do I remember how I learned to be tough."

"You said you were at the siege at Vicksburg. Where else did you fight?"

"I was only in a few battles, but they were so wretched. They struck such terror in me that I could barely function. I never ran, though. Deserting . . ." Shaking her head, Kylie went on, "Maybe running took more courage than I had. I froze more often than I fought. I . . ." She stopped again, swallowed hard.

Aaron saw the fear in her eyes. For a whole year after the war, he'd seen that same fear every time he looked in a mirror.

"I killed a man," she said. "I shot into a crowd of charging men. I don't even remember pulling the trigger. But a man got too close, and he had his bayonet fixed and was screaming as he charged straight for me. There was such hate, such rage in his eyes. I knew I'd die if I didn't fight back. My gun roared, and I saw the pain in his face. He didn't go down right away. He kept coming, and somehow I dodged that bayonet. Then he collapsed on top of me and died. I might have been unconscious for a while, I don't know. Maybe I was just scared out of my head. I just lay there, drenched in his blood. I was so shocked by it all, I didn't move. I spent the whole rest of that battle pinned under a dead man as cannons pounded around me and more men fell and died."

With a humorless laugh, Kylie added, "Yet I don't get to count my years of service when I homestead." She shrugged. "Maybe that's fair. I was poor at soldiering. Maybe I didn't earn that exemption."

"I don't know how to fix that. And I'm sorry you saw such ugliness." Aaron took one of her clenched fists and eased it open, threading his fingers through hers. "I'm sorry I saw it. I'm sorry anyone had to see it."

"We won that day, which was a good thing." She went back to her story. "If the Confederacy had won, I'd have been found and taken prisoner. Instead, the Union controlled those few yards of bloody grass, and they dragged me out from under that man and took me to the infirmary. I was so soaked in the man's blood, they assumed I was wounded. In all the chaos it took them a while to realize nothing was wrong, not physically. I was in such shock they didn't know what else to do with me, so they left me in a badly needed bed as long as they could."

Aaron lifted her fingers to his lips and kissed each one.

"I had nightmares of that man running his bayonet through me. I'd close my eyes and see him coming and hear him screaming. I finally pulled myself together and got out of the infirmary, but I was so afraid to go back. Everyone was, but I was determined never to go through that again. I marched into my commanding officer's tent prepared to admit I was a woman and demand I be sent home. Pa would've been so ashamed of me. I was already practicing my lie, how I'd lead Pa to believe I'd been found out in the infirmary and sent home, that it wasn't my fault.

"I got there just as a general was saying his right-hand man had been killed. I saw my chance and jumped at it.

I told the general I could read and write. I made sure he knew I'd come from the infirmary and let him assume I'd been wounded. I was always too good at leading people to believe a lie without saying a dishonest word. I'm finally old enough to be ashamed of that. But back then I considered it a handy skill. I played on his concern for such a young boy facing the horrors of war. They needed someone's help that very minute, and I got the job."

"You were manipulating people even then." Aaron couldn't help smiling.

"We all have our talents." With a sad smile that showed most of her spirit had returned, she said, "I always handled Pa better than my big sisters. I learned how to turn his attention, distract him, offer him food and a comfortable home, and with a great deal of subtlety let him know I'd have a hard time providing those comforts if I was running around wearing britches, plowing fields. No one can really handle Pa completely, but I did better than most. I used those same skills in the war. As the general's aide, I was kept behind the battle lines. Mostly."

"And you were a spy, too?"

"I was good at it for a reason none of my commanding officers ever realized. I'd leave camp as a sneaky young boy, change into women's clothes, and do my spying as a woman. Army men had a weakness for just the sight of a woman, and also a disrespect for their intelligence. So they'd talk in front of me while I brought them food or cleaned whatever house they lived in. They really should have been more careful. Then I could vanish completely by turning myself back into a boy. Using this trick, I ran back and forth between enemy lines many times."

Aaron sat beside her in companionable silence in the beautiful mountain meadow. He didn't know if she realized she was still on his lap, but it seemed like a good thing that she was so comfortable being there. It made it a bit easier to say what he wanted to, knowing he was asking for trouble.

"I think I have the solution to your troubles with your homestead," he said.

But that was the wrong way to speak of what he had in mind. He dug deeper and thought of a better way.

He drew her close and kissed her.

17

Kylie liked kissing Aaron a lot more than she liked remembering the war or the snakes or burning arrows or even flapping shingles. In fact, she liked it more than anything else in the whole world.

Yet she knew it was a mistake. He was headed for the mountains and would no doubt soon be as wild a man as Matt Tucker. She was headed for the East, though admittedly she wasn't heading there with any great speed.

And her kissing him, and most certainly sitting in his lap, not to mention wrapping her arms around his neck and hanging on as if her life depended on it, wasn't sending him the right message at all. Still, for something she knew with all her common sense to be absolutely wrong, she'd never felt anything so perfectly right and she couldn't stand to let go.

Finally, he straightened away from her. "Kylie, I want you to marry me."

"M-marry you?" Her voice squeaked in a way she'd never quite heard before. "I don't think—"

He cut off her answer by kissing her again. After far too long he spoke again, close this time, so that his lips moved on hers. "We have to get married."

"We do?" He sounded so sure that Kylie thought he might know better than she did.

"Yes, because I want to hold you for the rest of my life. I want us to be together. We'll find a life that makes us both happy."

But where? Was she to live the rest of her life in this hardscrabble country? Almost hysterically she had a vision of herself wearing buckskin and beaded fringe. She imagined Aaron with a wild full beard, his blond hair reaching halfway down his back. It was nothing she wanted.

Except she wanted Aaron's arms around her. She wanted him to stay with her and not leave her alone in the wild ever again.

She even wanted Gage Coulter to take that stupid pond back and leave her alone. If Coulter wasn't trying to scare her off, someone sure was. Once they knew they'd succeeded in making her run, they'd quit with the arrows and snakes and whatever other dangerous mischief they could devise.

"But what about—?"

His lips landed on hers again, longer this time, deeper. Every speck of sense in her muddled brain lost track of itself by the time he raised his head. "Say you'll marry me, Kylie. That's what a man and woman do who enjoy each other as much as we do. We can be together all day and . . ."

She saw his Adam's apple bob as he swallowed.

". . . all night." He kissed her again, soft and gentle, a kiss that woke up places inside her she hadn't known were asleep. Places she hadn't known existed.

He hadn't said they'd move east, but he said they'd find a life that would make them both happy. Kylie suspected happiness was too much to ask. Except right now was the happiest moment of her life. Could she be happy just to be held in Aaron's arms? Yes, she could, but happy enough? Was it selfish of her to want more?

A sad twist to her heart reminded her that he hadn't spoken words of love, most likely because he didn't love her. She suspected no men said such things. Her pa certainly never had. Love was something sweet but impractical, fit for fairy tales but not for real life. Kylie was a practical woman, and if it left an empty ache in her heart that Aaron couldn't speak of love, well, still he had to be a big improvement on Pa.

He was right. In fact, she suspected she had little choice. It felt like she was tearing apart inside, half wanting to stay beside him always, half wanting none of the life he offered . . . outside of his arms.

Married, she'd be safe. It may be wrong to marry for such selfish reasons, but she couldn't go back to that cabin. His hand slid down her back, and it was as if he claimed her, owned her. She couldn't long for a man's touch like this and not accept his proposal.

She opened her mouth to say yes.

Unshed tears closed her throat. To say yes was to give up all her dreams. To say no was to lose his protection and strength and being held in his arms.

She made up her mind. Fighting to steady her voice, she said, "Yes, I'll marry you."

Before the words were even spoken, she wanted to call them back, but he was kissing her again. More passionately than ever. And before he let her go, she had accepted what was to come. A fine man to protect but not love her.

Kisses that made her understand that to be a woman was a wonderful thing, even without foolishness like bonnets and tea parties and civilization.

A life she wanted almost as much as she already dreaded it.

"Snakes?" Coulter shoved back the hat he wore and scowled. "And you think I did that? A man who accuses me of turning snakes loose on a woman had better be prepared to draw."

"This has to do with you, and you know it." Aaron tucked Kylie behind his back.

"I'm not hiding from Coulter." With a shove, she stepped out of grabbing range, darted around her fiancé, and stuck herself right between these two bull elks. She dodged Aaron's outstretched hands. "And we're not accusing you of doing this."

She crossed her arms, daring Coulter to take his temper out on her. Of course, he'd never do it. She could tell Gage had that code so many western men went by that wouldn't let him hurt a woman—a code that whoever was attacking her apparently set no store by. But Gage had it, and she was in a better position to badger him than Aaron. There was no code about hurting other men.

Despite her dodging, Aaron got ahold of her and clamped both hands on her shoulders, but he didn't shove her behind him again.

Although he might have if Coulter hadn't waved his hand. "Leave her be. I want to punch someone, only it ain't gonna be either of you." Coulter jerked his buckskin gloves off and tucked them behind his belt, then removed his hat with a frustrated tug. He ran one big hand through his overly long dark hair.

"Listen, Gage, whoever's doing this knows you want that pond." Kylie was trying to be friendly and at the same time make some progress on this mess. "They're not doing it on your orders, but they might be doing it to gain your approval or maybe your attention. You say you're sure of your men, then who else could it be?"

His eyes flashed with temper as they shifted between Kylie and Aaron. "There's a good way to find out who's behind this, but I'm not putting up with it."

"What's that?"

"You move out and we see who claims your homestead. It appears someone wants it real bad." Coulter's jaw tightened, until Kylie worried he might break his teeth. "But if we do that, I lose the water again. I ain't letting that happen."

"We'd arrest whoever stepped forward." Aaron's hands tightened on her. "We wouldn't have to let them stake their claim."

"How could you stop them?" Coulter's cold eyes seemed to turn silver when he was angry. He looked from Aaron to Kylie, to the strong hands on her shoulders.

Kylie knew he was reading things about right.

"You'd have no proof they'd attacked Kylie. The first person who comes in to file that claim might not even be the one behind all this. You'd have about a minute to get to the bottom of it while they filled out that paper work. You can't stop them without any proof, and if you couldn't stop them, I'd lose that water hole."

Coulter's ice-bitten eyes turned on Kylie, and she felt the chill all the way to the bone. Aaron was right there, though, holding her up. She found his strength so alluring it was all she could do not to lean back against him and let him bear all her burdens.

"I want you," Coulter said, jabbing a finger at Kylie, "to move out."

Kylie wanted to move out, too.

"I'll be right there at the land office with you. You rescind your claim, and I buy up those acres."

Kylie took an angry step forward, knowing it was Aaron who gave her the courage to be bold, despite any unwritten code about women. "So you get what you want, and whoever attacked me goes free. All I get out of the deal is losing my property."

Aaron leaned over to her ear from behind her. "You're a lot braver around Coulter than you are around snakes." Which might be his teasing her. She wasn't exactly sure.

"If you and Masterson get married," Coulter said, his eyes lighting up, "you're gonna lose your claim anyway, Miss Wilde. As I understand homesteading laws, married women have to turn their property over to their husbands, and the husband then takes over proving up." With a smirk, Coulter looked at Aaron, standing so strong and tall, despite Kylie being in front of him. "So, judging by the way you've got your hand on this little missy here, I'd say my business is with you."

Something warmed deep inside Kylie to have Coulter

talk of her and Aaron together as a couple. She knew she should be offended by the way Coulter brushed her off as unimportant, but the notion that all her problems were soon to be handed off to Aaron was so appealing she could hardly stand it. Was this how things worked with men and women? Because this was what she really wanted—to be treated as a woman ought. To tend a home and let her husband see to making the living.

At the same time that she relished it, Kylie knew she'd been living by very different rules for a long time. She wasn't a tough westerner, and certainly not a man by any stretch. But neither was she going to be a properly demure little wife.

Coulter's dismissal of her was insulting, even if it did lift a crushing weight off her back. Was this how it was for men, always bearing this weight? Would she be able to just step back into her role as a quiet, submissive wife after so many years of living as independently as she had?

Honestly, she wanted all the good parts of both, leaving the bad parts for Aaron. That probably wasn't exactly fair, and Aaron most likely had his own ideas of how a marriage worked. If she didn't knuckle under to his ideas, would their lives be an endless battle? She'd been to war, and she never wanted to endure even a domestic version of it again.

Then Aaron flexed his strong hands on her shoulders, and she was reminded again that she had little choice in the matter. Whatever their future brought, she wanted more than anything to share it with him.

"Miss Wilde and I are going to be married. When that happens, her homestead is transferred into my name. But I have plans to move on and homestead elsewhere. As pretty as that stretch of land is that Kylie claimed, there isn't enough grazing on it to run a herd or the kind of land that would grow a crop, so it's not a practical place for us to get a start."

His hands tightened again as if apologizing for not liking her homestead, although he wasn't saying a thing she didn't already know. She'd picked the land mostly to annoy Pa, anyway. The water was good, but by itself, with no decent meadowland and the rocky soil, there was no way to make a living off of it. Pa had goaded her about that and tried to force her to take a different claim. She'd made it clear to him and her sisters that she'd claim the land and live on it for her required years, then sell out to them and leave. It would give her enough money to live in a city while she made other plans. It was the pond that gave Kylie's claim value, making it a good enough investment. But without that, the place was beautiful but worthless.

Her tormenting Pa had made signing up for that parcel of land even more attractive.

Coulter flashed a smile of satisfaction that goaded Kylie. "Let's ride to Aspen Ridge then and get this taken care of. And then if you've a mind to get married, I can stand as witness."

The thought of marrying Aaron without telling her sisters, and with this tyrannical land baron standing smugly by to take her land, was more than galling to Kylie. Yet she didn't dare tell Bailey and Shannon the news. Well, maybe Shannon would understand, but Bailey would put so much pressure on her to change her mind, she just might buckle.

Aaron might be pushing her to marry him, but at least he was pushing nicely. Coulter was pushing for that land, but at least he was straightforward about it.

But sisters knew all the right things to say. And Pa didn't bear thinking about. Which left Kylie with only one choice really. Do it quickly, before her family found out.

For one wistful moment, Kylie remembered weddings she'd gone to before the war. Not elaborate affairs, because all their neighbors were hardscrabble farmers just like the Wilde family. But the weddings had all been in a church. There were wildflowers wrapped into bouquets, and almost always the bride's pa walked her down the aisle to her waiting groom.

She'd always known she couldn't have that. Her pa was too cantankerous to do much but ruin a wedding. But she'd imagined it, even dreamed of it at times. Another dream died, and she knew her fondest dream—living in a city with lots of people and fine things—would die soon, too.

All she'd be left with was a foolish longing that everyone she knew considered frivolous and selfish. But was it? Was it so bad to want to be around people, around other women, who loved being who they were?

She'd never quite been able to figure out why her wants were so bad.

Aaron stepped up beside her, his arm strong on her back. That strength guided her to do exactly as others wanted . . . at the price of her own happiness.

"You live in the boardinghouse?" Kylie stopped dead in her tracks, most of the way out of the church where they'd had their hasty wedding.

Aaron almost stumbled at that question. He hadn't thought of where they'd spend the night. Oh, he'd thought of the night—Lord have mercy, he'd done little else but think of the night—just not the *where*. "Um . . . I reckon that's no proper place for us. The rooms sleep ten, and it's all men. Not a single woman or private room in the place."

They stood looking at each other. Coulter came up and stood next to them. He'd been trailing them out of the tiny clapboard church. At least Kylie had gotten her church. The parson was just behind Coulter and made something of a circle of the four of them.

Aaron didn't want a circle; he wanted to be alone with his new wife. And he sure wasn't going to manage that in the boardinghouse.

"For tonight, we can sleep at your cabin." Aaron realized when he'd thought of their wedding night, the location had been at Kylie's.

"I told you . . . I'm not going back there." Kylie nervously sucked her bottom lip just the littlest bit into her mouth. A distracting thing to do, and Aaron found himself watching her do that when he oughta be thinking.

"It's my cabin now, Mrs. Masterson."

Aaron liked the sound of "Mrs. Masterson" real fine, and he went back to thinking about Kylie's lips.

"But you're welcome to stay the night and clear your things out." Coulter's reminding them that he'd bought the land wasn't a welcome reminder. In fact, Coulter's entire presence here wasn't welcome. Aaron would be obliged if the man would just move along.

"She signed those papers, dropping her homestead," Aaron said, "and I signed the papers as land agent, selling you that stretch. We'll honor the law, so you don't need to push, Coulter." Aaron saw Kylie's shoulder sag, as if all of this was more burden than she could bear.

To the parson, Aaron handed a few coins. "We thank you for conducting our wedding service, Parson. We'd appreciate it if you had an evening meal at the diner, our treat. While you're at it, tell everyone who'll listen that Kylie's done with that claim, and Coulter now owns it. We want the word to get out, so that whoever's been attacking her will find out."

"I'll make sure and spread the word, too," Coulter offered. "If one of my men is doing this in some bid to get that land for me, they'll know by nightfall that they're wasting their time. You should be safe now, ma'am."

The parson thanked Aaron for the money and hightailed it to the diner to spread the news.

Aaron finally had everything arranged, and he could concentrate on his pretty new wife.

"What's goin' on here?"

Wrong again.

The squawk of rage told Aaron nothing was arranged after all. Cudgel Wilde stepped out of the general store carrying a heavy saddlebag. He saw them, saw the parson walking away, saw Kylie holding Aaron's hand, and must've figured it all out in a moment.

That didn't make him a genius.

He dropped the bag in the street and strode for them, teeth clenched, hands fisted. A wiry old man with years of bad temper cutting deep lines into his face.

"Hi, Pa." Kylie sounded more resigned than scared.

Aaron knew from their first meeting that Wilde made a lot of noise, and Kylie wasn't especially afraid of him. But no one liked their pa flapping at them like a bad-tempered banty rooster. Honestly, no one liked anyone flapping at them like a bad-tempered banty rooster—but least of all a father who was supposed to love and protect them. Despite those fists, Kylie didn't edge closer to Aaron or flinch away, which meant the old coot was more bark than bite.

While the barking wasn't upsetting Kylie, Aaron found himself mighty upset. He liked the idea of Kylie being out of her pa's reach now, at least legally. Emotionally, he could still hurt her.

"Your daughter and I just got married, Cudgel. *That's* what's going on." Aaron braced himself. Just because the old coot didn't hit his girls didn't mean he wouldn't swing a fist at a man.

Wilde didn't punch. He reeled back and choked. It looked like he was falling over backward, and Aaron shot out a hand and caught the man before he fell over his clomping boots. Up close, it appeared Wilde hadn't shaved for a few weeks. And judging by the smell, he hadn't bathed for far longer.

Kylie darted forward and slid an arm around her pa's back. "There wasn't time to invite you, Pa." She said it as if she had the intention of inviting him. Aaron knew better. "We decided to get on with it, and it's done." She smiled as if all the choking and stumbling and sputtering didn't have much effect on her. She was obviously used to her pa's fussing.

Cudgel steadied. Kylie let him go and moved back to Aaron's side. In fact, she moved just the littlest bit behind him before saying, "And after I relinquished my claim on the land, Coulter bought the homestead."

"You what?" Wilde seemed to be working up to blasting the top of his head off. His bristly face turned a shade of red that couldn't be healthy.

His eyes moved from Kylie to Aaron to Coulter, as if he needed to hit someone and was just trying to work out who.

Since he didn't seem inclined to swing at his daughter, and he wasn't quite crazy enough to take a punch at Aaron or Gage, despite his near apoplectic rage, he kept his hands to himself.

Kylie stepped forward, right into the teeth of her pa's fury.

Aaron's instinct was to put himself between Kylie and danger, but he fought off the need. Kylie had been handling her father for a long time.

"Pa, you've always known I'd have a hard time staying on that homestead. I was always the weakest part of your plan."

"You needed to hold that land! Bailey's got the grazing. Shannon's got water enough for her land but not enough for all Bailey and I claimed. The only reason I put up with you staking that claim was that pond. Our land was going to connect into something big, something worthy of Jimmy's memory. You wanted that pond when you should've picked something more practical, something with less water and more pastureland. I went along, gave you what you wanted, and now you've betrayed me and your departed brother."

"You only went along because I refused to sign for any other piece. Shannon and Bailey have enough water. You've got one good spring, and Pa"—Kylie's voice dropped to a near whisper—"none of us are ever going to forget Jimmy. We don't need a big old ranch to remind us."

"What all land has your family claimed anyway?" Coulter asked.

Aaron knew the truth and wasn't looking forward to Coulter finding out. The man had been busy with spring work and hadn't ridden out to the farthest parts of his land. He wasn't going to be happy with what he found.

Kylie was calming Cudgel down, but one look at Coulter told Aaron the man wasn't really interested in whether or not there was peace in the Wilde family.

"None of your business, Coulter. You ain't gettin' any of it." Cudgel bared his teeth, and with his unshaven face and deep lines, he looked like a cur dog.

Though Aaron wanted to scoop his wife up and take her home, he was afraid Cudgel would follow, and the man wasn't a good fit for a honeymoon. He hoped that if they talked long enough, Cudgel would either settle down or be so enraged he stormed off. Either way, Aaron would be done with this ugly scene.

"I'll find out on my own." Coulter yanked his gloves out from behind his belt buckle. "I've lost half a day's work over this, and it looks like there's more land I need to inspect."

Which probably meant he planned to get all his land back from the Wilde family and every other settler in the area, but he intended to pace himself.

Coulter looked at Kylie as he pulled on his gloves. "Thanks for the land, Mrs. Masterson."

As if Kylie had sold it to him, when in fact no money had changed hands. She didn't own it; she just abandoned her claim. Coulter had paid for it through the land office. But Coulter seemed to relish making Cudgel foam at the mouth and not care one whit if he caused trouble between a pa and his daughter.

Aaron didn't care much, either.

"Congratulations on your marriage." His eyes went to Cudgel. "Nothing's settled yet, Wilde. I've been busy sorting out your daughter's claim, because I needed that water hole and her land was closest to my dry pasture. I haven't had time to see who all else is nesting on my land. I'll turn my attention to that right soon."

"You want trouble, Coulter, I can give it to you," Cudgel snarled, deepening the resemblance to a cur.

Gage's harsh laugh said Wilde's threat didn't worry him one bit. "Don't get comfortable on your claim, old man." He tugged at his hat brim, strode toward his huge brown stallion, mounted, and galloped away, leaving a trail of dust behind him.

"Pa, don't you start on me." Kylie saw those eyes turn to her and wasn't putting up with it. "I'm a married woman now, and I don't answer to you anymore."

The very thought sent chills through her that were part terror, part excitement. What had she been thinking to marry in such haste? Had a couple of snakes really caused such recklessness?

Which reminded her. "And Aaron," she said, digging in her heels without taking a step, "I'll sleep on horseback before I spend another night in that cabin."

"Sunrise is clearing the snakes out. We'll be fine."

"We'll be snake food."

"We'll find another place, then." Aaron looked around the town as if trying to think of a place for them to go.

The boardinghouse was the only place that rented rooms.

Kylie wondered if they would end up sleeping under the stars. She'd bet there were plenty of snakes under the stars. "We can go to Bailey's."

"No we can't."

"You two stop talking nonsense about where to sleep and march right back to that land office. You're in the family now, Masterson, and you don't own no land. You can stake a claim. I'll show you where I wanted Kylie to homestead. Better stretch than what she picked anyway."

Aaron shook his head. "No—"

"I'm trying to build something out here, a legacy to my son," Cudgel went on, cutting Aaron off. "Kylie's got responsibilities to this family, and her gettin' married doesn't change that."

"It sure enough does." Aaron didn't seem to be one speck bothered by her cranky father. She felt a little jolt of love for her new husband, who was so casually batting her father's words away. This was going to be a good thing. He could fight with Pa all the time, so she wouldn't have to.

"Can we just ride out there, Kylie?" Aaron asked. "Maybe if you had some time to look around in the cabin, you'd feel safe."

Cudgel stomped right up to Kylie. Aaron made a smooth, solid move and blocked Pa from threatening her.

"You should never have left your daughters alone on their property like you did, especially when you've staked a claim too far away to protect them. You're a poor excuse for a father, Cudgel, and I'm not real interested in honoring the son of such a man."

Kylie's whole body was covered in goose bumps. It was pure joy. Her new husband was shaping up to be the best choice she'd ever made. Of course her life was just one lame-brain choice after another, so that wasn't saying much. Suddenly the snakes didn't seem quite so frightening, not compared to sleeping on the ground somewhere, for heaven's sake. Worse yet, sleeping in the boardinghouse with a bunch of other men in the room. The most frightening choice of all would be their staying with Bailey. She'd be so disgusted at Kylie for abandoning her claim it'd make snakes look warm and friendly by comparison.

It put her in a really cooperative mood. "Let's ride out to the cabin. If it looks safe, we can stay there tonight."

Aaron quit glaring at her pa, turned, and smiled down on her. "Good, let's go."

"We're not done here, Masterson." Pa slipped around Aaron and reached for her. She'd been dragged around by Pa a lot in her life and was used to it.

What she wasn't used to was having a husband.

Aaron's arm shot out as fast as any striking snake. He clamped his big hand on Pa's arm and stopped him. "Oh, yes we are."

Kylie wasn't going to be shaken or dragged by Pa ever again. Her heart lifted even higher.

Aaron, who seemed like a kindhearted, even softhearted man most of the time, spoke in a voice so cold it froze Pa right where he stood. With his great height and broad shoulders, Aaron leaned down until he was nose to nose with Pa.

"I'm not staking a claim here in Aspen Ridge, Wilde, and sure as certain not in a place of your choosing. Kylie has turned hers back, and Coulter bought it. Now we are going to get on with our married life together. There's no place for you and your mean mouth around us, especially not tonight. A *decent* father would take this moment to hug his daughter and wish her well. He'd shake my hand and tell me I'm a lucky man to get such a sweet, pretty woman to join her life with mine. But all you can do is talk about yourself. Well, I've had enough of it. We're leaving."

Pa stood sputtering in the street while Aaron boosted her up onto her gray mustang. He swung up onto his thoroughbred. He turned his horse, and Kylie gave Pa one last glance. It was a shock to realize as she looked at him—so diminished, a little man with a big mouth—that she felt sorry for him.

Pa had always been in charge of his girls. The neighbors back home had put up with him and mostly stayed clear of the whole Wilde family.

Bailey had cooperated, but she'd made it clear that she did it because she liked the outdoor life, liked wearing britches, liked pushing herself to see how tough she could be.

Shannon had worked hard out of her love for the animals, both tame and wild. She loved plants and enjoyed nothing more than hiking in the woods for hours. She was more at home in the outdoors than anyone Kylie had ever seen. And she had a knack for sneaking off into the woods and not coming back until she pleased.

Kylie had never stood up to Pa. She'd charmed her way around him, teased and flattered. She did whatever it took to get her way and she usually got it. But never by facing Pa down and saying, You're wrong, and I refuse to do things your way.

But Aaron had done just that, and watching him she

became a proud wife. What's more, Pa had backed down. And that reminded Kylie that Pa had two more daughters who might end up married someday—if anyone got on to their being women.

His troubles were just starting.

Even feeling a bit sorry for Pa didn't make her want to spend another minute in his company. Instead, she pushed her pity down deep and rode alongside her husband on the long trail to the snake house.

And wasn't that just going to be the most romantic place a woman ever spent her wedding night?

Aaron wasn't a man to think much about making a wedding night romantic. Truth be told, he wasn't a man to think much about a wedding night, period. He'd spent most of his time with men in recent years, and when he was young, with his sisters, whom he mostly lived to torment. Having Northern sympathies in the South had kept most of the girls his age away when he reached courting age, and it'd kept him away from them, as well.

And now here he was, married, and without spending much time with Kylie at all.

Oh, he wanted to be married to her. He had no regrets about that. But how did a man go on with a woman? Kill her snakes? Force her to hand over her land? Yell at her pa?

That didn't sound real romantic to Aaron, but then he had no idea what he was doing, so who could say? And killing the snakes had been heroic and that might count as romantic, except there'd been snake blood and screaming and Kylie had cried a lot. Not Aaron's idea of romance.

When they reached the cabin, dusk was settling in. Sunrise came out to greet them, and she quietly watched Aaron lift Kylie down from her horse.

He took his wife's hand and turned to the Shoshone woman. "We got married today."

Sunrise nodded.

"We let Coulter have the land," Kylie added.

That made Sunrise frown just a bit for no reason Aaron could understand. He saw his wife's eyes go between Sunrise and the cabin door. "Did you find more snakes?"

"No more. You are safe from snakes. And without the land, the attacks should end. Where will you live?"

"I'll have to figure that out, but for now we're staying here with Coulter's approval." Aaron was mighty tired of talking. He wanted to be alone with his wife.

"I left a meal." Sunrise walked away with no further talk.

Much as he liked the woman, Aaron wasn't sorry to see her go. He headed into the house, wife in tow. He shut the door firmly.

"I wonder why Sunrise didn't stay to eat sup—"

Aaron's kiss cut off Kylie's question. He pulled her hard against him, not a bit interested in supper. He slanted his head to deepen the kiss and engage Kylie's attention fully. The woman, with her worries about snakes and supper and her pa and flaming arrows, needed to pay attention to her brand-new husband.

He felt her hands sliding up his chest, slowly but steadily. Maybe he wasn't so bad at romance, after all.

"I've figured out where we're going to live." Aaron lifted his coffee cup and smiled at his beautiful wife, who'd just refilled it.

It was a pure fact that he'd been smiling pretty much nonstop all night and morning, and he didn't see himself stopping anytime soon. Being married was the best idea he'd ever had.

Kylie blushed as she peeked over her shoulder at him. She set the pot down on the stove with a clumsy little scrape of metal on metal that told him she was thinking about something else.

Him, to be specific.

Then she hurried back to the table as if she'd hated to leave his side, to walk all of five steps away to return the pot. She was smiling a lot, too.

Aaron's heart did something strange, something nice and heated that he'd never felt before. She sat down right around the corner from him without once taking her stunning eyes off of him. He knew that because he never once took his eyes off her.

His wife. He might never go to work again.

"Where?"

For a second he was so distracted by how happy he was to have her for his wife that when she said "where," a completely different notion popped into his head. He knew exactly where—and when. Right here. Right now.

Then he remembered about the cabin.

His heart felt a little less nice, because he knew she was wishing he'd say, I've decided we're going to live in Virginia. And he wasn't going to. He wasn't even going to stay here in this little cabin, not even for the day.

And leaving this place seemed like about the worst idea he'd ever had. He wanted to spend the day making love to her, talking with her, pampering her. Letting her know he was absolutely thrilled they were married, and it had nothing to do with her being in danger or whether or not Coulter wanted her land. It was because he cared about her, and because she was a sweet, beautiful, smart, interesting, and passionate woman. He was realizing more every minute that he was blessed to be given a chance to spend the rest of his life with her.

He'd spend every minute ridding her of all the nonsense her father had filled her head with all these years, as if being a son would have been better than the glorious woman that she was.

And they *should* stay here in the cabin, alone, getting to know each other better. There was nothing wrong with a pair of newlyweds having a honeymoon.

There was a good chance, now that Coulter owned the pond, that no one would try to kill Kylie or burn her out or scare her to death.

That'd make a nice switch.

Instead, they needed to get moving. Which brought him back to *where*.

"There have been so many folks coming west since the war ended that there isn't a single empty house in Aspen Ridge, and the only rooms to rent are at the boardinghouse, which is out of the question. But I've got to stay in the area until this land rush is over. I gave my word, and I'm meaning to keep it."

Her smile dimmed a bit. "What do you have in mind?"

"I'll build us a little cabin close to town. I even know the place. There's a clearing with a good spring only a mile or so out. It's not part of Coulter's grazing land, and it's not open to homesteading, but it is for sale—just a little acreage. No one will mind what we do there. I can get a simple one-room building up in a few days or so, and we can move in. I can't spend a lot of time making it nice right now, Kylie. I'm sorry. I'll give you a pretty house when we finally get settled. But for now, I need to finish up my land agent work here, which I hope to do before the snow flies. Then we'll get on with starting our life together."

"Deeper into the mountains." She said it in a steady voice. A calm voice, not unlike a person bravely facing her own hanging.

Aaron didn't respond to that. Instead, he said, "We'll ride out right now. We'll come back here at night until the new house is done."

Kylie nodded. Aaron knew she was a woman who spent most of her life putting up with not getting her way. Why should marriage be any different? She said, "Do you need my tools?"

They started packing, and Sunrise, in the mysterious way she had of being around when she was needed and vanishing when she was not, arrived to help. With her efficient hands, they had everything packed and were on the trail early.

As they left Kylie's clearing, Sunrise said, "I followed those who left snakes."

That stopped Aaron in his tracks. He'd been so busy being a newly married man that he'd forgotten all about those sidewinders who'd unleashed snakes on his wife. "What did you find?"

"Two riders. The woman again and one man. One man stayed away."

Aaron wanted to fire questions at her, but he held off. He knew Sunrise would tell him everything in her own time and in her own way.

"Different horses."

Sunrise fell silent.

It took Aaron a second to realize the significance. "Rented."

Sunrise gave him a muted smile, which on her was close to beaming. They'd just eliminated every person in town who owned their own horse. Few folks owned more than a single horse for themselves. A cattleman like Coulter had a remuda, but homesteaders and folks in town were doing well to own a single horse or maybe a team. Different horses meant . . .

"If I find out which women own horses and which rent, we might be down to a handful of suspects." Aaron heard the satisfied tone. "Maybe even just one."

"I thought the danger was over." Kylie had spent the morning sounding cheerful and calm and happily married. Now he was reminded that only yesterday she'd been in full-blown hysterics over those snakes.

"I'm hopeful your attackers will break off trying to frighten you, sweetheart. But that doesn't mean I'm not going to see them jailed. Burning arrows, even used as a scare tactic, is attempted murder." He thought of something else. "If one was wounded bad enough not to ride out with them, his injury is serious. We can use that to identify him."

"I find Tucker." Sunrise turned her horse toward Coulter's place. "My boy asks questions. You build."

"Let me give you directions to where we're putting the house," Aaron said as Sunrise reined her horse away.

This time Sunrise really did smile. "I will find you." She rode away.

Aaron chafed as the Shoshone woman rounded Kylie's cabin. He wanted to know more. He knew she'd seen more in those tracks, and now Sunrise would tell what she knew to Tucker and not him. But he didn't have time to investigate a crime right now. He had a wife and no home. They needed a roof over their heads. "Let's get on to town."

Kylie was riding beside him, and she leaned close and said, "I had a little talk with my sisters."

Having her close was enough to distract him from his frustration with Sunrise. He smiled at her, inhaled her. Being married was brilliant. "The fact that you're as good as whispering about this proves you don't believe anyone is going to think they're—"

Kylie's hand came up to shush him. Aaron supposed someone could be skulking around in the woods, listening.

He whispered, "No one's going to think they're women."

Kylie gave one of her shoulders a cute little shrug. "They'll handle their own lives their own way. My big sisters aren't exactly famous for taking advice from me, so I knew I was probably wasting my time, but I decided it needed saying. I told them it's time they chose an honest path. I let them know I was glad I'd admitted to the world I was a woman." Kylie gave him a broad smile. "And that was before I married you. Now I like it even more."

Aaron felt the smile melt off his face as he stared at the

woman he had married for practical reasons, heroic reasons even. To protect her. To do the right thing by a woman in danger. And because a man needed a wife, and a woman needed a husband. Because he respected her and wanted her.

All very practical.

But right now he was having a hard time being practical. Instead, he was finding all sorts of foolish reasons to be glad she was his. Reasons of the heart, of passion. Soul-deep reasons about finding the woman God had made for him. Even reasons of fun.

"What's the matter?" She sounded confused, uncertain.

Wondering what she was seeing on his face, he said, "You need to be mighty careful when you say that to me, woman."

"Why's that?" Now she sounded hurt.

"Because we've got a house to build, and right now, what's the matter is, all I want to do is drag you off that horse and kiss the living daylights out of you."

All Kylie's hurt was instantly gone, and those hazel eyes flashed as if they were fired by the sun. "I want that, too."

Aaron reined his horse to a stop.

It was their honeymoon, after all.

Kylie couldn't believe how much she didn't care what this cabin looked like. Honestly, she caught herself often daydreaming about how much she was enjoying married life. And that had nothing at all to do with building a house.

But the house was good, too.

It was just a larger version of the chicken coop, but unlike the coop, in the days since Aaron had started building, Kylie had helped very little.

Aaron never once scolded her for not grabbing an ax and hacking down a tree. When she offered to try to chink out the corners, he gave her a kindhearted look as if she were the sweetest thing in the world for offering and kissed her for far too long.

Aaron did ask her to sew some curtains. About the third day of their marriage—most of which Aaron had spent felling trees—Aaron took her to town. He'd left her several times to go work, but Sunrise was always close by. Never once had he left her on her own.

Kylie had ridden miles on end in these mountains alone without giving it much thought, at least not until she'd been attacked. But now she wasn't left alone for a minute. The tiny general store had very little, and the one piece of cloth was dark blue wool, so buying that took little time.

Afterward they went to lunch at Erica's Diner. She'd never been to lunch in town before. Pretending to be a man had made it a bad idea to let anyone see her. Which was just such obvious proof that it was a lame-brain idea she never should have agreed to in the first place.

Now she was being taken out to lunch, and it was thrilling to walk into the diner on Aaron's arm.

When a girl near Kylie's age brought them their beefsteak, Aaron didn't pass up the chance to make introductions and spread the news, in case it hadn't reached every ear in town already. "Myra, I don't think you've met my new wife. Kylie and I got married a few days back."

Their plates skidded.

Kylie was quick or she might have gotten a lap full of beef.

Myra gave Kylie a hard look. "I . . . I hadn't heard."

"Yep, Kylie homesteaded a ways from town, so she hasn't gotten to Aspen Ridge much."

Myra looked so dismayed, Kylie wondered if this pretty young woman had set her cap for Aaron. Well, that was a disappointment she'd just have to learn to live with.

"A woman homesteader, imagine that." Myra's voice rang false. Her gaze shifted to Aaron in a way that seemed overly interested. "So you're living out there now on her homestead?"

"Nope, Kylie's claim became mine on her marriage, but I've dropped my rights to it. Gage Coulter bought it. He was in for supper after he stood witness at our wedding. I figured he'd be crowing about it. He wanted the water hole on Kylie's place bad."

"Ma gives me a night away from the diner once in a while. Maybe he came in when I was gone. I didn't hear." Myra cleared her throat. "Well, congratulations. So you're planning to live somewhere else, then? Here in town maybe?"

Myra's voice steadied, and she sounded friendly. Maybe Kylie was reading too much into her surprised reaction to the news of the wedding. But the girl had just admitted to being gone the day Kylie got married—the same day the snakes were let loose in her cabin.

"We're building near town, but we won't homestead here," Aaron said. "I want to settle elsewhere after my land office work is done."

"Well, I've got more to serve. I'll refill your coffee as soon as I can get back." She bustled away.

A woman had been involved with the attacks on her place. She looked at Aaron, who arched a brow at her and gave Myra another quick glance. He was wondering the same thing.

Myra didn't speak to them again, not even when she poured more coffee.

Aaron was in a hurry to get back to building, or seemed to be.

The minute they were outside, Kylie said, "Why didn't we question her? That was our chance to—"

"Hush!" Aaron nearly dragged her toward the horses. He boosted her up, then vaulted into his own saddle. Kylie respected Aaron's instincts, so even though she wanted to march right back in there and shake some answers out of that girl, she followed her husband. Aaron didn't lead her back toward the clearing where the house was going to be; instead, he rode toward the livery stable and around back. Tucker was set up there with his own fire, roasting a hunk of meat.

"Myra at the café," Aaron said.

Tucker looked at Aaron; his eyes sharpened and veered toward the corral. "It fits. I've narrowed it down to three women, and that includes her."

"Marshall Langley's her pa, so have a mind."

"Her stepfather. And word is, he's got no use for her or her two brothers. They're all old enough to be out on their own. Myra Hughes is her name. She works in the diner, but she's past the age where she should've accepted one of the marriage proposals she's gotten. Looks as though no one's good enough for her. And the two boys, Archie and Norbert Hughes, are just pure lazy to the bone."

"Three of them?" Aaron said.

"Yep. I don't know much about the rest of Langley's family."

"I do. Their ma, Erica, is expecting a baby, and she's already got a little one. I didn't know Langley was her second husband, but it explains why the children are so far apart in age. I thought maybe the war separated Bo and Erica for years."

"Langley's back in town. I'll have a talk with him and tell him what we know. He's been out here since right after the war and he's a good man, mighty fed up with his layabout stepchildren. I'll ask him if one of his boys is wounded."

"How come I don't know those boys? It's a small town."

"I heard they spend their days in the woods. Both decent hunters, and they supply the diner with meat. That's the only reason Langley hasn't tossed them out on their ears."

"Good hunters? Like maybe good enough to know how to use a bow and arrow?"

Tucker arched a brow. "Could be."

Aaron jerked his chin in agreement. "I gotta get back to the cabin site. Come for me if you need any help."

Tucker gave Aaron a cocky smile that seemed to say he couldn't imagine needing help.

Aaron shook his head and looked at Kylie. "We might be getting to the bottom of this at last. Let's go on home."

When they got back, he found a comfortable stump for her to sit on, out of the wind and in the shade.

She got to work on the curtains.

He went on with building their little house and was seeing to her protection.

It was confusing. Aaron was shifting a lifetime of thinking. And all the more confusing, because she was pretty sure she was shifting her thinking from wrong to right.

She really liked being married. She set her stitches to the pulse of that swinging ax of his. As he chopped the trees back from the site, she was only slightly aware that he'd gotten a good distance away from her on the far side of the house.

He wasn't even visible when an unusual snap of a twig drew her attention. It reminded her of how Sunrise had deliberately broken that twig before she'd stepped into sight to let them know she was coming. Looking up, wondering if Sunrise had come, she saw nothing.

Then she heard, "Kylie." A whisper.

Staring, she thought she saw a shadow move, yet no one came into sight. Though Aaron was chopping the trees back, just as he had at the cabin on her homestead, there was still dense forest all around.

A chill ran up her spine. It reminded her of that night she'd stood alone on her porch and seen eyes watching her.

They'd just accounted for Myra at the diner. She'd been hard at work only hours ago. But she had two brothers, unaccounted for. But the land was sold now, which took away any reason for someone to attack her.

She opened her mouth to call for Aaron, and in a flash she was certain that whatever had frightened her was nonsense. Or gone now.

She thought of how she'd decided to be reborn into a grown-up woman who took control of her life. Even now, married and under Aaron's protection, she could do that. She gathered up her sewing and very calmly went around the house until she could see her husband.

"Aaron?"

He straightened from his chopping and swiped the back of his wrist across his brow as he turned to her. "Yes?"

She must have sounded calm, because he smiled. "I like working where I'm closer to you. I wanted to warn you I was moving. Where will I be out of the way of falling trees?"

His smile widened. "A very wise question, Mrs. Masterson." He pointed to a stump near the corner of the half-built cabin. "That one should be safe."

She nodded, then settled herself again. He went back to work. If she couldn't completely forget that odd whisper on the wind, she gave up her worries to God with a prayer as she stitched and watched Aaron work.

There weren't going to be any tea parties in her future, though. Probably not even any tea. Where they were in the mountains, tea was very expensive and hard to find, even if you did have coin enough to pay for it. As she stitched, she berated herself for being shallow and silly, and she distracted herself from foolish dreams by watching her extremely attractive husband chop down trees with a skill that made Bailey look like a shirker.

When he seemed satisfied with his new stack of logs, he set the ax aside and looked at the house, the walls about halfway built.

"I can help." Kylie knew building went better with two people, and her curtains were done.

"I'd appreciate that." He straightened, swiping his forearm across his sweating brow again. "I'm to the point where I need to put the windows in, and you can help hold things in place for me."

Kylie waited until he set a notched log on top of one corner.

"Hold this, please."

She hurried to do as he asked. He actually wanted less from her than she was capable of. They worked quietly; he barely had to tell her what he needed. He left gaps for the windows and talked while he built, so Kylie could see what he had in mind, and it all went smoothly.

It was about thirty feet square overall. As time went on, they finished erecting the walls and putting in windows, all the while talking and in most ways just being a good team. Then suppertime came and Aaron called it a night.

"Let's ride on back to your cabin."

"I don't mind making a long day of it." Kylie knew the relentless pace her sisters always set.

"Well, I mind, darlin'." Aaron smiled and kissed her until she forgot all about the house.

"Sunrise said your sisters are coming over to help build, is that right?"

"She saw Bailey yesterday and told them we got married." Kylie nodded as they got back to work the next morning. "She stormed around some, but she said she'd get Shannon and come over to help. They're good carpenters. They'll be a big help."

She looked at the house, raised to where they could start on the roof.

"Good. I need to go do some land agent work. If you don't run into any trouble, we might be able to sleep here tonight." Aaron exhaled. "No chimney yet, dirt floors, and we won't be able to stay if it looks like rain and we don't get the roof closed up, but that's the way in a new land—folks building under their feet and over their heads."

The sound of hooves drew their attention.

Though Kylie assumed it would be either Bailey or Shannon, Aaron moved to stand between her and whoever approached. His hand went to his six-gun, which he always wore on his hip.

Tucker trotted out of the woods on his wild gray horse.

"I'm having trouble with Langley." Tucker leapt down

off the grulla mare with its long black mane. "Langley's got his wife's children figured to be lazy no-accounts but not outlaws. He won't make an arrest on my say-so of events. He wants to talk to you and Kylie." Tucker looked over at the cabin. "You want me to stay and put some time in on it?"

"I want you with me, Tucker. I don't want Langley to have any doubts about this, and he trusts you. I don't blame the man for not liking to hear his stepchildren accused of something so low-down. Help me saddle a horse for Kylie."

Aaron strode toward the horses, where they'd staked them out just minutes ago to graze. Even in a hurry, he didn't expect Kylie to do men's work. In this case, she'd have been glad to do anything to get in there and look those varmints right in the eyes.

Kylie headed for her rapidly-being-saddled horse, thinking that while she might want to be in all ways womanly, no one needed to forget she'd been to war. And Marshal Langley's stepchildren were going to learn that, too.

Bo Langley was solid, in temperament as well as build. Well suited to being a lawman in the unsettled West. He looked mighty grim as Aaron laid out the evidence against his wife's children. He'd heard it all from Tucker, and he'd had time to think about it while Tucker rode out for Aaron and Kylie.

"I haven't seen Bert since the day of the arrow attack. Haven't heard a word out of him. Of course, I've been gone mostly. But I got back last night, and he's never late to the table morning, noon, or night, and he missed every meal since I've been here.

"Hiding a wound would explain that. I've known they were lazy youngsters, but I've hoped they'd grab ahold of something and start pulling. Figured a man's gotta grow up sometime. And Myra, she's a decent-lookin' gal and smart enough. She works hard in the diner, along with Erica. Figured she'd say yes to one of the men who've asked for her hand and she'd move on west, be someone else's problem. But she never has. She's got a sharp way about her, not wanting to build a life with hard work. Taking a shine to Coulter is about what she'd do."

Shaking his head, Bo went on, "They grew up with a no-account pa, who liked his liquor, accordin' to my wife. They had an arrogant old grandpa with too much money in the old-money South, who helped the boys shirk from the war. They took to hiding in the swamp in Alabama. I can't say I even blamed 'em much. Nasty war, but it might've made something of 'em. Reckon the boys will do some time in the territorial prison. Don't know what we'll do with Myra, but her time in my home is over. Let's bring 'em in."

Tucker had picked himself out a comfortable chair and settled in. "I don't reckon you need any help bringing back three foolish kids, one wounded, one a girl. I'll just wait here."

Aaron followed Langley out of the jail. They went around to the back of the diner.

"Our living quarters are mighty cramped. I plan to build a house, but I've refused to do it. I've wanted Myra and her brothers uncomfortable in the hopes they'd move on. I guess they'll go now." Langley led them up a flight of stairs to a small set of rooms. It was suppertime in the diner. Voices and the clanking of plates and utensils sounded through the floor. A single small room served as the only room for the family to gather. A couple of doors off must lead to bedrooms. Langley was right that it was cramped. *Tiny* was a better word for it. Six people lived here, and with a baby on the way.

Aaron smiled. Bo Langley was a stubborn man. How could three adult children stand this? Why hadn't they found some way to get out on their own?

Bo went straight to a closed door and swung it open. Aaron was right behind him, and he saw a young man stretched out on a pallet, wearing a long-sleeved shirt. The way the kid sat up, favoring his arm, was as good as a confession.

"Go on, Bo. I'm resting."

"Bert, get out here. You too, Archie."

Another kid, full grown but still scrawny, sat in the corner, his knees drawn up to his chest. He gave Bo a sullen look and seemed to be thinking about whether to mind the man who housed and fed him.

"Just get up, Archie." Bo's voice rang with disgust. "Both of you move. Now. Didn't either of you give a thought to how bad your ma was going to feel when this came out? Were you so foolish you thought you could get away with it? Well, you didn't, and now she's gonna live with the shame of knowing her children are in prison for the attempted murder of Miss Kylie Wilde."

Aaron stood behind Bo and was tall enough to watch over the bulky man's shoulder. Kylie trailed him, but she couldn't see in. He heard her gasp. It was awful to hear those words spoken so bluntly. Aaron slid his arm around her waist and pulled her to his side. She leaned on him, and it was the sweetest thing in the world to support a woman and know she welcomed it.

He saw the fear on Archie's face. What color there was in Bert's face quickly drained, until Aaron wondered if he'd be able to stand. It was late enough that Myra should be done downstairs anytime now.

"Can we wait until Erica and Myra come up, Masterson?" Langley asked. "I know the whole town will hear about it tomorrow, but for tonight, can I break the news to my wife privately? Give her one night to get past the shock of it?"

Aaron nodded. "Let's get these two locked up. I've got questions for 'em. We can come back for Myra."

Archie didn't tell them much. He was a mix of sullen and terrified, which came down to utter silence. But Norbert confessed everything, including that he'd shot the arrows. As that was the most dangerous thing that'd been done, and he was admitting to it, Aaron wasn't sure just what crime to even charge these two young fools with.

They went for Myra an hour later, and she came in. Erica stayed back at the diner with her baby, a one-year-old who stayed on her hip while she worked all day. With another baby soon to come, the woman was worn to a frazzle by the end of the day, and the news of her older children being arrested shook her badly enough that all she could do was sink wordlessly into a chair.

Langley didn't put Myra in the cell with her brothers. Instead, he let her sit, white-lipped, on a hard chair in front of his desk.

"I wanted to marry Coulter. I've been interested in him ever since we settled here." Myra stared at her hands. "There were rumors about Coulter wanting that land. I thought if we scared her off . . ." Myra glanced up at Kylie, then back at her hands.

"I'm the one who came up with the idea." Archie finally spoke up. "I'm not letting you take the blame for this, Myra. I heard someone say Coulter might marry Miss Wilde to get that water hole. I told Myra we oughta get the claim for her, and then Coulter would marry her."

Myra shrugged one shoulder. "I've tried to gain his attention and never had any success."

Archie sat on a thin cot in the single jail cell beside Bert, looking hopeless. "I thought if we scared her, Myra could homestead and he'd marry her. We were trying to run you off is all, Kylie, not kill you."

"Her name is not Kylie to you," Aaron said. "And it's not Miss Wilde. We're married now, so her name's Mrs. Masterson. I suggest you call her by it."

All three of the youngsters looked up in such comic surprise, it underlined their resemblance to each other.

"With Mrs. Masterson married, the claim became mine. I released it and Coulter bought it. It's all settled."

"Like I said, it was my idea," Archie said. "Norbert was just helping. He's best with a bow. Myra promised Coulter would hire us once she married him."

"You could have killed Kylie." Aaron was having trouble seeing this young lady locked up in the territorial prison. He was having trouble seeing any of them there. "At the very least, you could have burned down her cabin. And using arrows could have stirred up trouble with the

Shoshone. Don't you care if you start a war between whites and Indians?"

Archie jerked his head up. "Isn't there already trouble between whites and Indians? I didn't think it'd hurt if there was a little more."

Aaron's eyes closed on the pain of this kid's ignorance.

Tucker erupted from his chair so hard the chair flipped over backward and crashed to the floor. He moved like a striking snake toward the cell.

Tucker always smiled. He always looked amused by life. Sure, he went around heavily armed, but Aaron had never seen him upset, let alone angry. But right now, Aaron saw how the man could survive in a brutally hard country for years on end. Matt Tucker was a hard man, fast and mean, and no one you wanted to cross.

Aaron would have thrown himself between Tucker and the boy if iron bars hadn't stood between them already. Aaron's stomach twisted at the thought, because there wasn't much doubt that in any fight between Aaron and Tucker—between just about anyone and Tucker—Tucker would come out the winner.

"I was raised by a Shoshone woman." Tucker's voice lashed like a whip. "The Shoshone are good people. Abusing a woman is bad enough, but trying to foist off the blame on someone else makes you the worst kind of low-down coward. No man can do that and still call himself a man, not anywhere, and sure as certain not in the West. Gage Coulter is a hard man, but he'd never get roped into the trap you were setting for him." Tucker looked at Myra. "He'd never have married any woman he didn't respect just to get himself a water hole."

Aaron hadn't known Tucker long, but this was the most talking he'd heard the man do. In fact, he'd just said more words in one long rant than he'd probably said total in their acquaintance, and Tucker wasn't done.

Tucker's eyes, usually friendly if a little wild, flashed with cold rage as they moved to Archie, then Bert. "And he'd've taken one look at the two of you and read you like a book. Neither of you would've spent one hour working for him. What's the matter with you? You're full-grown men. Where's your pride? You should be ashamed of living off your ma like a batch of pups still on the teat. Instead of heading for the hills to live off the land or staking your own claim to a homestead, you're plotting against a woman and an honest man."

Tucker stormed forward and grabbed a bar of the jail cell and looked to want to tear it loose. "Now you're headed for prison, and it's all for want of the simple sense to get an honest job. A job that wouldn't be a bit more work than it took to get yourselves into this mess."

A mountain man took care of himself and expected others to do the same. It appeared that such a man held those who didn't in contempt. And involving Indians, when he'd lived with Sunrise most of his life, was too much.

Tucker turned to Marshal Langley. "Anything you need from me to lock these three no-accounts up, you've got. I read their tracks and I know they attacked Mrs. Masterson with burning arrows. Later it was two of them, without Bert, who broke into her house and put the snakes in. Circuit Judge Blodgett knows my word is good, and I'll be glad to testify. Now I'm leaving before I do something to get myself thrown in there with 'em. Because no one here wants that to happen."

Tucker stormed out. He slammed the door so hard the glass in the window rattled.

Silence reigned, broken only by the sound of galloping hooves as Tucker rode out of town.

Finally, Langley said, "I ain't locking Myra up. You got a problem with that, Masterson?"

Aaron hoped Tucker didn't. "Nope."

"You boys will stay here until Judge Blodgett comes through, and he's overdue, so I hope it'll only be a few days. I don't reckon what you done will amount to prison time, but when you get out, don't figure on coming home. And don't stay in the area, or anywhere you might run afoul of Matt Tucker. You're on your own. I'm ashamed of myself for making you force my hand. I should have said no when you traipsed along with me when I headed west, and I should've said no again when you moved into that little room with your ma and me. I let myself believe putting up with your laziness was worthwhile, because having men around was good protection with me gone so much.

"Well, now I'm saying no. You'll not sleep under my roof for one more night. And, Myra, the next cowpoke who asks for your hand, you'd better say yes, because your days in my home are numbered." Langley looked at each of his wife's children, burning his eyes into theirs. None of them met his gaze for long.

He nodded toward the door. "Head on home, Myra. I'll be right along."

Myra stood from her chair. When she reached Kylie, on the other side of the marshal's desk, she stopped. She stared at the toes of her boots for a long moment, then finally she raised her eyes. Aaron saw the guilt in them and was glad the girl had enough sense to feel it.

"I'm sorry for what we did, Mrs. Masterson. It was cowardly and stupid. I never meant any harm to come to you, but I know what we did was dangerous. I hope someday you can see your way clear to forgive me, but I'll understand if you don't." Dropping her gaze, she hurried from the building without waiting for a response.

Langley turned to Kylie. "I reckon your troubles are over, Mrs. Masterson. I'm mighty sorry my family was a party to all of this." He looked at his stepsons. "Have either of you boys got the decency to apologize to Mrs. Masterson?"

"I'm the one who hit your house with the arrows, Mrs. Masterson." Bert was curled up on the lone cot in the lone cell. He looked to be suffering, but with no doctor for a hundred miles, there wasn't any help for that. "We ran wild in the swamp and woods in Alabama during the war, and I got good at bringing in food for the family with my bow. I should've used that skill to strike out on my own in the mountains. I know how to live off the land. But Arch and me got it in our heads that we'd find some easy life like we had when we were kids and Grandpa had the plantation. There are some big spreads around, like Coulter's, and they reminded us of the life we had back home, living high off the hog. I reckon we forgot we were kids when we lived so easy. We only remembered Pa and his drinking and how he carried on."

Bert's eyes went to Langley. "I'll hit the road as soon as I'm loose. You're right that we need to get a move on. I'm sorry, Bo. We've been poor sons to our ma. Maybe when I've made something of myself, I'll come back for a visit."

Langley managed a half smile. "Sounds good, Bert."

Archie wasn't so polite. Aaron got the feeling he was the most like his pa and the furthest gone down the path to worthless. He said to Kylie, "Sorry we brought you trouble, Mrs. Masterson." But he sounded less than sincere, more like he was sorry he'd gotten caught.

Kylie nodded, stood, and moved toward the door. "I think we're done here, Aaron. Can we get back to our new cabin? We can get more work done before the sun sets if we hurry."

Aaron took her arm and led his wife out of the jailhouse.

"I thought to take you out for supper, Kylie, but I'm not much in the mood to take a meal at Erica's Diner tonight if you don't mind."

Kylie smiled. "I think I'd rather eat grass with the horses."

"Maybe all our troubles are finally under lock and key." As Aaron boosted her up on her horse, though he wasn't a superstitious man, he regretted saying that—like he was begging for more trouble to land smack-dab on top of his head.

Tucker kicked his horse into a full gallop and was halfway to Masterson's new cabin before his head cleared enough to even know where he was going or why.

Sunrise.

He was going to see his ma. She'd be there. He knew her as he knew no one else on earth, and she'd taken Kylie under her wing. So she'd be at the cabin, building it, making sure a chick she'd decided to claim had a snug nest.

And those varmints in town had tried to make it look like Sunrise and her people were attempting murder. Things in the West were touchy enough. What they'd done could've flared up into killing with not much to ignite the blaze.

Those kids were too stupid to know the damage they might've caused, but that didn't make Tucker any less furious. He bent low over his horse and rode like a bat escaping the fiery depths of Hades.

Finally the drumming of the grulla's hooves penetrated his anger, and he let the forest in. He'd been riding like a fool. Tucker wasn't a man who ran around blind, and not paying attention was as good as blind.

Now he listened and it soothed his raging soul. He eased his mare to a trot and then to a walk. Resting his hand on his mustang's sweating shoulder, he let the wiry animal's strength soak into him and silently apologized for working the loyal critter so hard. This was no way to treat the best horse he ever had.

The breeze sighed through the lodgepole pines. The aspens quaked until he could drink in the peace of their flutter. A sudden quiet rush of activity overhead drew his eyes up to see a falcon swooping away from the regal tip of a fir tree, its narrow peak dipping gently.

It all helped.

This was his land, his heart. He understood how this world worked. It was people that were a mystery.

Give him a grizzly bear or a wolverine and he knew just what to do. Let him stumble onto the edge of a glacier or find himself hungry in the middle of a Rocky Mountain blizzard, and he'd handle it without much worry.

But people. Tucker dragged one hand over his eyes. Those three young whelps trying to steal a claim when they could as soon work for their own. Trying to trick a good man into a marriage he didn't want.

What kind of fool woman wants a man who'd only marry her for her land? What kind of worthless kid wants a job wrangled by his sister?

Thinking of it got Tucker riled again, so he went back to patting his horse and enjoying the woods, hoping he'd find Ma at Masterson's house.

He loved that woman. He reckoned he owed her his life,

because Pa would've probably made a bungle of raising him. And he sure as certain owed her for his love of this beautiful mountain land.

He checked the powder horn and knife strapped crosswise on his chest, the gun holstered at his hip. The knife up his sleeve, and the two in his boots. His rifle was across his back, his whip was hooked on his belt, and he had a second pistol tucked into the small of his back, with a stiletto—needle thin and razor sharp—slipped into a hidden pocket in the seam of his pants.

A man didn't wander this rugged land without being prepared to defend himself, and the more prepared he was, the less trouble he faced.

All of his upset was gone, and his usual cool head was back in control as he neared the clearing where Masterson was building. He shook his head, wondering why anyone would want to live this close to the noise and smell and bother of all those folks in Aspen Ridge. He'd talked a bit to Masterson and knew this wasn't permanent. Why then was he building at all? Was the man so narrow-minded he couldn't think of a teepee? He was killing trees and clearing land for a place he'd only live in a few weeks or months maybe. Certainly he had no permanent plans to stay.

Tucker liked his ma's way of living better, and although Tucker had a cabin in the high-up hills, he'd thought long and hard before he'd picked the spot. He'd tramped a lot of miles and lived in caves and teepees and out under the open sky for years before he'd settled.

Emerging from the woods, he saw movement on the roof of Masterson's nearly finished cabin. A pair of eyes turned and locked on him. Something in those eyes drew his attention in a way he couldn't quite explain. He couldn't look away. Then that head with its dark curls ducked out of sight.

Masterson had killed back the trees to make a decent-sized clearing, which Tucker was just entering. He was probably forty or fifty feet from the house, and he'd only seen those curls and those eyes for a moment when he knew he'd never seen them before. And he knew he wanted to see them again.

Words he couldn't make out passed between two people behind the house. A skinny young man with blond hair peeked around the corner, then quickly disappeared.

Tucker touched his holstered gun, wondering where Ma was. Then he saw her. She walked out of the house, where a door had been neatly hung. He swung down and noticed a hitching post had already been put in place in front. He smelled something cooking and heard a fire crackling behind the house. Beef. Ma didn't go hunting for beef, so someone had brought it over. Probably one of these visitors.

Scanning the place, Tucker saw a corral finished behind the house. The house wasn't closed up yet, but there were split aspens laid overlapping each other about halfway up on all four walls. Probably a bigger job than could be tackled today, but it didn't look like rain. If it suited them, Masterson and his wife could sleep here tonight.

A lot had been done since he'd come out here to get Aaron and Kylie. Ma was a mighty handy woman, yet she sure hadn't done all this. Who were the folks building on the house?

Hooves pounded away on the far side, and Tucker knew

whoever it was, they were hightailing it. He had a momentary stab of worry for Ma just as she stepped out of the house, looking just fine. Jumping off the grulla, he stripped off the hackamore bridle and let the mustang roam.

"Howdy, Ma." He jogged up and hugged Sunrise, lifting her off her feet as he often did. She slapped his shoulders and smiled. It was their usual greeting. "Who was helping you?"

"That was Kylie's family. All but her pa."

Tucker quit smiling. "I've met Cudgel Wilde. I had a run-in with him in the woods. He told me I was on his property and threatened to fill my backside full of buckshot if I didn't move along. A sour old goat who doesn't deserve to have a pretty young daughter." He thought of that head of dark curls. Those eyes. He waited for Ma to tell him more, not wanting to get caught showing interest.

"Shannon and Bailey are good builders. They came to help with the house. They are not ones to mix with folks, so when they heard you, they headed home."

"I remember her brothers were at her house the other day. Is that the whole family?" That hadn't looked like a brother up there. Except what woman had short hair like that? "They wouldn't come out of Kylie's house when Coulter and I rode over. I understand keeping to yourself. I like that as well as any man, but it don't make no sense to be quite so standoffish."

Sunrise waved a hand. "It is their way. Now you help."

Ma hadn't answered his question about Kylie's family. Was there a sister? Shannon and Bailey sounded like men. "Masterson had a few more things to see to in town before he could come home. Let's see if we can surprise him."

There was a nice pile of aspens ready for the roof. They were neatly done, and it was all new, since Tucker had been here just a few hours ago. Must've been the brothers' work. The Wildes were skilled woodsmen. A nice change from the Hughes family.

Tucker looked up at the roof and pictured those dark curls and bright eyes. He'd bet he could get Kylie to tell him about her family. He bit back a grin as he leaned a long row of split logs on end against the wall, then headed for the corner of the house and scaled it. The corners were logs notched and crossed so they stuck out like steepled fingers, a perfect ladder.

He pulled the first log up and set it in place.

Over the years he'd helped his ma build a barn, and they'd re-roofed that and her cabin a couple of times. Sunrise didn't like admitting any white man's ways made sense, but Pierre had himself a cabin, so that was where she lived and she'd finally let Tucker build her horse a shelter in the winter.

Sunrise was a lot younger than her husband, and as Pierre had aged, Tucker had done a lot for them. He and Ma knew how to work well together.

There was plenty left to do before the cabin could be called finished. Building the chimney, hanging the windows, chinking the cracks, and Masterson would probably want to lay a floor.

But with his ma's help, Tucker was setting the last log in place on the peak of the roof when the Mastersons rode into the clearing. Kylie and Aaron could sleep here tonight.

Kylie saw Tucker straddling their roof. She smelled food cooking. The people after her were locked up. She had a handsome new husband who showed signs of real decency. Except he wanted to move farther into the wilderness.

It was all she could do not to cry.

And if they weren't completely tears of gratitude, well, she had no intention of letting them fall, so what difference did it make?

Tucker hailed them and then turned his attention back to the roof. He was right at the peak; he had it all enclosed.

Sunrise waved from the ground, where she picked up scraps of log. "There is stew around back."

Aaron helped her down from her horse and kept a supporting hand on the small of her back as he led the horses toward the corral.

Why, she was being waited on hand and foot. She might as well be a princess.

They sat on the dirt floor of the roughly finished house. Tucker ate with them.

"I saw your brothers today, Mrs. Masterson."

"Oh, call me Kylie, for heaven's sake. Mrs. Masterson takes too long."

Tucker grinned. Kylie couldn't help remembering him with all that wild fur on his face. He looked much more civilized now, though the long hair and full beard was probably more who he truly was. A kind, hardworking, decent man, but only half tame.

He nodded. "Obliged, Kylie."

"So you got to know Bailey and Shannon a bit, then?" Aaron asked.

Kylie could hear the amusement in his voice, even if he was doing his best to keep it under control.

"Nope, I barely caught a glimpse of 'em. The dark-haired

one on top of the roof and the fair-haired one working on the ground. They rode away the minute they saw me. I never even spoke to 'em. Your brothers are mighty unfriendly." Tucker might have stressed the word *brothers*, but Kylie wasn't sure and wasn't going to mention it.

"Shannon has dark hair." Kylie looked around. "I can see Bailey's been working here. Bailey has a lathe and some other fine woodworking tools. I haven't seen them since my wedding. I reckon they're upset that I gave up my claim, but still they came, prepared to help. That sounds like my family."

"Does it?" Tucker got up, empty plate in hand, and carried it to a basin of hot water set on the dirt floor. He crouched beside it and made short work of washing his plate and fork. "Well, then you're lucky in your family, lucky indeed. I am going to make a point of getting to know them, despite their standoffish ways. Good night, everyone." Then he left the cabin.

Kylie had no doubt he'd meant those words as a warning. Her sisters were going to have to watch out.

"I moved in bedrolls and clothes from your homestead cabin today, nothing large or heavy," Sunrise said. She made that announcement and was gone moments after Tucker.

Kylie was alone again with her husband.

"I'm sorry we didn't get the rest of your things moved, Kylie. Your bed and stove and your rocking chairs. For tonight we'll have to make do with a bedroll on the ground."

Kylie smiled and caressed Aaron's face with her open palm. "That's fine. I never dreamed we'd be sleeping here tonight. I can't believe the house is so close to done. I came west in a covered wagon, Aaron, so I slept on the ground for months. And before that I slept in a tent. I've slept in muddy trenches. I've crawled across battlefields with cannons exploding around me. I've—"

Aaron reached out and touched her lips with one finger. "We need to talk about that. I'd even like to share war stories." He gave her a sad smile. "But I hate knowing you've seen such ugliness. I wish I'd have known you then and been able to shelter you from such hard things."

Kylie kissed that callused fingertip. "Thank you, but I don't think I carry it around with me the way you do, Aaron. Maybe in some ways, the fact that I was pretending to be someone else, a man, makes it easier to leave it all behind. And Pa was already planning to take advantage of our service exemption, so we headed west as soon as we all got home. Bailey was the slowest getting there. I'm not sure why. She never would talk about it. But she returned months after Shannon and I did. Then, just days after she came walking up our lane, Pa told us our disguises would have to stay on. He loaded us in a covered wagon and we headed west. We weren't leaving much behind. We always had a miserable little farm that didn't produce much. And we were all pretty beaten down by the war. Letting Pa take charge was easy enough. We weren't giving up a nice place like you did, with a long, prosperous family heritage."

Aaron pulled Kylie into his arms and kissed her. By the time he let up, she was breathless. Aaron rested his forehead against hers.

"The war is going to rage on there in the Shenandoah Valley, in small, vicious ways until the entire generation is gone. I wish I could take you back to the beautiful place I grew up, but I can't do that just by going there. I have to go back in time, too. Into the past. Because the place I love no longer exists. I'm sorry, Kylie. Can you be happy out here in the mountains?"

Kylie saw in Aaron's expression that he was truly grieving, for his family and for his home. She realized then that her dreams were the same as his. She was pining for exactly what he'd lost. For her to want what he would love to give her but couldn't made him feel like the worst kind of failure, a man who couldn't make his wife happy. That was how marriages became laced with bitterness over a lifetime. Hers wasn't going to be like that.

"My home is where you are, Aaron. I'm happiest when at your side. We'll find our own place and make a life together." She smiled and made sure he saw only acceptance in her eyes. If she sometimes pined for nicer things and gentler ways, she wouldn't be the first woman to give up a few bits of comfort in exchange for peace at home.

There was hope in his eyes, and it made her heart sing. Her respect and caring for him grew into something different, something deeper, which both pained and stretched her heart in ways she hadn't known before. It was the most beautiful ache in the world.

She knew nothing about womanly love for a man, but she wondered if she might be falling in love with her husband. He kissed her, and she decided that she'd just go ahead and decide it was exactly that.

"Kylie, can you be happy out here? I wish I could give you that old life. I know that's what you want, but—"

"Right now, an old life isn't what I want at all, husband.

What I want is you." She silenced him as her arms tightened around his neck.

She felt the world tilt, and suddenly she was lying on the pallet with Aaron above her. He brushed her hair off her forehead as his lips caressed her eyes and wandered across her cheeks to find her mouth once again.

21

The next morning, Kylie served him a surprisingly tasty breakfast cooked over an open fire. He knew she didn't particularly like doing it, but he was already learning that his wife was competent at many things, including a lot of manly chores. Just because she liked things civilized didn't mean she wasn't capable of roughing it.

It made him want to give her the comforts of a settled land all the more. He needed to get her stove moved over, but today he had to make some headway on the land rush.

He stepped out of the cabin with a list of things to do and looked back at her, worried. "I don't like it, Kylie. I just finished promising you and myself that you weren't going to be alone in the wilderness."

His kind smile lit him up and touched her all the way to her heart. "Riding with Bailey, Shannon, and Sunrise isn't the same as being alone. That's why you said yes."

"I know." They'd hashed this out last night, and he'd agreed, yet now that he was leaving it seemed like a bad idea.

"I can ride the few miles to Shannon's without an escort, Aaron. I've made the trip dozens of times. And now that Myra Hughes and her brothers are taken care of, I'm all right on my own."

"I'll ride along. That's proper and that's how I'll do it, Mrs. Masterson." Aaron laced his words with a smile, but he wasn't letting his wife hare off alone in these woods, no matter if it'd save him some time. Sunrise had gone back to Kylie's homestead to sleep, so she would meet them there.

They were on the trail to Shannon's within minutes.

"Bailey will come to Shannon's," Kylie told Aaron, "and we'll meet up with Sunrise at my old cabin. Once we're all together, we'll stay together. Bailey helped me move the stove to my place. She complained about it nonstop, because no wagon could handle the narrow trail. My big sister makes a lot of noise, but she always gets done what needs doing. She built a travois, and we pulled the pot-bellied stove along the trail that way. I'm sure we'll move it to our new home that same way."

Aaron tugged at his hat in frustration. He should be doing this. But he was already guilty of shirking his job. His negligence wasn't honorable. When they were within sight of Shannon's holding, Aaron pulled Kylie's horse to a halt and gave her a sound kiss. "I probably won't see you until near sunset. I'm sorry to leave this all to you."

"You've done precious little work this week, Aaron. Moving what's left of my things isn't that big a chore. Now stop worrying." Kylie, looking demure, which didn't fit on her face very well, said, "I'll see you tonight at our place."

Narrowing his eyes, Aaron said, "Just see that you don't wait there alone." He kissed her one more time, then rode away while he still remembered why it was a good idea to leave his pretty wife's side for even a minute. And he regretted being separated from her for a lot of reasons. Worrying about her safety was only one of them.

Aaron had gotten in a good morning of work. He could see the land rush was already tapering off. The worst would be over before the snow cut the area off, but Aaron had to accept that he and Kylie would be spending the winter in the house they'd just built. Moving on would have to wait until spring.

He wanted to be higher in the mountains, so that meant a late start because the mountain passes didn't open early, and . . .

The door to the land office slammed open, and Myra Hughes rushed in. She was taut as a drawn bowstring, but then when she saw Aaron, she seemed to relax a little. "Good, y'all are here."

"What's the problem?"

"A man, he said some strange things. At first it didn't worry me, and then this morning I thought I'd better tell you."

"What is it?"

"A man came in the general store yesterday, asking after you. I didn't even think about him being anything but a homesteader. He asked about the land agent, and I told him you'd gone home. He was right friendly at first and seemed to be a talker. He mentioned that he knew Kylie. But he sounded so friendly, I told him some about Kylie and her family and how you'd built a cabin and she'd given up her claim. This morning I got to thinking. He seemed to know too much about you for a homesteader just coming into the country. You haven't had any trouble, have you?" Myra wrung her hands nervously.

"No." Aaron moved to the door and stepped outside. He looked around at the quiet little town. Strangers came and went with little notice, if they didn't cause any trouble. "He knew too much. You mean like he'd been asking around?"

"Y-you know what I did to Kylie. I only mention that because of the way he said her name, like he was familiar with her."

"How did he say her name?"

"It was strange is all. He whispered it, real soft, until a body might think she was hearing a breath of air instead of a name spoken. It was strange. 'Kylie.' He said it twice. Then he started muttering about the war and left the general store real sudden-like."

"But who was it? Did the man have a name?"

She nodded. "He made a point of telling me to say hello if I saw you. He said to tell you to be watching out for him. Said his name was Neville Bassett."

Aaron was stunned, stumbling against the open door.

Kylie. Like a name spoken on a breath of wind . . .

Memories of his childhood friend raced through his mind. Nev swimming with him, climbing trees, chasing bullfrogs, riding horses, dreaming about working their land and marrying the pretty girls who lived nearby.

Playing war as boys. Playing a life-and-death game of war when they came home.

Then he thought of Kylie. Riding with her sisters and

Sunrise. Thinking the people threatening her were locked away. All her troubles were over.

Nev, standing in that cellar doorway, had said before going for his rifle, "*I swear before God that if you had any family left, I'd shoot every one of them and make you watch.*"

Aaron ran for his horse with only one thought: get to Kylie before Nev took his hate out on the woman Aaron only this moment realized he loved.

If you could get married and not tell us, how come you couldn't move and not tell us?" Bailey liked to complain, but that didn't stop her from throwing her back into shoving the potbellied stove across the floor of Kylie's cabin.

They'd emptied everything else out first and strapped it on the backs of the horses. Bailey had arrived at Shannon's with a string of her mountain ponies. Bailey didn't like admitting it, but she was a really nice big sister.

Kylie smiled through the curls that'd come loose and now dangled in front of her eyes. She blew a particularly annoying one aside. "This is the last of it. We can get going for my house and have the whole place set up in time for when Aaron comes home. Tonight I can make him a nice dinner on my own stove."

It hadn't taken much nagging on Bailey's part to get Kylie to change into her britches. It made all the bending and hoisting much easier, and the ride was sure to be more comfortable. Much as she loved feminine things, Kylie dearly loved some of the more practical parts of dressing and acting manly. Kylie would have to figure out how to give that bad news to Aaron, because she didn't want to give it up entirely.

They shoved and lifted until they got the stove in line with the door, and then Bailey, who was always thinking, tied a rope around it while it was still inside, lashed the rope to her horse, and used the horse's muscle instead of their own to drag it outside and down Kylie's steps. It took a little more maneuvering before they had it on the travois, along with the stovepipe, hooked up to the gentlest of Bailey's mustangs.

Sunrise had worked right alongside them, saying very little. But what she did say reminded them clearly that she considered it all foolishness. She thought the ways of white people with their cumbersome stoves and houses and beds and clothes and possessions of all sorts were all very odd.

"The fire I started is still hot, and the coffee is warm," Sunrise said. "I kept the cups out of the packs so we could use them. A fire that took minutes to build and did not need four women and a strong horse to haul, unlike your stove. The sun is overhead. It is time to stop for food."

Shannon searched in her saddlebags. "I didn't think we'd want to cook a meal, so I brought biscuits and cookies."

Bailey rolled her eyes at Shannon. "I figured you'd want to feed us and that you wouldn't have the heart to serve us up one of your lambs, so there are some roast beef sandwiches in my saddlebags."

Shannon smiled unrepentantly and sat on Kylie's porch,

facing the pond, her legs dangling between the spindles she'd worked on so hard. She handed out hard biscuits while Bailey shared her sandwiches. Sunrise poured coffee.

Kylie drew in a long breath, scented with pine and the sweet smell of lake water. The tin cup of coffee sat beside her on the porch. She threaded her legs through the porch spindles and swung them as she took in the scenery.

"This is a beautiful place." She took a bite of the roast beef sandwich and chewed Bailey's good hearty bread and tender beef.

"It is a good place," said Sunrise. "I have told Coulter I mean to live here. We are in agreement."

Kylie gasped and choked on her sandwich. Both rocking chairs had been tied to the packhorses, so Sunrise sat leaning against the cabin wall next to Bailey. Sunrise shifted and pounded Kylie on the back.

When she could breathe again, Kylie turned to her friend. "He's letting you live here?"

"Yes."

"Then why wouldn't he let me live here?"

"He would have."

Silence seemed to spread between all four women as Kylie looked at Sunrise, and Sunrise looked back as if she had no idea what Kylie was confused about.

Finally, Bailey said into the silence, "I reckon he just wants the water. If you'd have given him clear title, he'd've let you live here. He don't care if someone's in the cabin. At least not if they don't cause any trouble. And I'm sure he trusts Sunrise. He probably figures having her here is a good thing."

"So Aaron and I didn't even need to build a house?"

Kylie thought of the work they'd done, and how heavy that stove was.

"Well, Aaron needs to live a lot closer to Aspen Ridge than this, so yes, you needed to move."

Shannon probably deliberately waited until Kylie took another bite before she asked, "What can you tell us about being married?"

Kylie choked again.

When Sunrise quit pounding her back, Kylie looked at Shannon, who had an innocent expression on her face. Like maybe she hadn't meant to ask about the first thing that came into Kylie's mind. So the fact that the more personal side of marriage had come to mind said more about Kylie than it did about Shannon. Then there was a glint in Shannon's eyes, and Kylie didn't think she was mistaken at all. But the only time Kylie would talk about that would be on Shannon's wedding day, at which time she might have a talk with her sister.

Kylie decided to discuss something else instead. "Aaron is really worried about protecting me. It's a wonderful feeling. Pa has really done wrong by all of us, making us dress and act like men. Sending us off to war, thrusting us into the middle of an army full of men. It's terrible we were put in that position. Pa oughta be ashamed of himself. I'm really hoping you two figure out real soon you can't go on living the way you are."

Bailey narrowed her eyes and kept chewing. Shannon smiled her pretty dimpled smile, and Kylie could only roll her eyes at how pretty and feminine they both looked.

"When Coulter came to this cabin, neither of you went outside to greet him. That's because you knew he'd immediately recognize you were women. And yesterday, when Tucker came to help build the house, both of you ran for home for the same reason. Do you really think you can keep hiding for the rest of your lives? You're admitting you don't believe anyone will be fooled by your britches and short hair, and you know Aaron changed your paper work. So why are you doing it? I'd say by now it's just an old habit. When are you two going to grow up and start behaving like the women the good Lord made you?"

Bailey finished her cookie and took a long drink of her coffee. "I wouldn't want to try and break a mustang wearing a skirt."

"Somehow it seems shameful for a woman to wear trousers. If we're pretending to be men, it's not so bad." Shannon shrugged. "That's nonsense, I suppose."

"It's all nonsense," Sunrise said, gathering up the cups. "This is the West. Live as you please, but live honestly."

Kylie took the last bite of her food and wondered if Aaron would let her wear her britches part of the time.

They stowed the cups and coffeepot and made sure everything was ready. Bailey swung up on the lead horse, leading a remuda of four mustangs strung together, each of them heavily packed. They carried bed slats, her bed tick, and her rocking chairs, as well as her table and chairs, tools, pots, and the few other things she owned.

Sunrise followed the line of packhorses with what load her horse could carry. Shannon followed, riding the horse pulling the travois with the heavy stove. Bailey had trained the horse Shannon rode, and it was the steadiest of any of their animals. While Bailey was the best at breaking and training, Shannon had an almost magical touch with any animal, including keeping this horse steady as it pulled the unusual load on its back.

Kylie brought up the rear to make sure the stove didn't tumble off the travois. Her horse was also loaded down. They set a snail's pace, so that the stove wouldn't bounce and startle Shannon's horse.

They had the whole of the afternoon, though, and it was a beautiful day in the dappled shade of the woods. The people terrorizing her were taken care of, and Kylie didn't have a care in the world. As she rode through the heavy forest, Kylie thought of Shannon's question about marriage. Her thoughts went right back to where they'd gone at that question, and she looked forward to seeing her husband again soon.

The distinct crack of a twig in the forest caused her to turn in the saddle in the direction of the sound. She heard the wind breathe her name again.

"Kylie."

This time she couldn't convince herself she'd imagined it. She opened her mouth to tell everyone to stop. She was going to find out what or who that was.

A hand covered her mouth.

Not even a whimper escaped.

She was lifted off her horse by arms that made her feel as if she weighed nothing. Her horse shied a few steps, but she was whisked away so fast and quiet that her horse resumed walking after the others with barely a missed step.

With the utter hush of a ghost, she was swept into the woods. Only that one warning snap. It reminded her of the times she'd felt watched, the times she'd jumped at shadows.

As he dragged her deeper into the woods, farther from rescue, he leaned so close his whiskers brushed her face. "Kylie," he whispered with rancid breath.

He moved with complete silence just as he'd stood in the woods, just as he'd watched her. She realized he'd stood in those woods very near where they were attacked by the arrows. But neither Sunrise nor Tucker had noticed the tracks of another man, besides the three from the Hughes family.

This man was better than either of them. And now he moved with a skill that might make him hard to follow, which meant she was at the mercy of someone who knew how to make himself invisible in the woods.

He'd just used his talent to make her invisible, too.

Aaron was practically lying down on his gelding's neck. He'd raced to his cabin first, hoping he'd find the Wilde sisters there. They hadn't arrived. He'd then charged on toward Kylie's homestead. They'd be on their way by now if Nev hadn't gotten to them, killed them already.

The thought drove him with crazed recklessness. He closed the distance between himself and the place he prayed Kylie would be, the whole time asking God how he could have been such a fool as to think distance had anything to do with hate.

He should have stayed.

He should have ripped that rifle out of Nev's hands and held him down until he came to his senses.

He should have talked of their memories and reminded him of their friendship.

He should have sown love where hate bloomed and thrived.

If he had, that land could have born a new crop of faith and goodness. But Aaron had been too weak. No, that wasn't true. He'd been too filled with his own hate to sow those seeds. And now he'd led his private war out here, and Kylie and her sisters might die as a result.

"Forgive me, God. Forgive my own failure. Make me new again." He thought of the way Kylie had cast off those britches and put on a skirt. She'd let her hair grow long before she'd met him. His mixed-up little wife, who talked of wanting fussy things, was braver than he was. "She had the courage to start over, to begin again. Help me to be a new creation in you, God."

In the midst of the worst terror of his life, because he had no one to turn to but God, he let the love of God pour in. It pushed aside his fear, even as it deepened his determination to get to Kylie and protect her. And then together they'd make a new life together, pleasing to God and to them both.

Finally, he saw Bailey ahead. She smiled and glanced over her shoulder as if knowing he'd come looking for his wife.

She reined her horse to a halt, drew her gun, and hopped to the ground. "Kylie!"

Although he was still a ways off, he heard the urgency in her voice. She was shouting something he couldn't make out.

A string of heavily laden ponies were behind Bailey. Past them, Sunrise swung off her horse while Shannon behind her dismounted.

And behind Shannon was . . . a horse ridden by no one.

Where was Kylie? There was only a saddled horse without its rider. Aaron didn't pull up until he was nose to nose with Bailey's horse on a trail too narrow to pass. He leapt off his horse and sprinted toward the back of the caravan.

Sunrise was already down the trail. Not running, yet moving fast. Bailey was trailing her.

At last, Aaron caught up with them. "How long has she been gone?"

"I don't know," Bailey replied.

Grabbing her by the shoulders, Aaron said, "That's not good enough. What were you doing, leaving her behind like that? Why weren't you watching her?"

Her sisters would be coming. Kylie had no doubt about that. Coming right into the teeth of danger.

That was all it took. The ground was steep, broken up, sloping downhill, and studded with boulders. She slammed her bootheels into the dirt. Her kidnapper stumbled, and they both fell. She wrenched away and dove forward down the unforgiving slope.

Falling, then scrambling, then falling again, she heard the man roar behind her. Not so silent now.

She clawed her way to her feet and knocked loose a rock from where it clung to the wooded mountainside. Dirt kicked up the beginning of a small avalanche. The man tackled her, and together they rolled and careened into a tree.

Her battered body stopped. He leapt on her just as her hand, gripping a stone the size of her fist, came at him and crashed against his head. It stunned him enough that she was able to wriggle free. She used both feet to kick him in the chest, a move that sent her hurling back down.

Getting to her feet again, she saw what lay below—downhill for hundreds of yards, all in the wrong direction, away from her family and safety.

She ran up. He was only a few paces behind her. She grabbed an aspen as she rushed past and used her weight to spin around. She heard the kidnapper stumble on past. Dropping to her hands and knees, she scrambled.

He was coming. She heard him. Every inch she gained was one step closer to her sisters and help. And the end of whoever this watcher was who'd added to her torment. She recognized a faint trail cutting along the side of the mountain. She dodged aspen trees and boulders, praying with every breath. He'd most likely catch up, but she saw no reason to make it easy for him.

Heavy footsteps pounded behind her. He'd gained the trail. Ahead was a fork in the path. She sprinted toward what she thought was the direction of safety, taking it just as his weight slammed her facedown in the dirt.

Where all defeated foes end.

With brutal strength, he flipped her over, this time careful to keep her hands under control as he pinned her to the ground. She kicked her feet but gained no leverage. He panted as he leaned down, his gaping mouth only inches from her face, so that she couldn't avoid his stinking breath.

She saw cruel satisfaction in his eyes as he watched her squirm. His lips twisted into a grotesque smile, and he whispered, "Kylie."

"Enough." Sunrise didn't yell, but her quiet order cut through Aaron's nearly out-of-control rage. "I need quiet."

He realized he was on the verge of shaking Bailey.

"I'm sorry." Aaron took Bailey into his arms and hugged her. "I'm so sorry."

She froze as if she'd turned to stone.

"None of this is your fault. I should never have blamed you. Forgive me."

Bailey reached up with halting movements and gave him a pat on the shoulder. "Sure, Aaron. Y-you can let me go now."

Finally, he released her and stepped back. Bailey watched him with wide eyes. She hadn't been this unsettled when he'd been rough with her. Aaron wondered if her father had ever touched her in kindness before. He turned to look at Shannon, who was studying him as though he'd grown a second head.

Quietly she said, "You were in a panic when you came riding up. You know what's going on, don't you? Did the Hughes family break out of jail? Is that what's got you scared to death?"

"Not the Hughes family. No, they were all pranks compared to this. This is about the war and a hatred that has stretched across a continent. And it's all my fault, none of it yours."

"Come." Sunrise cut off Aaron's need to blame himself more. "Leave the horses. No trail big enough to ride. The man who has her moves fast, but he is on foot." Sunrise strode into the woods while Aaron, Bailey, and Shannon rushed to catch up, leaving their horses ground-hitched.

"Who's doing this, Aaron, if it's not the Hughes family?"

Bailey asked. The ground slanted sharply downward, so narrow they couldn't make good time. They had to duck branches and step around boulders. It looked as if nothing bigger than a deer had gone this way before them.

"It all goes back to the war and an old friend who fought for the South. I found out this morning he came here to get revenge for the death of his family. He blames me for all of it. He can't be in his right mind."

"He's sane enough to track you down, find out you're married, and slip silently through the woods. I think that makes him responsible for whatever crimes he commits. Is he planning to kill Kylie?"

"From what I hear, he's planning to kill every one of you. Then kill me."

Nev's words echoed in his mind. *"I swear before God that if you had any family left, I'd shoot every one of them and make you watch."*

Was it possible Nev wouldn't kill Kylie until he got his hands on Aaron? Did Aaron dare to hope for something based on the ravings of a madman months ago?

"Your old friend?" Bailey said with a frown.

"Yep," Aaron replied.

Bailey nodded, a determined look on her face. "Sunrise, let's pick up the pace!"

Her urgency scared Aaron even more than he already was, and that was saying something, because he was terrified right down to his bones.

He dragged her to her feet, and she screamed like to peel skin off someone's hide. The man just smiled and pushed her back against a massive tree. He wasn't particularly rough; he didn't gag her or hit her. In fact, she had the sense that he wanted her to scream. Which was the reason she stopped.

He was a living scarecrow, dressed in rags, skinny as a stick. His hair hung like filthy brown straw, and his tattered black hat sagged over eyes which gleamed with hatred and soul-deep pain that reached to where no medicine could heal.

"Who are you?" she asked.

He smiled, his teeth green, his face skeletal beneath a scraggly beard, close enough that his foul breath was nearly overwhelming. "Scream some more, Mrs. Masterson. I want your husband to come running to save you. I want your sisters here. I want Aaron to watch his brand-new family die, just like my family died." The man inched closer, and the stink of his body pushed aside the odor of his breath. His face was lined, each line creased with dirt. He couldn't have washed in months.

Kylie remembered the stories Aaron had told her of his family dying during the war and knew somehow this man came from that part of Aaron's life. "Are you Neville Bassett? Aaron's neighbor?"

The man laughed, a mockery of humor. "That's me."

"Aaron said you were his best friend."

"I was until he and his Union Army killed my family." Neville spat the words. "I was until he and his Union Army starved me half to death in a prison camp. I was until his Union Army demanded I swear allegiance to the tyrants who'd tortured me for over two years. I was his best friend until he and his Union Army left me to walk home, even though I was so sick I could barely stand. I was his friend, Mrs. Masterson, and now I'm his enemy. I tried to kill him back in Shenandoah, and I've been after him ever since. He got off easy while my whole life was destroyed." He laughed again, a sound as ragged as his clothing.

"I'm going to kill him and everyone he loves." He pointed at her with one bony finger. "Then I can rest. Then the nightmares will stop and the bombs will quit exploding in my head."

Neville reached his hands up to press against his ears, as if he were hearing explosions right now.

Kylie saw the gun.

In one trembling hand, his finger on the trigger, Neville held a '58 Remington, Army model. Kylie had seen this same revolver a lot in the war. As it was a Union Army gun, she was surprised this loyal Son of the South had one, but apparently hating the North didn't stop him from knowing a good firearm when he saw one.

"When I heard you were moving today, and your precious husband was finally going to let you out of his sight, I staked out the trail knowing I'd finally get a chance at you and your family. Because you're the only family Aaron has, and I mean to take that away from him."

The only thing that kept her from screaming was what Neville had said about wanting her to. If she screamed, her sisters might come, and this man meant to kill them. She knew they'd be coming anyway. But if she didn't scare them into bursting in hard, they'd be careful.

What's more, Neville knew too much about her. He'd asked around somehow, finding out that she and Aaron had gotten married. He'd been watching her from the first night Aaron learned she wasn't a man, the night Coulter's cattle had trampled her rock garden.

That was the first time he'd spoken to her from the forest. She vowed then and there to never again doubt the instincts she'd been given by God.

But to know her name and to say that he heard she was moving, he'd heard that only last night, because they'd only decided to move yesterday. If he'd done that, there was a chance Aaron got wind of it and he'd be coming, too.

All Kylie had to do was stay alive. Help was close at hand.

And she had an edge. Neville had kidnapped a woman who'd been to war. Even though she liked being feminine, Kylie knew how to live through terror. She'd done it before, plenty of times. The feeling, awful as it was, was familiar. The war had prepared her for this moment, and possibly for the first time ever, she was grateful to have gone through it.

Yes, she was frightened. Honestly, she was in the clutches of an armed madman; only an idiot wouldn't be scared. But she could function, just like she'd functioned on her stupid roof in that rainstorm.

She realized that the only reason she'd let those snakes shake her so badly was because Aaron was there, and she didn't have to be strong. Before he arrived, as crazed with fear as she was, she'd been fighting them off. Once he came, she'd let him take over and turned into a proper damsel in distress.

Yet maybe she could do more than function. Maybe she could help. She looked at Nev, a shadow of a man. Scared as she was, her heart broke for him. She'd heard of the horrors of prisoner-of-war camps and could only imagine all he'd been through.

"Neville, the war is over. The killing is over. Why would you want it to go on?"

"Nothing's over. It's in my head. I live with it. The war's with me all day long and it haunts me at night."

As if God whispered to her that it was the right thing to say, she told him, "I fought in the war disguised as a man."

Neville's head reared back, and some of the hatred was replaced with pure amazement. "No one would believe you were a man. Not for two minutes."

Kylie sniffed and tossed her head. She even fluttered her eyelashes a bit. As a woman, she had a few wiles of her own, and she decided to try them out on him. "I believe you've just insulted me. Aaron said one minute. Or maybe he said ten seconds, I can't recall, but it was definitely less than two minutes."

It couldn't be called a smile exactly, but Neville's lips seemed to soften a little, and he looked a tiny bit more human.

"Masterson always had a way with women."

Maybe she could touch him with talk of the old days. "He said you were his best friend. You know he lost everything, too. His parents, his brothers and sisters. Why can't the war be over? It was a mad thing. I was in the middle of those battles. Decent men killing other decent men. The blood and bullets, the cannons and death. I spent an entire day trapped under the dead body of a soldier I'd killed. It was a horror that I still see in my dreams, just like you."

Neville stared at her as if he wanted to see deep inside her mind and know her thoughts. "How could a woman be in the middle of that?"

"My brother Jimmy died, and my pa stirred up in me a desire to go fight in his place. He convinced me I needed to fight for Jimmy's sake, to get revenge. But once I was there, it was only ugliness. I don't understand war, do you?"

Neville shook his head slowly.

"Afterward I came out here, still disguised as a man. But, Neville . . ." Swallowing hard, Kylie reached for him, not for the gun but for the shoulder on his other side.

His eyes widened as he watched her hand approach. "What?"

She touched him and felt nothing but bones, the poor man. Just some rest and some good food would help him so much. "I found the courage to put it all behind me. God tells us we need to be born again."

Neville sneered, and then some of that faded to misery. "To go back to the life I had before the war, to be born back into that beautiful place . . ." He gave his head a violent shake. "That's impossible. It's all gone, and the people I love are all dead. Killed by your husband."

"We can't go back. We can't begin that old life again. We need to start a new life. And you need that, Neville. You need to get it all out of your head and off your shoulders. You need to clean out your mind and soul and begin again. God helped me do that, and He can help you, too."

"If only that were true. If only I could get rid of what haunts my thoughts day and night." A longing unlike anything she'd ever seen crossed his face, and he lowered his gun. Kylie thought the fight was gone out of him. Then she heard the brush of fabric.

Neville's head jerked up. He grabbed Kylie and yanked her in front of him. His arm came around her neck in a grip so tight it cut off her air. His gun pressed to her temple, his back to the massive tree, shielding himself well.

Aaron stepped out of the woods, gun drawn and aimed straight at Neville.

Bailey stood a ways behind him, off to his left. Kylie couldn't see Shannon or Sunrise, but she knew they were close by. She hadn't a single doubt. Shannon was the best of the Wilde sisters in the woods, and Sunrise was better than all of them. Those two would be ghosting around, looking for a way in from the side or from behind.

"Aaron Masterson." Neville said the name, then spat on the ground, right over Kylie's shoulder. He cocked the gun just inches from Kylie's ear. "You're lookin' prosperous."

Kylie had never been so happy to see anyone in her life. At the same time she wished they'd all waited. She'd almost had this mess under control.

No one ever let her handle anything.

Neville's gun swung away from Kylie's head and aimed at Aaron.

Kylie watched that muzzle as it pointed straight at Aaron's heart. She knew the revolver, fully loaded, held six bullets. It could kill them all and Neville would have a bullet to spare. And a lot of men carried with them a second loaded cylinder. If he did, he had six more shots that he could have ready in seconds.

They were all just one wrong word from death. One last massacre, thanks to that awful war.

Aaron could breathe again. Now that Nev's gun was aimed at him, Aaron had every hope the women would survive, because Bailey, Shannon, and Sunrise would gun down Nev before he killed Kylie.

Nev might get one shot away. But that shot would be at Aaron. And Nev wouldn't fire a second time. Sunrise was already behind him with her bow and arrow drawn. Shannon was nowhere to be seen, but he'd listened to Kylie talk about how good her big sister was at slipping around in the woods. She'd vanished and was closing in, getting in position to help.

"Nev, you talk like I profited from that war, but I lost everything. My family is gone. I was driven off my land. You're out of Camp Douglas, but you're still in prison. Why do you hate me?"

"The North took everything and you fought for them."

Nev was a walking skeleton. His clothes were in shreds.

"Both the North and the South did terrible damage, and they took everything from me, too."

Nev laughed. It was a broken, mad sound. Aaron wanted to go to him. Hold him. Find the old friend. And just like that, the memory of Aaron's decision to start anew washed over him and it was right. Right for Aaron and right for Nev, too.

Aaron lowered his arm. He wasn't going to shoot his friend, not for any reason. Nev wasn't ready to meet his Maker, and Aaron would have no part in ending his life.

Besides, with Kylie between them, there was no possible way for Aaron to take a shot. It was too risky. Without taking his eyes off Nev, Aaron holstered his gun.

Nev's gleaming blue eyes followed the gun, and a furrow formed between them. "You think I'm also gonna put my gun down now?"

Aaron shook his head. "That's not why I did it." He took a step closer, then another.

"No, Aaron, stay back," Kylie pleaded. She seemed to understand that Aaron was giving up on winning a gunfight.

"I would rather you shoot me than I shoot you," Aaron said calmly. He had a better chance of surviving if he stood back. Every inch he moved closer raised the chances of a bullet finding his heart.

"You think I won't?" Nev extended his gun.

"I hope you won't." Aaron kept walking. "I hope you remember how much we loved each other. We were like brothers." He walked very slowly, making no sudden moves that would startle a man on the fragile edge of reason, that might make him flinch and fire his weapon.

"You and I, we're enemies." The muzzle trembled.

"No, we're friends. Old friends. I know you're tormented by the war, but can't you take one moment before you pull that trigger and remember what good friends we were?" Aaron stepped closer. "Do you remember the first raft we built? You and I were seven years old at the most. We took nails from both our fathers and used them to keep a bunch of saplings together. Then we lashed it with vines. We almost drowned when we tried to float the thing on the river. We left the ax we borrowed from your pa and the hammer we borrowed from mine in the woods. Remember? And we went home soaking wet, and both of us got in trouble."

Nev's arm seemed to loosen on Kylie's throat. "We found out the hard way that the vines we used were poison ivy."

Aaron nodded. "We spent the rest of the summer shoveling out horse stalls and scratching. And the worst was that I didn't get to see you for over a month. A whole month of summer and I didn't see my best friend. I loved you then, Nev, and I still do. I refuse to let that war stop me. I would rather die than live the rest of my life knowing I killed you. I couldn't bear to have that on my soul. I fully believe that if I died today, I'd stand before God and be judged as one of His people. I'd be allowed into heaven. If you pull that trigger, well, the Lord tells us that we have to lose our lives to gain life with Him. So I'll go be with my heavenly Father in glory if you send me there. But you're carrying so much hate, I'm afraid for you. I don't want you to meet your Maker today, Nev. I know it's not our place to judge, but I'm sorely afraid that if you went today, you wouldn't be ready."

Nev blinked, and the grimy arm around Kylie's neck eased some more.

"I don't want him to die." Aaron's voice rose. Now he spoke to Sunrise and Shannon and Bailey. They were capable women and could overpower Nev without killing him.

Nev seemed to come out of some state, some deep hole his mind had gone into. Maybe he was remembering that he'd snatched Kylie from a line of riders, four riders. Not including Aaron. And now he only saw the one he held in his hands and the one behind Aaron. He looked sideways, left and right.

With each step, each second that Nev's gun didn't fire, Aaron's hopes grew that maybe, despite the hate, the war, and the sickness, maybe Nev didn't have it in him to kill one of the last remnants of his childhood.

"I'm in hell already," Nev said, his eyes fastened on his gun. He spoke as if only he were there. "The nights are never-ending torment. The days are full of haunting memories."

"So long as you're alive, Nev, and no matter how bad life is, there's hope. Things can get better. You can still find happiness in this life and prepare for peace in the next."

"How is this hellish life any different from being turned away from the pearly gates?" His gun turned.

For a sickening moment Aaron feared it was aiming again at Kylie. He gathered himself to lunge at Nev.

And then the muzzle turned toward Nev himself. "I can't live with it anymore," Nev said, and his voice broke. "I . . . I don't know any other way to make it end."

"Your death won't end what torments you, Nev. It will just make it permanent."

The gun rested on Nev's temple. His finger tightened on the trigger.

Aaron bolted forward. His hand lashed out and knocked the gun up. It fired into the air. He tore it out of Nev's hand and threw it aside at the same time he yanked Kylie free and thrust her at Bailey, who was at Aaron's side instantly.

He pulled Nev into his arms. "I love you, Nev."

"No, you shouldn't have stopped me. You should hate me. If you knew all I've wanted . . ." The words trailed off as Nev's arms wrapped around Aaron, and sobs closed his old friend's throat.

"There's been enough hate," Aaron said. "We'll find a way back. We can be friends again. We can start over. We'll get through the memories and nightmares. I have them too, but I've managed, with prayer and time, to lay them down. You'll stay with us, and we'll find a way to hand the old life off to God and begin anew." Aaron glanced around.

Kylie was there, her beautiful hazel eyes shining with tears. She nodded. He reached out his hand, and she caught it and held it.

Their life together was part of all that was new.

Aaron thought now he had a chance to help Nev heal. As he looked at Kylie, a hot, wet drip cut past his vision and splattered on their joined hands, staining their fingers crimson.

A scream ripped through the air, the kind of scream that cut a man all the way to his bones. He saw Kylie staring overhead and followed her gaze.

Shannon was dangling from a fat oak branch fifteen feet straight up. She was unconscious, her face covered in blood.

Kylie saw no way up. The tree was huge, the lowest limb that Shannon was on far out of reach. Her belly was draped over the thick branch, with her arms dangling down on one side and her legs on the other. From where she stood on the ground, Kylie couldn't tell where the branch began.

"Get a horse over here!" Aaron said, his voice cracking through Kylie's panic. Out of the corner of her eye, Kylie saw Sunrise hurry away.

Bailey circled the tree. "Shannon got up there, so there has to be a way."

The trunk was so wide that Kylie's arms couldn't reach even halfway around it.

"Over there." Aaron rushed for a tree about a dozen feet away. It was a much younger oak with its bottom branches lower to the ground. In a flash Aaron was up it, scampering like a squirrel. "Nev!"

In her panic, Kylie had forgotten about Aaron's lunatic

friend. But there was Nev, the one whose actions had led to Shannon being shot, right behind Aaron, climbing.

And Bailey was right behind Neville.

"Stay down, Bailey," Aaron called. "Get under her. I'll lower her to you."

The fact that Bailey obeyed him was a shock. Later, Kylie would have to find out how in the world Aaron had managed to get obedience out of Bailey Wilde.

Aaron got up to the level where Shannon was and crossed to the bigger tree, walking upright on the branches. Was he that confident in the tree or was he in just too big a hurry to be careful?

At last he reached Shannon. Aaron touched her so gently it made Kylie's throat ache as she craned her neck, watching, wishing she was up there to help her sister.

"Let me at her, Aaron," Nev said. He said more, but it was muffled as Aaron moved aside and Nev stepped carefully among the branches to offer a hand. Soon he was bending over Shannon.

"Is she alive?" Bailey asked, her voice wracked with fear.

"Yes," Nev answered, though he didn't say more.

Aaron crouched but stayed back. Kylie's stomach twisted to see that troubled man hovering over her injured sister.

Nev said something to Aaron, who quickly slid back over to Shannon. With his hands around her waist, Aaron gently lifted Shannon and eased her forward, her head down.

"Be careful of her arm," Nev called down to them. "I think it's broken. The head wound is just a cut on her scalp. It knocked her cold, but the wound isn't serious."

Kylie considered getting shot in the head serious, no matter what some Reb said. Especially the one who'd fired the shot!

Inch by inch, Aaron continued to lower Shannon, with Nev taking her legs and lowering her some more. It was still a long reach to get Shannon to the ground.

Sunrise returned with a horse just as Kylie was trying to figure out what they'd do now. Bailey swung up on horseback and caught Shannon around the shoulders. Aaron lay on the branch on his stomach, still hanging on to Shannon.

"I've got her!" Bailey said.

Aaron let go. With Sunrise's help, they eased Shannon the rest of the way to the ground while Aaron and Nev rushed down from their perch.

Everyone circled Shannon.

"Let me get a better look," Nev said, pushing past everyone.

Bailey blocked Nev. "Get away from her!"

"I can help. I worked some as a medic in the war."

"You're a doctor?" Bailey couldn't have sounded more skeptical without just plain calling him a liar.

"I'm not claiming that. What I did was rough medicine, but I learned some things. I can help." Nev added more quietly, "I'm so sorry. I didn't mean to hurt her."

"No, you meant to *kill* all of us."

"She's still bleeding. Please, let me help."

"I'm right here, Bailey," Aaron said, "and I won't let him hurt her." He had that implacable tone in his voice—not quite as sharp as when he'd given Bailey an order earlier, but hard to disobey just the same.

Kylie didn't trust Nev either, but she trusted Aaron. She touched Bailey's arm. "Let him doctor her."

"I'm sorry," Nev said again. "Let me make this right."

Only distantly did Kylie realize that Nev was saying "her." He had been all along. He wasn't fooled into believing Shannon was a man. Bailey either, most likely. The disguises were worthless.

Bailey gave way.

Nev dropped to his knees beside Shannon. Sunrise moved to the other side before Bailey could. The older woman pulled a pack open that must have come from her horse. She had bundles of cloth and other things Kylie didn't recognize. Along with every other skill, Sunrise had them beat at doctoring.

Bailey knelt at Shannon's head, while Aaron went to Kylie's side. He slid an arm around her waist and pulled her close. They watched together. Nev talked quietly as he bandaged her head wound, then turned his attention to her arm.

Nev looked up at Aaron. "I hope the arm bone isn't broken. A bone broken by a bullet is often shattered and rarely heals well. In fact . . ." Nev quit talking so suddenly, Kylie's eyes riveted on him.

"In fact what?" she asked.

Nev shook his head and went back to winding a long strip of white cloth around two sturdy sticks Bailey had scrounged up to be used as a splint on Shannon's upper arm.

Bailey caught Nev's arm so hard he winced. "In fact *what*? Tell us!"

Nev became shaky again. He'd been handling things well, but it came back to Kylie real hard that only moments ago he'd been on the verge of killing them, then himself. This wasn't a strong man, mentally or physically.

Finally, Nev looked at Kylie, then at Bailey. "Most gunshot bones d-don't heal. Most end in . . . in amputation."

Bailey's eyes went wide. "No!"

"You're *not* touching my sister with a knife," Kylie said, her expression firm.

Aaron's arm tightened on her waist. She wasn't sure if he meant to comfort her or hold her back.

Neville's eyes flickered fearfully between Bailey and Kylie. "It doesn't look like the bone needs to be set, but I can't be sure of anything until we can wash the wound thoroughly. I'm splinting the arm just to keep it still. When I'm done, we'll need to get her home and in bed. Aaron, you and Kylie figure out a way to move her."

"Our house is closest," Aaron said.

"The travois," Bailey said to Kylie.

Kylie nodded. "We'll leave the stove."

Shannon moaned and tossed her head, the first sign of life. Kylie wanted to cry with relief.

"Are you done, Nev?" Aaron asked. "If so, I'll carry her to the main trail." He waited until Nev gave him a nod before gathering Shannon up in his arms.

"I've done all I can here," Nev said. "Let's get moving."

The man sounded confident, with no trace of the hatred and killing rage that had driven him out here. Where had it gone? Would it come back when they least expected it?

Kylie looked at Bailey. Their gazes caught, and they both nodded. They wouldn't leave this man alone with Shannon. They'd let him care for her—they could see he had doctoring skills—but that was a long way from trust. One of them would stay with her at all times.

Kylie and Bailey headed for the travois, with Aaron right on their heels carrying Shannon.

Aaron's new cabin was now a hospital. And the doctor oughta be a patient.

By the time Nev finished cleaning and binding up Shannon's wounds, he decided her arm wasn't broken, and she'd regained consciousness enough to start fretting about her sheep.

Sunrise left Nev to his doctoring once she was satisfied he was capable. She brought down a buck and before long had stew ready for all of them. Even vegetable-loving Shannon had a bowl of the stew.

"I will get to work on this deer hide. We can make a pair of pants and a jerkin for your friend," Sunrise said to Aaron.

A good thing, because Aaron had burned Nev's clothes. He also saw him through a desperately needed bath, which showed Nev's body to be riddled with old scars and newer unhealed sores. His body would be months healing. Aaron wouldn't give up until his friend's mind was healed, too.

The haircut Sunrise gave Nev reminded Aaron of the one she'd given Tucker. Sunrise had a talent for taming wild men, or at least for taming their hair.

They got Nev into bed, and with two people in the hospital ward there was now nowhere to sleep. Bailey had led the rest of her remuda here and dumped everything on the floor. The stove was still back on the trail. Bailey had run home to do her chores and then returned, determined to keep a wary eye on Nev, which Aaron understood. Sunrise also looked to be staying the night.

Seeing his chance to get his brand-spanking-new wife alone, Aaron volunteered to do Shannon's chores and sleep at her cabin. A fair trade, even if it did mean he'd have to face down a smelly flock of sheep.

Holding her hand, Aaron led Kylie to the corral. He grabbed her saddle, and she grabbed his.

Scowling, Aaron said, "Let me do both saddles. This is man's work."

Kylie gave him a pert smile. "I agree, and I like it that you want to take over the manly jobs, but I want to get on down the trail. So, if you don't mind, rather than stand by and watch while you do twice the work, I'll saddle a horse."

Aaron wanted to be alone with her mighty bad. "At least do your own. The saddle is lighter."

"Gladly." They switched horses and were on their way in half the time.

As they rode into the setting sun, through the dappled light of the forest, Aaron wondered just how worn out she was. She'd worked hard all morning, packing up her cabin, before all this trouble started. And the day wasn't over yet.

It was late enough when they got to Shannon's that even her sheep came in with little coaxing. They didn't need to be carried in each night, after all. Shannon was obviously babying them.

Heading for the house at the end of a dreadful day, Aaron took Kylie's hand. "I figured something out today, sweetheart."

She turned to him and smiled. Her hair was all jumbled, spilled down around her shoulders. There were dark circles under her eyes. Getting kidnapped and tending a bleeding sister made a mess of a woman.

And yet she was still the prettiest thing he'd ever seen.

"What's that?" she said.

"I've got a lot more work before this job is done. Shannon is going to need some care before she's healed up, and I can't abandon Nev until I'm sure he's all right. I don't know how long all that will take."

"However long it takes, we'll take it."

Aaron's grip tightened. "I do know that when we're done with it all, when Nev is better, I want to go home."

"That's fine. I can be happy at a ranch in the mountains, so long as I'm with you."

She always knew that this was what it meant to marry him, even if she hadn't liked it. There'd been no other way, so she'd agreed. But now here she was, willingly saying she'd follow him and be happy about it. A woman did that for a man she loved.

"So if I decide to go home to the Shenandoah Valley, you'll come with me." He led her inside another well-built Wilde cabin.

Kylie gasped. Her eyes brightened. Despite her exhaustion, she suddenly looked wide awake. "Really? You've decided to go back? But I thought after today, after seeing how ugly Nev got, even though he seems to have decided to move on past his hate, you know there will be others who—"

"But that's what made me change my mind," Aaron interrupted. "The fact that he'd come all this way made me realize I need to go back. I realized while I raced for you, terrified he'd get to you before I did, that I hadn't left all that hate behind. It followed me. I was giving up all that was good about my home in exchange for peace. But in the end I had no peace and no home. I decided then I'd take you back to Virginia. I knew that two people who truly loved each other, with God on their side, could make a new life together."

"Two people who love each other," Kylie said. "Are you saying you love me, Aaron?"

"I am, Kylie Masterson." Aaron pulled her close. "I knew it before I saw Nev with a gun to your head. As he held you there, though, and I thought he might kill you, the depth of it almost tore me apart."

She rested her head against his chest. "When you holstered your gun and took that step forward, I knew what you were thinking. I saw in your eyes you were willing to lay down your life for your friend. The goodness and decency stole my breath, Aaron. And wonderful as it was, if your crazy friend hadn't had me by the throat, I'd have kicked you right in the backside. I already thought what I felt for you was love, but that's when I knew for sure, because the thought of you dying was unbearable."

Aaron lifted her chin and kissed her until the frightening memory faded, and then he kissed her some more.

He was a long time saying, "We'll stay as long as we need to."

She said in a rather bewildered voice, "Here? At Shannon's?"

He laughed. "No. We'll stay here in Aspen Ridge. Then we'll go on to Shenandoah. It won't be civilized, not at first. But with time I hope I can give you your dream of tea parties and bonnets and . . ."

Aaron stopped talking and broke into a laugh. He took her by the shoulders and pushed her to arm's length.

"What's so funny?" A furrow of annoyance appeared on Kylie's smooth brow.

"I just realized you're wearing britches." He laughed again.

Kylie looked down at herself and back up, blushing. "I forgot I even had them on. I let Bailey convince me to wear them while we moved." She smiled. "I really do want to live near civilization, Aaron, but there are a few things about living a more manly life that are quite convenient."

Aaron shook his head and chuckled.

"You can quit laughing at me now."

He let go of her shoulders and scrubbed both hands over his face. "Don't you see? I'm apologizing to you for the rugged way we'll have to live when we rebuild, and all the while you're standing here in britches and I didn't even notice."

He kissed her long and hard. "I think that civilized world you want so badly back in Virginia is never going to be the same after it meets you, Kylie Wilde Masterson." As he drew her toward the bedroom, he added, "I know I never will be."

Keep reading for a special preview of

Now and Forever

WILD AT HEART, BOOK 2

BY MARY CONNEALY

Coming June 2015!

AUGUST 1, 1866
ASPEN RIDGE, DAKOTA TERRITORY/IDAHO TERRITORY BORDER

Matt Tucker could take people for only so long and then he had to get up into the mountains. All the way up—where he was more likely to run into a golden eagle than a man. He'd wander in the thin, pure air for a week or two, to clear his thoughts. Forget the smell and behavior of men.

He slung a haversack over his shoulder—the pack contained everything he needed to live—and rambled up a trail that'd scare the hair off a mountain goat. He'd left his horse behind, wanting to travel light and go places even his tough gray mustang couldn't go.

This time it wasn't men driving him to the high-up peaks. This time it was a certain head full of black curls and a pair of shining blue eyes. Not a *man*—though no one would admit it—which was so odd he almost turned around.

In fact, he wanted to turn around so badly he walked faster.

That hair and those eyes were why he wasn't paying attention, which was a good way to get a man killed in wild country.

He scooted past a boulder on a trail as narrow as coal-black lashes on bright blue eyes, then rounded a curve as tight as black curls—and stomped on the toe of a bear cub.

A squall drew his eyes down. A roar dragged them up. He looked into the gaping maw of an angry mama grizzly. He hadn't heard her or smelled her. Honestly, that was so careless and stupid he almost deserved to die.

She swung a massive paw, and he had no time to dodge. She knocked him over the side of that mountain. Not a cliff, but the next thing to it. He slammed into an aspen. He bounced off. Dirt flew around him, and he gasped from the pain and sucked a mouthful of grit into his lungs. He plummeted.

He hit the next aspen so hard his ribs howled in pain. He grabbed, trying to stop his plunge. Branches cracked, and he lost hold. Loosened stones pelted and clattered, falling along with him.

He snagged. His arms, legs, and torso whipped forward, but his haversack held. It had saved him.

He heard a roar that brought his head around.

The mama wasn't satisfied with knocking him off a mountain. She was coming and coming fast, finding a way down somehow. She was running almost as quickly as he'd fallen, closing in with teeth bared. He had no time to think up any crafty plans.

With sickening inevitability, Tucker had no choice but to tear the sack's strap loose from the tree and let himself fall on down, with no idea where the bottom was, only knowing stopping made him grizzly food.

He rolled on, hitting one tree after another, grasping at trunks, trying to slow his fall. One tumble landed him on his back, and he gained his feet, ran a few steps, tripped over a stone, dove face first, and twisted into a shoulder roll to keep from breaking his neck.

A long, high yell ripped from his throat. Tucker saw no point in being quiet about this.

He hit his head hard enough he thought maybe he heard angels singing, or birds tweeting, or maybe both or neither. That bear roared above the music, and Tucker kept on falling. Finally he slammed into level ground and stopped, sprawled flat on his back. He flicked his eyes open, knowing he had to get up and run. The bear was bound to still be coming.

His blurred vision filled with a cap of black curls and the prettiest blue eyes he'd ever seen.

Well, no. Not *ever*.

Because he'd seen them before on the roof of Aaron and Kylie Masterson's cabin. He wanted to just lie there and look at those eyes forever.

And then that dratted bear roared and those blue eyes, looking at him all worried, glanced uphill and the concern turned to horror.

The pretty little filly reached down, grabbed Tucker by the front of his shirt, and hauled him upright. What was she going to do, throw him over her shoulder and run? He didn't think that was going to work. He was about six inches taller and outweighed her by one hundred pounds.

But Mama Grizz was coming, so someone was going

to have to do something. They couldn't stay here, and Tucker wasn't sure he was up to moving on his own. Of course he'd only had about two seconds to think about it. He hadn't really tried.

"Hang on!" She shoved him backward, clinging so tight it was like he'd gotten a second pack hooked on.

She screamed.

They flew. There was no more rolling. No more aspens. No more rocks. They soared.

Tucker saw the walls of the cliff rushing past and knew where they were. Worse yet, he knew where they were going to land. "Are you crazy?"

He'd just been killed by a woman as wild as he was. Well, he wasn't killed yet. But it was only a few seconds ahead of them.

The bear roared overhead.

The black-curled woman shouted, "I hope Bailey's not too stubborn to tend my sheep!"

"I hate sheep."

They hit the water so hard it was like slamming into granite.

The water took over trying to kill him as it swept him forward, pulled him under, and slammed him into a wall all at the same time, then threw him over another cliff.

The Shoshone called this the Slaughter River.

Those little black curls that had him so curious—and the woman they were attached to—had just thrown him into the worst stretch of water maybe in the whole Rocky Mountains. What did Tucker know? Maybe in the whole world. A stretch so wild Tucker had never heard of anyone riding through it alive, though he'd heard of a few dead bodies being fished out on the far end.

They hit the roiling foam at the bottom of the waterfall. The first of seven. Each one worse than the one before.

All he could do now was hang onto the woman and try to keep them both alive, which he very much doubted he could do.

He grabbed the whip he kept on his belt and lashed them together. It seemed like the gentlemanly thing.

He slammed up against a rock and was dragged under and took her with him. His attempt to save her might get her killed. Maybe he oughta let her loose. Before he could give that plan much thought, they went flying again. She screamed in his ear fit to leave him deaf for the rest of his life. Of course, his life probably wasn't gonna be all that long so what did it matter if he was deaf?

Blast it, all he'd wanted was to go see a few golden eagles. Was that too much to ask?

Matt Tucker. Shannon Wilde had figured out who he was while he was still falling down that mountain. She'd recognize the good-looking wild man anywhere. That he was two paces ahead of a frothing-at-the-mouth grizzly had kept her from giving his looks much thought at the time.

She'd have climbed a tree—she had plenty of time to get away from the bear—except she had to wait for Tucker to fall the rest of the way and take him with her, and that, plus his dead weight, cut tree-climbing out of her choices. And that left her with one option only: dive over a cliff.

A miserable option if ever she'd ever been given one.

She'd grabbed him and jumped, glad she didn't have much time to think about what she was doing.

They'd lived through the cliff.

They'd lived through the first, second, and third waterfall.

They'd lived through two stretches of water churned white as snow and studded with rocks.

And now, though the river was still racing like mad, when she thought she might be able to flip Tucker onto his back and drag the poor, battered man to shore, he'd tied her to him with a whip of all things, and she couldn't get away and swim.

She should've let the bear have him.

"Tucker, no. Untie me."

He wrapped his arms around her, as tight as the whip, as if they weren't tangled up enough already. She knew they'd never get to shore this way. She'd had some experience in the water, thanks to her experiences during the Civil War, and knew how to rescue a person.

They were going under, so she drew in a chest full of air and sank. The world bubbled as they raced along. Under the icy, clear water, she stared at him, and he looked right back.

He kicked heavy boots, rapping her ankles. But she was protected by her own boots, so no damage was done. She matched those few swimming moves and they surfaced, face-to-face. Gasping for air, rushing along, she tried to be rational.

"I know how to swim. Take this whip off, and I can get us to shore."

"No you can't."

"Yes I can."

"Shore is a hundred feet of sheer rock, straight up. There ain't no shore to climb out on for miles and miles. Hang on for the ride, Miss Wilde."

She hadn't been called *Miss* Wilde in years. It was a reminder that she was supposed to be masquerading as a man. In all the fuss, she'd forgotten that. Here she was in britches, with short hair and a man's shirt and boots, and yet Tucker didn't seem to have one single doubt in his mind that she was a woman. For some reason—some reason she didn't understand at all—right this very second, she didn't want to be anything other than a woman.

She looked up at the sheer canyon walls they were being swept past and saw he was absolutely right. "I seem to have no choice but to hang on, Mr. Tucker. Your whip has made it impossible for me to do anything else."

"We'll do better if we don't get separated. I'm familiar with this stretch of river."

"Is the worst over?"

Tucker gave her the biggest smile she'd ever seen. Of course she didn't think she'd ever been this close to any man before. His animal-like white teeth looked ready to gobble her right up, and she wondered if the grizzly bear might have been safer after all.

"What's so funny?"

"The worst, Miss Wilde? You think that was the worst?"

"You don't have to call me Miss Wilde."

"So you're still claiming to be Kylie's brother, huh? You expect me to believe you're a man?"

"I'm Kylie's sister." Shannon was glad for the britches, though. It was much easier to swim in pants than a skirt.

Tucker smiled a little wider.

"I said you don't have to call me Miss Wilde because, considering what we're going through together, you can call me Shannon."

There was a long pause while they looked at each other, and then she called over the noise of the water, "So there's more to come, then?" Her voice sounded uncharacteristically hoarse.

"They call this the Slaughter River, and I am mighty afraid there is a lot more to come for you and me."

We hope you enjoyed this sample of *Now and Forever* by Mary Connealy. For more information on this book, please visit www.maryconnealy.com or www.bethanyhouse.com.

Mary Connealy writes romantic comedies about cowboys. She's the author of the acclaimed TROUBLE IN TEXAS and THE KINCAID BRIDES series, as well as several other series. Mary has been nominated for a Christy Award, was a finalist for a RITA Award, and is a two-time winner of the Carol Award. She lives on a ranch in eastern Nebraska with her very own romantic cowboy hero. They have four grown daughters—Joslyn, married to Matt; Wendy; Shelly, married to Aaron; and Katy—and a little bevy of spectacular grandchildren. Learn more about Mary and her books at:

maryconnealy.com
mconnealy.blogspot.com
seekerville.blogspot.com
petticoatsandpistols.com

More From Mary Connealy

To learn more about Mary and her books, visit maryconnealy.com.

The Civil War may be over, but the adventure has just begun for this ragtag group of soldiers who became friends while held captive in Andersonville Prison. When they cross paths with three one-of-a-kind women, there's going to be trouble in Texas!

TROUBLE IN TEXAS: *Swept Away, Fired Up, Stuck Together*

In the town of Dry Gulch, Texas, a good-hearted busybody just can't keep herself from surreptitiously trying to match up women in dire straits with men of good character she hopes can help them. How is she to know she's also giving each couple a little nudge toward love?

A Match Made in Texas: A Novella Collection
by Karen Witemeyer, Mary Connealy, Regina Jennings, and Carol Cox

You May Also Like

Brilliant but reclusive researcher Darius Thornton is not the sort of man debutante Nicole Renard could ever marry. But can she stop her heart from surging full steam ahead?

Full Steam Ahead by Karen Witemeyer
karenwitemeyer.com

Zayne Beckett and Agatha Watson have always been able to match each other in wits. But will unlikely circumstances convince them they could also be a match made in heaven?

A Match of Wits by Jen Turano
jenturano.com

After three failed attempts, Everett Cline is not happy when another mail-order bride steps off the train—a woman he neither invited nor expected. But is she the wife he's been waiting for?

A Bride for Keeps by Melissa Jagears
melissajagears.com